FAIR GAME

BY

TORIAN GOODEN- COLON

Sendy Stoffner,

Thank you for the

support.

God Bless!

Torian Colon

2003

Lillophelia Publishing
9211 West Rd. Ste. #143-242
Houston, TX 77064
E-mail: lillophelia@yahoo.com

ISBN   0-9743014-1-8
Library of Congress Control Number   2003095298

Cover designed by Brenda Smith with Creations to Life, New Jersey

Photography on cover by:
Bill Gordon with First Impressions, Houston
Model on Cover: Harry Colon

Printed in the United States of America

Pictures Change

My understanding of the problem came from my picture. My
  picture of me and what I believe.

My understanding of you is in my picture. My picture of me
  and what I believe.

My understanding of the problem can change when I change
  my picture. My picture of me and what I believe, and
  what I believe about you.

Pictures Change
Change Pictures!

Dedication

This novel is dedicated to my three favorite people:
Harry, Hayli, and Havyn

With Love,
Nino

Acknowledgements

First, I must thank God for guiding me through life, and blessing me to complete this project. It was rough at times, but you allowed me to finish the task.

Harry, without your support, this wouldn't be. Thank you for your patience and for the information you provided me to create this story. I love you.

Hayli and Havyn, my precious angels. Thank you for trying to be understanding while mommy wrote this novel. One day you will be of age to read this piece, and hopefully be proud of me.

Richard and Faye Gooden. Thank you for being the best parents a woman could ever ask for. If it weren't for you, I wouldn't exist. Thank you for raising me to be a goal oriented woman.

Carolyn Gooden, thank you for your support and encouraging words.

Toya Gooden, you are the strongest sister I know. Thanks for reading and editing all those incomplete drafts and not complaining. Your feedback was valuable. You were prompt and positive. I love you for that.

To Lillian Thomas and Ophelia Mosley, my grandmothers: LillOphelia Publishing would not exist if it weren't for you. I hope you are proud!

Brenda Smith, you are the best! What can I say but thank you for believing in me and spending numerous sleepless nights graphic designing, editing, counseling, and all that you did to help me get this book done. You believed in me more than anyone else. I love you girl!

Valerie Muhammad, thank you for assisting in editing this project. Your advice was appreciated.

The BIGGEST thanks goes to my friends, especially those who did a weekly check to see how I was doing with this book.

Robyn Ayers, you have supported me since birth. Thank you for always kicking in. It's nice to have a friend who is real and doesn't want anything in return. I'll never forget all that you've done. (Much love, Kaseem)

Tommia Johnson, my big sister. Thank you for the support and for your positive spirit. You always have pleasant, encouraging words. Thanks for asking every single day how the book was doing. (Much love, Rob)

Laundria Perriman, girl, what can I say but you are the BOMB! You stroked me and listened to me cry when I had nothing left in me. I don't think you know how much I leaned on you for encouragement, and of course more of your brilliant ideas. Thank you. (Much love, Brett)

Keith and Angela Ogburn, thank you for your support. Keith, you are the brother I never had. Thanks for reading that first draft, and inspiring me to keep going.

Leonard and Toni Gant, thank you for checking on me and my writings. Leonard, your calls, giving me support inspired me to keep pushing. I couldn't ask for a better friend.

Lashae and John Kimbrough, thanks for being great friends. Shae, thanks for looking out!

Tonya Mitchell, thank you for your support on everything! You read Fair Game when it was first born. Thank you.

Kenyetta and John Thomas, thank you for being good friends. Kenyetta, you were one of the very first editors for this project and you gave me great feedback and editing. Thank you for all of your support.

Janine and James Wilson, thank you for reading and giving me great feedback. Janine, if it weren't for you, I wouldn't have entered into the Tavis Smiley contest. Thanks for delivering empowering words when I needed to hear them. Your words were very uplifting.

Rhonda and Byron Doxey, thanks for being long lasting friends. Rhonda, we've been together for a while, and our bond is unbreakable!

Kennette, and Les, we have that CMSU connection. I love you guys and thank you for your support. Kennette, you are my illustrator. You don't believe me.

Angie Malone, thank you for your support.

Joycelyn, Natalie, and Dezzi, my L.A. connection. All three of you are wonderful women, and I'm glad we have such a great relationship. Joyce, thanks for helping with the book. Much appreciation.

Liwaza Smith, girl, we have been through it and back. We could never explain our connection. You are one creative sista'! (Much love, Nate)

To my family members, the Mosley's, Ballard's, Gooden's and Colon's. I'm glad I have wonderful relatives like you. Thanks for the support.

To my childhood friends, who I share wonderful memories with:

Keith Ogburn, Hank Hampton, Jakima Hampton, Shad Williams (rest in peace), Chase Murphy, Felicia Wilhite, and Nico Lee. I expect you guys to buy every book I write!

To my Central Missouri State friends, those I can find, and those I can't. What great memories!

To the Ladies of Delta Sigma Theta Sorority, thank you for the love and support.

Tracy Scott and Stephanie Perry Moore, thank you for your advice, and keep writing great novels.

Dr. Loyce Caruthers, Tami D., Laura Haug, Tracy Tousant, Shaun Smith, Michelle Murphy, and Jennifer Malonson, thank you for great feedback.

Mack and Sarah Smith, thank you for being great consultants on this project.

Pearl Book Club in Houston, thank you for the love and support. Deborah, C.C. and Akilah, thank you for reading in the very beginning. Much appreciation.

To my NFL crew who I share wonderful memories and experiences with,

Santo and Damaris Stephens, Antonio and Gloria London, Brett and Laundria Perriman, Derrick and Stephanie Moore, Robert and Kim Porcher, Darryl Wallace, Darren and Vickie Carrington, Cestaine and Kevin Glover, Pamela Evans, and Mickey Washington. It was a blessing! Thanks for the support.

If I have forgotten anyone, please forgive me. My next novel will be dedicated to you.

Love,

Nino

Prologue

We stood at the altar, and a wave of emotions hit me that nearly knocked me off my feet. I turned slightly to see if anyone noticed my sudden movement, but the audience was still all smiles and some misty eyed. If they only knew what it had taken to get us here, the pain and sorrow, or the times we almost didn't make it, rivers of tears would be flowing in this church.

My Aunt Erma would be shouting for the Lord, and if the whole story was told my Aunt Joyce may just get the Holy Ghost and start speaking in tongues as she ran up and down the aisles. I, of course, would suffer a severe case of embarrassment causing me to faint on the scene bringing the ushers to my rescue with their Martin Luther King church fans and smelling salt.

I could relax though, because they didn't know the truth about the struggle I had to get here. All I can say is, thank you Lord. Very few knew how we made it. My diary was the only keeper of the truth.

I know it may be strange for a woman my age to keep a diary, but oh well, I do, and to be honest, I write in it every chance I get. See, writing frees my mind of things that are troubling me; it's kind of therapeutic in a sense.

i

If it weren't for my writing, I would have lost my mind with all the drama my girlfriends and I experienced this past year. It was almost like writing the daily news. It became difficult logging all of the incidents down as they unfolded, but I managed to get every last detail the best I could.

When my life settled down, I looked through my notes, recapped the situations and I laughed, cried, and analyzed them with a clear mind.

My diary became another best friend. I wrote things in her that I didn't share with my girls. Then I decided to share it all with the world in a book.

I explain how it all happened. How he came into my life. I don't know exactly when, but I do know ever since that day, he has consumed my thoughts. Never have I been so strung out over a man like I was over him.

As I stand at this altar before God, my family and friends, I'm still shaking my head at the road we took to get here. I must say my friends and I had a hard time putting the pieces together and we struggled to hold on to our relationship. This story I am going to share with you, detailing our struggles over the past few months, tested us all!

1
Happy Hour

Jada

December 2001

"*I*t's some fine, fine brothers in here tonight!" Deidre Carol announced as she licked her fully glossed lips. "Check out the bar, there are about ten cuties over there without rings on."

"Well that sure as hell doesn't mean they're not married," I said, rolling my eyes.

"I know, Jada, Ms. Goody—Two-Shoes. Don't you think I'm aware that most of these brothers are in here walking around faking like they don't have a wife and children at home? But do you think I care? Hell, no! That's not my problem. That's the woman's problem if she keeps letting her husband out of the house. The way I see it, these women shouldn't turn their men loose on Friday nights if they don't want anybody to mess with them. I figure they need to make sure they stay at home, especially if he's fine as hell."

"There you go with that bull again," Mara said, shaking her head. "Girl, the longer you go without a man, I swear the more ruthless you become."

1

Mara and I laughed and D.C. ignored us.

"You do know I'm not thinking about either of you?" she said as she rolled her eyes.

"We love you, Dee," I smiled.

****

Mara and Deidre Carol, better known as D.C., were my girls. We'd been inseparable since kindergarten at Turner Elementary School, in Houston, and we were still close at thirty-two years of age. Nothing or no one could come between the Ladybugs, that's what we called ourselves back in the day. In our eyes, we were the cutest girls in our class, and we were always buggin' out and acting crazy.

We spent kindergarten through fifth grade together until Mara's dad decided to walk out and leave the family. That's when our lives changed. Mara and her mom sold their two-story home, which was directly across the street from ours, and moved into an apartment on the Southwest side of town.

We all lived in Third Ward, a predominantly black area in Houston, and we were distraught when we were broken up. We were used to seeing each other every day whether for two minutes of quick gossiping or a few hours of playing beauty shop.

I'll never forget the summer we were going into the sixth grade. No more than two weeks after Mara and her mother moved, D.C.'s mother filed for a divorce from her second husband, and that meant D.C. was going to be leaving too. I was lost because now D.C. was moving to Missouri City, a suburb of Houston, and she too would be a nice little piece away from me.

After that summer, it seemed like everybody's parents on our block got divorced, leaving my family, the Ballards, the last family together.

****

Pappadeaux's, a restaurant off 610, was our spot. D.C., Mara, and I met there for happy hour every Friday night. It was the place to be if you were single, black and had a little change in your pocket. Plus, we all loved seafood, and in my opinion, Pappadeaux's has some of the best Cajun seafood in Houston.

No matter what Houston's unpredictable weather was like, the three of us were there. Even when Hurricane Allison blew in the flood of the century, wiping out thousands of people's homes and cars, we were at Pappadeaux's gossiping and chatting away about how men weren't worth a dime and how bad we needed one. It's amazing how God watches over fools, because the night of the flood, we were so into our conversations, that we never realized the seriousness of the situation until our cell phones started ringing with our mothers and friends asking our whereabouts and telling us of what was going on in the city. Thank goodness we were able to pile into Mara's BMW and coast our way to her house. Fortunately, we didn't reach too much high water and her car didn't flood.

"These crab cakes are delicious," I said as I chewed slowly, trying to devour every bite.

"Jada, you say that every Friday night. I'm starting to think they're slipping you something in them."

"Whatever, Mara." I answered as I chewed slowly.

While Mara and I were discussing our entrees, D.C. was still sitting prim and proper trying to slyly locate every interesting man in the restaurant. Her posture was erect as usual, and her long brown layers rested perfectly against her back. Every last strand of her blonde streaks were in place, like Oprah's hairstylist had just finished it.

D.C. was a very sophisticated woman, with a strut that let the world know she thinks she is the shit! She is about five feet eight inches tall, with a shape that can kill, thanks to her strenuous workouts at 24 Hour Fitness. Her gray Vanessa Williams eyes and the long eyelashes that frame them are very enticing. Most women would say she has it all. Her smile shows her pearly whites, she has flawless skin that glows, and cheekbones she accents daily with her favorite MAC products. D.C. is always together from head to toe, as were all three of us; but she is the prissy one in the group.

I am more on the laid back side, and I feel most comfortable wearing jeans and more relaxed outfits. If D.C. puts on a pair of jeans, there is definitely a pair of heels to go with them. To top that off, her attitude is at another level. She puts the 'C' in cocky, and Mara can't stand that! She thinks D.C. behaves the way she does because she is mixed and feels she can pull anybody she wants, since her mother is white and her father is black. D.C. is a soft caramel complexion with hair like Halle Berry's. You know the kind that can be styled without three cans of hair spray or gel. The bottom line is D.C. is attractive, and she works her looks.

****

It was around seven thirty when I glanced toward the bar, noticing the finest man I've ever seen! Standing tall and built, like Morris Chestnut, there was this chocolate brother with a flawless smile. I stared as he laughed and talked with another guy. His teeth were straight and sparkling white, and the turquoise fitted shirt he was wearing hugged every ripple of a muscle he had. The brother was a legend!

While he continued laughing and talking, I sat in a trance. I tried often to shift my eyes around the room so it wouldn't look too obvious, but I didn't do a good job because Mara caught me and asked, "Damn girl, who are you staring at?"

"No one," I blushed.

"Yes you are heifer. I've been sitting here watching you. You haven't even finished that last bite of your crab cake yet."

"Well, why are you watching me, and not your food?" I said trying to get the heat off of me.

"Look Jay, we know that trick." D.C. butted in "Don't try to change the subject. We know you were watching somebody over there, so you might as well tell us so I can make sure I didn't have my eye on him too. I'm not trying to fight you over my man."

"Heifer, you don't have a man!" Mara laughed.

"Humph. That's what you think."

I wouldn't reveal to either of them who I had my eye on, especially D.C. because she was notorious for starting drama. I remember one time she boldly told this brother we'd seen in the Reggae Hut that one of us had our eye on him. That pissed me off! I had just given her the heads up to take a peek at him when he entered the small Jamaican spot. Before I could grasp my thoughts good, she was up talking to him. I hadn't even looked the brother over for a second time before she embarrassed the hell out of me.

Needless to say we exchanged numbers, and he became another fatal attraction on my long list of ruthless men. From that day forward, I swore I'd never let either of them know when I was interested in someone. Plus, that wasn't my style. I liked to play it cool. I couldn't approach a man. He had to show interest my way first.

"Ooh, Girls," Mara blurted "I have to tell you about my quickie I had with Colin after work today."

D.C. and I looked at each other and shook our heads. Mara always had sex on the brain. She did things I couldn't imagine. I mean in all kinds of positions, and in the weirdest places.

"I know you didn't bone that man in the clinic, Mara?" I asked.

"No, I didn't, but we almost did."

"That means she did" D.C. laughed.

"Shut up, Dee," and listen." She continued. "Ladies, Colin has it going on. I'm telling you! He has really put it on me, and I'm not lying. That man knows what to say and what to do in the bedroom."

"Colin?" I asked in a surprised tone.

"Yes, Colin. He is the bomb! Let me tell ya'll what we did the other night."

"Please, Mara." D.C. interrupted, holding her hand up in Mara's face. "Can we discuss this later after my food has digested?"

Mara ignored her and continued.

"This man spread whip cream all over me from my neck down to my toes, and you know with me being a full bodied woman and all, that was a hell of a lot of cream for him to spread," she laughed. "Anyway, Marvin Gaye was playing, and candles flickered all around the room. It was making me horny as hell, as I laid there waiting to see what he was going to do next. Finally he proceeded in removing every last drop of the cream with his tongue, making sure he covered certain areas slowly, if you know what I mean."

D.C. made a gesture like she was about to throw up.

"Don't hate now," Mara smirked. "I'm telling you, Colin knows how to treat a woman, and he sure as hell knows how to give a sista' a workout."

I laughed at Mara while still sneaking a peak over at the bar where my fine chocolate friend was getting ready to leave. There were two women snickering and slinging their hair in his face, but he and some friends seemingly ignored this and made their way to the door.

"Girls, it's time we got out of here," D.C. announced. "So what's up for tomorrow?"

"I'm doing a little shopping at the Galleria," I answered. "Y'all can join me if you like."

"No, no not me," Mara cut in. "You are not taking up my entire Saturday. I know how you shop. You get a kick out of buying things on sale, which means you're going to bounce from store to store, and you know that gets on my nerves. Plus, I have too many errands to run and definitely too much studying to do. You know I take that bar exam again in a month, so I'll have to holler at you guys later."

"What about you, D.C." I asked. "What are you doing?"

"I'll call you in the morning after I finish my work. I have some paperwork to catch up on and that's about it. You know I'm always down for some shopping."

"You have to work on the weekend?" Mara chuckled. You're a pharmaceutical rep, you don't work during the week, let alone the weekends. All you do is drive around looking cute in that company car, talk on the phone, and go to lunch all day."

"You don't know what you're talking about. For your information, I get most of my work done on the weekends and secondly don't hate 'cause I got the bomb job!"

"Yeah, right" Mara mumbled as we prepared to leave.

As we stood in the restaurant parking lot saying our good-byes, a black Escalade with polished rims pulled directly in front of us. There were three men in the truck. The one on the driver's side had his window down and we could see how fine he was! I couldn't see the passenger or the backseat rider too well.

"Hey ladies, do you fine women mind hanging out with us tonight? We're new in town and we don't know where to go."

"Well how'd you find your way here?" D.C. responded flirtatiously.

The driver smiled.

"We asked around, and somebody told us we would see you here, so I made sure I found my way."

I could hear his friends in the truck laughing.

"Listen to this fool," Mara said. "He just doesn't know who he's messing with. D.C. can talk shit all night."

"Well today must be your lucky day, Brother, because you found me, and we were just talking about heading downtown."

Mara and I looked at each other. "What the hell is she doing?" I mumbled.

"You lead the way baby," he said staring D.C. down from head to toe. The lust in his eyes was so intense you could feel it. He couldn't take his eyes off of her, and his smile stretched a mile. I knew instantly he was going to be her next victim.

"Come on ladies," D.C. whispered to us. "I'll drive, leave your cars here."

"Hold up, we didn't say we were going with you. Mara snapped. "This is your bull, not ours. Go by your damn self."

"Come on now, Mara," D.C. pleaded. "Look at him. The man is fine, and from what I can see in that truck, so are the other two. It's only nine thirty. We can still be home at a decent hour."

"What you think, Jada? You in?" D.C. asked with innocent sad eyes.

"I don't care. I just don't want to be stuck, so I'll have to drive myself."

"See Mara, Jada's going. Will you PLEASE go with us?" D.C. begged.

"All right. Damn, I'll go, but I'm driving my own car too. I don't trust you."

We split off in separate directions heading for our cars. I turned to see if D.C. was getting her strut on like she always did when people were watching, and she was switching and twitching like never before.

2

Manipulated

I hadn't quite figured out how D.C. had convinced us to follow her and some strange men downtown, but she had. It was like she'd cast a spell on us. Ever since we were kids she could lure us into the strangest situations.

Every tight spot we've been in together Mara and I started off with a firm 'No', but then D.C's. persistence would win every time. It took me years to finally realize that she was a con artist and we were her main victims.

****

I wasn't in the mood to be at Nicolett's Café. Although it is a cool little club in downtown Houston, it was no place for Mara and me to be trying to entertain two men we didn't even know, and I hated myself for not sticking with my answer when we were at Pappadeaux's.

Unbelievably, when we arrived we found parking on the street. If we hadn't I would've really been in a foul mood. It was always so packed downtown on the weekends. You usually couldn't find a spot on any of the one way streets.

9

I pulled my pearl white Three thousand G.T in back of Mara's black Three twenty five BMW, and D.C.'s hunter green Lexus coupe. We looked like a little gang as we got out and clicked our alarms. The guys parked farther down the street, and I could hear and feel the bass in their truck, which let me know instantly I wasn't feeling them. I mean I liked music, but damn, I wasn't trying to roll around with a man that was still into blasting his music like we did in college.

"You ready, ladies?" D.C. said with confidence as she patted us on our backs like we were her children.

"Whatever," Mara answered. "I'm not going to be here all night with you, so let's get that straight now."

"You are always fussing Mara." D.C. laughed. "Can you please just relax and have some fun. There are three fine men in that truck over there, and who knows, maybe one of them is going to be your husband."

"I doubt that!" Mara snapped back. Jada and I don't even know what those other brothers look like."

Just as Mara was finishing her statement, the passenger's side of the truck opened, and out stepped Mr. Chocolate from the bar at Pappadeaux's.

There he was looking like he came right out of GQ Magazine.

"Damn, who is that?" Mara loudly mumbled.

Neither of us responded because the men were walking our way. The one D.C. had her eye on was fair skinned, very built and dressed in hip hop gear. He had on a pair of blue jeans, a colorful Coogi sweater with a matching hat that was turned backwards, and a pair of Timberland boots. He kind of resembled L.L.Cool J especially his lips and that dimple.

I saw when he smiled. He was very handsome, and by the way he licked his lips and checked us out, I could tell he knew it.

The other guy was tall and slender. He didn't appear to be as muscular as the other two, but he was well dressed in a black on black suit. He didn't have on a shirt and tie. Instead, he was wearing a beige sweater that was neatly tucked inside his pants. He looked like some sort of businessman.

The guy I had my eye on, was like something I can't explain. He had a beautiful mocha complexion and perfect goatee. Sexy was all that came to mind when I looked at him. His hair was faded, and he had a suave, Denzel walk. Everything about him was flawless. The man was wearing black pants with a sporty turquoise sweater. The sweater went well with his outfit and so did the leather jacket he was playin' that had just a touch of mink around the collar. I knew by looking at the jacket he couldn't have been from Houston. Our winters aren't cold enough for that kind of attire.

The diamond in his ear sparkled against his skin making him sexier.

"Ladies, I would like for you to meet some friends of mine." D.C. announced while we were standing in the parking lot.

Mara and I looked at each other with confused looks on our faces because we thought she didn't know the guys.

"Umm, Courtney, Michael and Duwayne, these are my girls Jada and Mara."

Mara and I shook their hands and said the usual, "It's a pleasure to meet you."

When I shook "Mr. Chocolate's" hand I felt a nervous flutter shoot through my stomach. He was so damn breathtaking! He had all the features a fine black man should have. His hair, goatee, eyebrows, and even his eyelashes looked like they could've been dipped in a bottle of jet black hair rinse by Clairol. His eyes were mesmerizing too. They were those full, yet slightly slanted bedroom eyes that could make a sista' weak at the knees.

D.C. and the Courtney guy walked ahead of us laughing and talking like they'd known each other for years. He even had his hand around her waist as they entered the club, and she softly giggled as he whispered in her ear. By the way she was acting I could tell they had more going on than a first date. Matter of fact, it all made sense to me now why she wanted to desperately follow, the so called strangers downtown to Nicollet's. Her sassy behind knew them all along and was apparently waiting for him to drive up when we were at the restaurant. That slick heifer had tricked us again!

Once at the door of the cafe, a tall man with dreads greeted us. We happened to get a big table in the back corner far enough away from the band where we could at least have a conversation. Since Nicolett's was a jazz set and restaurant, there was a little bit of everything going on inside. Folks were eating, dancing, and some just sitting around drinking, trying to enjoy the music.

We all took our seats, with Courtney scooting his chair so close to D.C., she might as well have sat in his lap. This left Mara and me in an awkward position. I was sitting next to Michael, and Mara next to Duwayne.

"So, where are you guys from?" Mara asked, trying to break the silence. D.C. and Courtney had their own thing going, whispering in each other's ears, being rude as hell.

"Oh, I'm from Chicago," Michael answered with a deep voice, and what about you ladies? Are you both from here?"

"Yes, actually we are all Houstonians," I chimed in.

"Houston has some very nice looking women," Duwayne replied with a sly smile.

"Yeah, you just happened to be sitting with the finest," Mara responded. We all laughed.

"And where might you be from?" I asked Duwayne.

"Oh, Baby, I'm from L.A., the land of the Lakers and so is my boy, Courtney."

"Oh really," Mara said excitedly like she was from there as well." I have some cousins that live out there, and I go every chance I get. What do you think about Rosco's chicken and waffles?"

Conversation was flowing between Mara and Duwayne, but nothing was happening for Michael and me. We both sat quietly, offering a smile here and there but no dialogue. *Every time I was given the opportunity to leave my mark, I'd screw up and get shy.*

"So, do you come here often?" he finally asked, saving me from having to think of something to say to him.

"Not too frequently."

Again there was silence.

The band seemed to get louder, and more people arrived out of nowhere and started dancing on the small dance floor. D.C., Courtney, Mara and Duwayne all got up, but Michael and I were still sitting.

He's obviously not interested in me, or he's got his eye on somebody else in here, I thought to myself. I looked down at my outfit to evaluate it. My size five Polo jeans were hugging my body, with my lavender fitted DKNY turtleneck. My waist length leather jacket was tied at the waist and my black leather Via Spiga boots added the finishing touches. I am not one to wear much make up, so I had on my usual black eyeliner, which accented my slanted dark eyes, and a dab of mascara.

I was pissed I had my hair pulled back into a ponytail, which was my favorite do. I had contemplated the night before on whether or not to hassle with washing and wrapping it myself, but I changed my mind because it was so time consuming. My hair is too thick and I hate dealing with it myself. That's why I usually let Toya fix it. She is the owner of the beauty salon that I frequent. She's sure to have my hair looking good in less than an hour.

I've been contemplating cutting my hair to my shoulders, because I can't style it any way except the ponytail. I must admit, the ponytail makes me look nice and sexy, like Sade.

"You wanna dance?" Michael finally asked as he admired how much fun the others seemed to be having.

"Sure," I said, as I took my jacket off.

He grabbed my hand and led us through the crowd to the dance floor as the band played a version of Janet Jackson's "That's the way love goes."

He had some nice moves. The cologne he was wearing turned me on. It smelled like my favorite fragrance, Burberry.

"Nice," he said as he checked me out from head to toe.

"Excuse me?"

"Oh, I was just saying that you look nice."

"Thank you," I replied nervously.

I really didn't have a clue if he meant I looked nice, or my dancing was nice, and I was too shy to ask. Hopefully he was thinking I was nice.

After the song, we walked back to our table, where Mara and Duwayne were already seated and talking. D.C. and Courtney were nowhere to be found. I looked around and didn't see them. I was relieved I'd driven my car.

"What time is it Jay?" Mara asked

"Almost midnight."

"Ooh, girl, we'd better get out of here. We have to drive clear to the other side of town and you know Houston ain't the country. Freaks come out at night, and there are plenty of them waiting to grab beautiful women like you and me."

I knew then that Mara wasn't digging Duwayne because if she were, our asses wouldn't have been going anywhere.

Mara reached for her coat, and so did I.

"Come on now ladies, just stay a little longer," Michael politely asked "If you do I promise, we'll personally escort each of you to your front doors to make sure you get in safely."

"Now you're really reaching, Mike," Duwayne butted in.

Mara turned and gave him one of her nasty looks. It definitely should have let him know he wasn't worth any more of her time.

"What do you want to do?" I said to Mara.

"I don't care." She replied

14

I was taking my coat back off, when one of the young ladies I saw in Michael's face at happy hour reappeared. She approached him from behind, wrapped her arms around his waist and whispered something in his ear. She was tall, thin, and dressed in a black fitted skin-tight dress, like the ones the group En Vogue used to wear. She appeared to be mixed with something because her skin was bronze, and her hair appeared to be a soft, silky texture.

Michael was trying to squirm his way out of her firm hold, but she held on tight. I read her lips while I stood behind them, not knowing what to do.

"Come on, Babe, you know you miss me," she said in his ear.

"Excuse me, Jada," he said in an aggravated tone and turned to begin a very unfriendly discussion with her. That's when Mara grabbed my arm and led me toward the door.

"Come on, girl. We don't have time for this kind of bullshit! Plus, I can't bear to hear anymore of that idiot Duwayne's lies."

I walked away in silence. I really didn't want to leave. I wanted to get to know him because I felt something. What it was, I didn't know? It just wasn't in my code of ethics to stick around while a man argued with another woman. I wasn't desperate!

"Where the hell is D.C.?" Mara asked once we got outside.

"I don't know. I think she left with that Courtney guy."

"I knew that girl knew him," Mara said with her hand on her hips, shaking her head like she was D.C.'s mother. Well come on, I'll follow you until we get to my exit. Put your seatbelt on, and have that cell right by you. I'll be calling" Mara instructed, like she was my elder.

"Ok, Girl, I'll talk to you later."

"Oh yeah, why did that lying ass Duwayne try to tell me he was a sports agent?" Mara said with an attitude.

"An agent for who?"

"Hell, I don't know. I'm sure he was lying about that too! See that's what I'm talking about with these sorry men. They are always lying, trying to impress somebody, in hopes of getting laid."

"So you think he was lying?"

Mara turned her lips up at me. "What do you think, Jay? Did that skinny little man look like an agent to you? I mean, don't agents dress a little classier than that?"

"I don't know. I've never met one before."

"Well, whatever. We're not going to even worry about it because I'm not interested. Be careful girl."

I drove off, desperately wanting to turn back. I wondered about the woman. As I was driving away, I looked in my rear view mirror. I saw him standing outside the club looking for someone. Was it me?

I slowed down, and almost made a u-turn to go back, but something wouldn't let me. Maybe it was the fear of rejection that made me keep going, so I shifted gears and sped off.

3

Christmas News

*T*he Galleria was undoubtedly my favorite shopping spot, especially at Christmas time. The decorations in the mall were creatively displayed. The gigantic fifty-foot Christmas tree that stood in the middle of the ice skating rink was phenomenal. It was always exciting to see the ice skaters gracefully swirl around it. The tree was sturdy and never swayed. I couldn't understand as a little kid how they got such a huge tree inside the mall, nor could I figure out how the decorator perfectly positioned each ornament.

For a Saturday afternoon it wasn't as crowded as I'd expected. There were lots of people at the mall, but not too many to where I couldn't maneuver in and out of the stores quickly. I had last minute gifts to purchase. Christmas was less than two weeks away. I was in a panic trying to get finished. It seemed like the closer Christmas got, the more people I added to my list.

As I was leaving the Coach store, my cell phone rang. It was D.C.'s number flashing on the screen.

"Hello."

"Jada, where are you?" she asked, sounding out of breath.

"I'm at the Galleria in the Coach store, and where the hell did you disappear to last night?" I asked.

"I'm in the Galleria too. Now, to answer your other question, Girl that's a long story. I'll have to tell you about it later.

We agreed to meet at Saks in the shoe department. She had something to show me. I couldn't imagine what since she was always full of surprises, or like Mara says, full of shit! Knowing her, she probably had purchased a ridiculously priced handbag and she needed my opinion. D.C. spends money like it grows on trees.

When I arrived at the shoe department, there she sat with boxes of shoes surrounding her.

"Hey girl!" she greeted, dressed career like, in black slacks, a white crisp blouse with black heels.

"What did you buy from the Coach store?" she asked

"Just a little something for Momma. She's been looking for another purse and I think I found one she would like."

While I was talking, D.C. was prancing around in a pair of dark brown Stuart Weitzman heels. She walked back and forth to the mirror checking them out. She didn't appear to be interested in what I was talking about at all.

"So what did you have to show me?" I asked, while showing my frustration.

"Girl, I have so much to tell you about last night. First of all, I think I'm in love with Courtney."

"Here we go again," I thought. I wasn't trying to hear another one of her love at first sight stories because she has a new saga every other month. D.C. falls in and out of love every time she meets someone, especially if he has money.

"Well, it was quite obvious you've known him for a while by the way the two of you were all hugged up. Why haven't you told us about him?"

"I don't know. I guess I was a little apprehensive, with him playing in the NFL and all. I didn't want to broadcast it until I knew where we stood.

"What – the NFL?"

"Girl, let me tell you," she said pulling my hands for me to have a seat next to her. "I met him at Morton's Steakhouse last month when I was there having lunch with a client. He came up to me and asked if we could talk after I finished. I was so impressed with his presentation and looks that I ended up saying bye to my client, and spending two hours talking to him. Jay, girl, I'm telling you, it was love at first sight. This man knows how to lay the wood and I must say I am sprung. I do mean in every way. Look at what he bought me.

D.C. held out her hand and there on her pinky finger was an elegant diamond band with ten perfectly round diamonds in it.

"Girl, it's platinum. I already had it checked. I know he spent at least a grand on it, because he got it from Torneau, you know, that expensive jewelry store here in the Galleria."

"D.C. **that** is sweet! I said with my mouth wide opened. "I can't believe he bought you something so soon."

"Actually he gave it to me when we were in Cancun last month, but I just got it back because he had to get it sized."

"Cancun?" I said surprised. "When did you go there?"

"Girl, that's another long story. I'll have to fill you in later on that one. Anyway what do you think?"

"I don't know what to say. What kind of brother is he?"

"One with some money, Baby, and that's all that matters. I think he makes at least a million a year, well that's what he told me, but I don't know if he is telling the truth or not. You know me though, I will find out. That is very pertinent information to this relationship."

"Dee, you've got to be kidding."

"Would I kid about something like this? You know I don't play when it comes to money. I'm telling you Jay, I'm not letting this one go. He's the right one girl, and as far as I'm concerned, he just met his match."

An NFL player was perfect for D.C. She wants to be in the spotlight. She'd already dated a couple of the Oilers before they left Houston six years ago and became the Tennessee Titans. If I'm not mistaken, she dated a few of the Rockets, as well. I don't know how she always ends up meeting high profile guys, but she does. Mara thinks D.C. is a groupie. I don't necessarily agree. I know she likes athletes, but I don't think she has to have one. In my opinion, Dee wants a man with money, whether he makes it running a ball or not.

Back in the day, she did date a football player in college named Dominic. He went pro and turned buck wild. He came back to visit her after his rookie season and I guess he thought he could say and do whatever he wanted. Dee cursed him out. In fact, she blacked out on him and threw so much shit at him that one of her neighbors had to call me to come and calm her down. By the time I got there, the place was torn up. The door was wide opened. Dominic was pinned in the bathroom with D.C. on the outside of the door swinging a butcher knife. I'd never seen her go that crazy.

"So what happened with you guys last night? Did either one of ya'll hook up with one of the guys?" she asked as she went to the register to buy the five pair of shoes she meticulously selected.

"Nothing happened. I don't think Mara particularly cared for Duwayne too much. I did think Michael was interesting, until this chick came up and whispered something in his ear, and they started having what sounded like a heated discussion, so I left after that."

"You left! Why did you do that? Did he ask you to leave?"

"No, I just wasn't going to stand there looking stupid, waiting for him to finish whatever he was doing with her. You know that's not me."

20

D.C. was looking at me like I'd said the most ignorant thing she'd ever heard.

"You never cease to amaze me Jay. As pretty and as smart as you are, you have no backbone. There is no way in hell you were supposed to leave that man talking to her. Did you at least leave him on a good note—meaning, did he get your number?"

"No. I told you I left, and he didn't see me leave. I walked away when his back was turned."

D.C. stopped walking, and stared at me. "Are you crazy? That brother is fine, and might I add rich as hell too. Matter of fact he's more well off than Courtney."

"What—He plays ball too?"

"Does he play ball? Hell yeah he plays ball, and he's been playing for about nine or ten years now. You've never heard of Michael Riley, from the Oakland Raiders?"

"Girl, you know I don't watch football."

"Well, he was one of the Bulls first veteran picks. I know they had to have paid him at least a million to sign. Not to mention, he might make around five million a year. Oooh, just thinking about it makes my mouth water. I can't imagine what his contract looks like. There's going to be all kinds of women on his tip. We can't let him slip away."

"Well, I'm not about to chase a man. I don't care how much he's worth. Damn it, I'm worth a lot too."

"I'm feelin' you, 'Sista'," D.C. agreed, holding her hand up for me to high five her. "But don't be no fool. You can't let shit like that slide by."

****

When I returned home from the Galleria, I went in my bathroom and looked at myself in my full-length mirror. I was attractive enough to be with an NFL player even though I wasn't light skinned or white like the women I'd seen them with on TV. I am, if I must say so my self, a very pretty brown skinned black woman.

I took my hair out of the usual ponytail and fluffed it with my hands.

Then I turned around and checked out my back view to see if it was still perfect. My back and arms were toned from all the weight lifting I had been doing. My tight round butt was just what any man would want. I was very satisfied with my physique, as were all the men I dated.

I unbuttoned my blouse just a little where I could see more cleavage from my 34B breast size. I re-fluffed my hair, and took one last look in the mirror. I liked what I was seeing, I always had. That man had missed out on a fine brown sugar!

4
Home Sweet Home

Sunday was always my day to relax. I usually tried to make it to early morning church service, and then run the few errands I hadn't completed on Saturday. I never did too much except for when it was time to make my twenty-minute drive to Third Ward to visit Momma.

Third Ward is my favorite part of the city. Not just because I grew up there, but because it is so full of history, history from Texas Southern University on to the University of Houston. It was always strange to me how they built a black and white university right next to one another, dead smack in what most would call the "hood."

Parts of Third Ward are now considered the "ghetto" to those who don't know any better. There is still a lot of history and black revenue in the area. Most of the professors used to live there and still do, as well as other prominent people. The homes in the area are sturdy and complete with amenities like real hard wood floors, and crafty crown moldings. You can look at them and tell they are worth a fortune, opposed to their dollar value fifteen to twenty years ago.

It's funny how everyone in Houston, who has any knowledge of the city, is trying to reinvest money back into this particular community. People are moving to the inner city, renovating the older homes while downtown is being redeveloped. The economics of this urban development plan connects the Wards boundaries to downtown, increasing their value as well.

Momma couldn't leave the neighborhood. I remember a few years after Daddy passed, she considered selling our two story home. I begged her not to sell it, so she leased it to a woman that was working on her doctorate at Texas Southern University. She bought Ms. Jackson's one story house around the corner because she didn't want to leave the neighborhood or her friends and she couldn't handle the maintenance of such a large home.

My parents, both professors at TSU were married for thirty-six years and spent over half of those years in that home. They never considered moving due to the fact that the university was located right across the street. Momma was known in the education department where she'd been for thirteen years, and Daddy was considered the best history professor the school had to offer. Needless to say, they were both very popular in the community, and when he passed, we were shown much love and support.

****

When I got to Momma's subdivision it was about six o'clock in the evening and everyone's Christmas lights were on. It was beautiful to see the entire neighborhood lit up, a yearly tradition. Everyone competed in the annual contest. They even had tours of the houses. The public could purchase a fifteen to twenty dollar ticket from one of the black organizations in Houston and enjoy a tour of the beautiful Christmas décor of the homes on the inside and out.

Man, the memories are coming back.

I smiled when I got to our house because it looked like the house Chevy Chase decorated in National Lampoon's Christmas Vacation. There were lights everywhere! Don't get me wrong, it was out of sight, but too much for me.

Momma had white lights on the roof, in the tress, up the sidewalk, and outlining the landscape. To top that off, there was a Santa perched on the roof with a spotlight on him, looking like he was going down the chimney.

"Momma, I'm here!" I announced as I let myself in with my key.

"Hey, Baby," she called back "Come back here to the office."

The inside of the house was gorgeous. There were red Poinsettias, Garland, and Holly all over the place. Her collection of black Santas were everywhere, and the smell of her favorite cinnamon candle filled the place. I stopped to admire the nine-foot Christmas tree as I walked to her office. It was the best I'd seen. She had it covered in white lights, with crystal red and green bulbs. These weren't your average bulbs though. These were the rather expensive ones you find in a department store. You know the ones a lot of us walk right past, but later try to find an imitation.

Everything she purchased was top of the line. If she couldn't get the best, she didn't get anything. Settling was not an option. My mother was a proud, intelligent woman who did not believe in half stepping on anything.

"Hey, Sweetheart," She said, joining me at the tree and giving me a kiss on my cheek. "Do you like it?"

"Momma, this is beautiful. Who helped you do this?"

"Well, your Aunt Erma came by last weekend and gave me a hand, and Girl, we had a time getting this big thing in here and putting all those lights on," she laughed.

"You guys did a great job. This is the best one you've ever done."

"Well, thank you, Baby. How do you like the outside? You already saw that last week didn't you?"

"Yeah, but I didn't see that Santa up there."

"Honey, your Uncle James put him up the other day for me. Isn't he cute? You see he painted his face black," she giggled.

"Why doesn't that surprise me?" I smiled.

Momma walked to the kitchen and I followed. She had a full spread on the stove, and I peeked in the pots. There were black eyed peas, collard greens, roast beef, macaroni and cheese, and of course my favorite, cornbread.

"Momma, you cooked too much food. It's just you and me."

"I can't help it baby. I'm just used to cooking all that food for your daddy. You would think with this being the third year without LaVell, I would have cut back by now, but I can't. He liked big Sunday dinners and that's just tradition. When I have some grandkids, it will be just fine," she smiled.

I was sick of her hinting about grandkids. Hell, I didn't even have a man, so how could I have kids.

Things were different without Daddy, but we were adjusting. My parents were everything to me and I never imagined that Daddy would be taken away from me before he could walk me down the aisle and give me away.

He and Momma were in a car accident one rainy day coming from visiting my aunt in Jacksonville, TX. He apparently fell asleep at the wheel and was thrown from the vehicle.

Momma sustained a few broken ribs and a broken arm, but unfortunately Daddy didn't survive. Thank God it wasn't both of them or else I really would have been devastated.

It was a shock for all of us, especially since he had just retired, and was starting to relax and enjoy life. He was golfing on a regular basis, and he also had been spending a lot of time with his best friend Mr. Shad, fishing on the weekends.

Daddy was a hard-working man, and I adored him. He treated me and momma like queens. He took us to fine places, opened doors, took care of our home and made sure we had money. We never wanted for anything!

LaVell Ballard was a real good man. The kind of man I hoped to find someday.

After Momma and I ate, we sat down in the family room and she slipped in my favorite movie "Claudine" with Diane Carol and James Earl Jones. Momma found a record shop where she ordered all of my favorite old movies and CD's.

"So how are your buddies doing?" she asked as she stretched out on the couch.

"They're fine. I was with them Friday night. Mara is still a smart mouth, and you know D.C. is definitely still arrogant" I laughed.

"D.C. just met a football player about a month ago, and now she's head over heels in love with him."

"She's always in love, isn't she?" Momma said smiling with a hint of sarcasm. "I would figure she would try to catch an athlete. A teacher or a man with a regular job would not be able to support her."

I shrugged my shoulders because deep down I hated I even mentioned it to her. I knew where this conversation would lead.

"Her momma is the same way. I tell you that white woman has dated more black men than I have. I mean look at her, she's been married two times to two different Negroes, and both of them had money. Now what makes you think D.C. wouldn't go for the same lifestyle. She's doing what she knows. The apple can't fall too far from the tree, you know."

I had never thought of it like that. Momma had the tendency to bring light to different situations for me.

"Momma, I met one of the football players last night as well. He is a nice guy and very attractive. He…"

"Jay, Baby," Momma interrupted "Don't judge a book by it's cover. Just because he is nice looking and appears to be nice doesn't mean a thing. These women around here are going crazy over this new team, and I don't want to see you getting hurt fooling around with somebody that isn't going to be truthful. You don't need all of that in your life, Baby. You just don't."

Momma discouraged me from telling her the rest of the story. She was such a no nonsense person, that it was difficult to get advice from her about anything concerning relationships, so I just forgot it, and continued to watch my movie.

5
The Clinic

*H*onestly, I don't know how she pulled it off," I said to Dr. Rotsworth, as I flipped through the article on Andrea Yates, the Houston woman who drowned all five of her children. I'm telling you, the woman has got to be insane to do something like that. I mean, how can you drown your own kids? Five of them at that! How the hell do you feel sorry for a woman that took five babies' lives, especially her own?

We both became silent.

"I do know one thing for sure," the Doc added. "The media needs to stop trying to make her husband out to be some kind of hero. I'm sick of looking at him every time I turn on the television. It's like one minute I feel sorry for the man, and then the next, I'm mad at him for not paying attention to his wife. If he had been watching, then maybe those children would still be alive."

****

I love my job at the clinic and I especially adored my boss, Dr. Richard Rotsworth. He is the owner and founder of

Rotsworth Rehabilitation Clinic. He's a very intelligent man and he knows the occupational and physical therapy field exceptionally well. He graduated from Baylor University in Waco, Texas and continued at the University of Houston to receive both his Masters' and Doctorate degrees.

The Doc is "the man" in my eyes. He has traveled all over the world working on research projects. The man is unbelievably intelligent! His clinic on Martin Luther King Drive comes highly recommended in Houston by all races. His business is in the inner city, but he treats patients from all over the world. It was an honor when I landed a job with him because everybody in physical therapy at Texas Womens' University wants to work for him.

Even though the Doc is one of the best in his field and is well respected in Houston, he is still your typical man. He always has at least three relationships going on at the same time.

The problem with him is that he is too nice looking to be sixty years old. He's about six feet tall, with smooth dark brown skin. He kind of puts you in the mind of Jim Brown, except he has salt and pepper hair. I know exactly why all the women in town want a piece of him. He's single, rich, fine, and that six series Benz he drives makes him even more irresistible.

****

"What's up everybody?" Mara asked when she entered my office.

"Good morning." I greeted. "Hey, what do you think about the woman who drowned her children?"

"Oh, her again. I'm sick of hearing about it. Every time I turn on the television, I have to look at her pitiful looking behind. They need to quit wasting air-time on her because I don't care what anybody says, if her family had been paying close attention to her, they would've picked up on something. You know?"

"I know. That's what the Doc just said."

"It's a sad thing. Can you imagine how terrified those children were?" Mara said softly with tears in her eyes.

It was interesting to me how Mara could be so cold one minute, and then teary eyed the next. Throughout our years of friendship, I finally figured out who and what could soften her personality. Those things included her mother and her love for children. Mara had an undying love for kids, especially under privileged and sick ones. Why? I didn't know, but there was definitely a soft spot there. Mara faithfully volunteered at our old neighborhood youth center and to my surprise, she even became a big sister for The Girls and Boys Club. I admired her for trying to make a difference.

Mara had been working at the clinic for a couple of months to help the Doc legally prepare for his next clinic opening. She has a degree in Law, but has not passed the bar exam yet. For some reason she refused to work anywhere near a law firm until she has completed the bar. In her eyes, she didn't feel legitimate until that requirement was fulfilled.

The Doc needed legal assistance so I encouraged him to recruit her to help out with the phones and other matters for a couple of months. He was always trying to help a sista' out. It has been a real pleasure having her around, and since there are only four therapists, including myself, adding her aboard completed our little family.

"Good morning, gang" Colin greeted, as he entered the building.

Colin was one of our four therapists. He was the new kid on the block and he thought he was the man! He attended Duke University where he graduated at the top of his class. He is supposedly super intelligent, but of course I wasn't too impressed because he hasn't done anything special to make me think that. I graduated at the top of my class as well.

The Doc insisted that Colin was brilliant, but to me he appeared to be just another know it all pretty boy.

Mara, on the other hand, thought Colin was the man! She liked the geeky look he tended to portray. I was shocked because for some reason she was usually attracted to the rough neck type brother. Colin was hardly that. His work gear was a pair of Dockers and a crisp white Polo shirt. Mara had her eye on him from the first day she started to work with us.

"Good morning, Colin" Mara said in one of her seductive tones. I smiled and shook my head as I watched him blush.

Mara was extremely forward and a lot of people couldn't handle it. She was one of those beautiful full-bodied women who looked like she came out of a fashion magazine all the time. Her makeup was always in place, matching to a tee, and not a wrinkle in her clothes. Her hands and feet stayed manicured. She may have been a little thick, but trust me, she had no problem getting a man. She **kept** a man, and the funny thing is that they were always thinner than she was.

I laughed as I watched her maneuver around my office pretending to be doing paper work. She was strutting every which way, and Colin was trying his best to pay her no mind, but every once in a while I'd see his eyes cut in her direction from underneath his glasses. I knew the two of them had been screwing around for a while, but I never said a thing. Mara thought I didn't know until one day we were out to lunch, and I came straight out and asked her. You should have seen her face!

"How did you know?" she asked, still looking surprised that I had busted her.

"Girl, I *peeped* you two a long time ago and I know how you roll. So—can he bone or what?" I asked, making her choke on her drink.

She smiled, showing off her flawless teeth.

"Since you know how I roll—do you think I'd be wasting my time if he couldn't?"

****

"Jada, can you do me a favor tomorrow?" Colin asked.

"What?" I answered "You already owe me from about ten other favors," I reminded him.

"I know, I know, but this is serious. I have this football player that just got traded from the Raiders, and he has knee and back problems. He's trying to get ready for camp in July and he really wants to be healed before that time comes."

"So why do you need me? It doesn't take two people to work out one person," I said, shutting down his offer.

"It does when you want to be as thorough as I'm trying to be."

"Come on now, Jada. Help a brother out. You know I'm trying to build my clientele to only athletes, and this is my first big one, that is my first big time African American one. You know it's hard to work with these ghetto athletes. That's why I only try to stick with the white boys because I don't have to deal with the late arrivals, no payments, and no shows. But this guy seems to be altogether different. I've heard he is very intelligent, and dominates the field. He might be the *baddest* veteran player the Bulls picked!"

I flashed back to the guy I'd met at the club on Friday night, and became irritated again.

"Jada! Snap out of it! Can you help me or what?" Colin asked again, breaking up my flashback.

"Yes Colin, I will but you'll owe me big time, and I swear the first time he says something ignorant, I'm going off! I just got rid of that crazy ass Shakeem after almost a year, and I don't want to be bothered with anybody else trying to holla', talking slick!"

"I know Jada, and trust me I don't think this guy is like that. Actually I think he's a little shy?"

"Whatever, Colin. I doubt that. Let's not forget that you're the man that still thinks O.J. is drug free."

"Here we go with that again" he said, throwing his hands up in the air like he was giving up on arguing with me.

"Are you going to do it or what?"

"I said I would, but you just better be ready to treat me to lunch for an entire week."

"Don't leave your girl out now," Mara smiled over at me, and winked at him.

"Oh yeah, Mara, has to come too," I added.

Mara and I looked at each other and laughed.

6
The Client

When I got to work the next day there was a black Jaguar parked in my spot. I wondered if Dr. Rotsworth had driven one of his women's cars because it was too early in the morning for any clients to be here. It was only eight in the morning, and most of us didn't usually have appointments until around nine or nine thirty. Colin's red Navigator was there and so was Janine's Volvo, but they are always early.

I pulled in next to the Jag and turned off the Yolanda Adams CD. I enjoy listening to her in the mornings. It helps to get my mind right. I know I need to designate my morning drive to music that keeps me in tune with God however, sometimes I slip, and my radio is blasting 97.9 or 102.1, Houston's popular black stations.

The Jag was irresistible so I couldn't help but take a peek at the inside. The beige leather interior was blemish free with not a crack in sight. I imagined the new car smell that I like so much as I continued peeking.

"Ooooh. You are sweet," I said, as I stepped back and checked out the rims. At that point I knew the vehicle belonged to a man and not one of the Doc's women.

I walked in and didn't see or hear anyone, so I went straight to my office to check my messages. Shakeem called three times, begging and pleading for me to come to a bar on Richmond Avenue to hear him play. No way! Once I'm done, I'm done! He is crossed off my list. I can't explain why I ever started a relationship with a man, whose dream is to start his own band at the age of thirty-five. In my opinion, a brother his age should be focusing on investments and retirement, not what his next gig will be.

Since Shakeen couldn't keep a job and insisted on trying to be Mr. Playa', I had to cut him loose. True enough he is fine as wine, but the brother needs some benefits.

My other messages were from clients canceling their appointments.

"Jada, I didn't know you were here," Colin blurted as he peeked into my office.

"Damn, you trying to give me a heart attack, sneaking up on me like that?"

"I need your help in the pool. My client is here. You know the one I was telling you about yesterday."

I let out a sigh, letting him know I wasn't in the mood.

"Come on Jada. You promised."

"O.k, I'm coming. Where are you guys again?"

"IN THE POOL" he answered in his usual smart alecky tone. "So get your stuff on."

I put on my navy Speedo bathing suit with swim shorts on top because I wasn't trying to flaunt anything in front of this man. Plus, I thought it was more professional to be covered up at work; that way I wouldn't have any trouble. I put my hair up in a high ponytail, slipped on my flip flops and headed toward the pool.

Colin and the client were taking laps when I got there. It looked like they were racing.

The guy appeared to be tall, very tall from what I could see. I walked to the end where they were due to finish and put my feet in the water. It was warm, which let me know Colin had come in early and heated it up. As the guy got closer to me he started to look familiar. I couldn't help but admire his toned physique as he neared me. When he finished and raised his head out of the water, I nearly passed out when I realized it was my man from Friday night. The tight bodied sexual chocolate, Michael.

He cleared the water from his face, and when he focused in on me, he gave me the same mesmerizing smile he'd given me the other night, making me weak at the knees all over again.

I couldn't believe he was in my presence.

Okay. Jada, calm down, you're breathing too hard.

Colin was reaching the finish line when we started talking.

"Well, well, well if it isn't the mystery lady" he smiled.

His voice made chills shoot up and down my spine. I was still on cloud nine and I knew the smile I displayed let him know I was more than elated to be in his presence.

"Oh, Jada, this is Mr. Michael Riley" Colin panted.

"Colin, Man, I've already had the pleasure of meeting Ms. Jada," Michael announced, still staring and smiling at me.

"Oh, really," Colin answered with a confused look on his face.

"We met the other night through a friend," I added.

"Well good. We can skip all the introductions and get to work."

Colin could be so corny at times.

"You're not going to pull a disappearing act on me again like you did the other night are you?" he asked, walking closer to where I was sitting.

My stomach started rumbling. I was positive he could hear it.

"No, I'm not."

"You sure?"

"Yes, I'm sure" I smiled.

I sat in front of him, looking at his chocolate chest as water dripped off of him. His muscles were bigger than I'd imagined.

****

Colin and I gave him a good workout. We raced him in the pool swimming and walking. We stretched and worked his body thoroughly. I was glad I was able to help. Matter of fact I wished he were my client because I didn't totally agree with the regimen Colin had developed for him. Colin was one of the best, but I was better.

Michael had previously blown out his right knee and you could see the surgery cuts around it. He needed to do a lot of work to strengthen it before the season started in eight months. I couldn't see how he was still playing because of his back and neck troubles. Poor guy. His NFL career had really banged him up.

****

I wasn't sure whether Michael was going to still be at the clinic when I came out the ladies room, but just in case he was, I put on a little lip gloss and a touch of eye liner so I wouldn't look too worn out. I slipped on my jeans, and my white Rotsworth Rehabilitation staff shirt. It wasn't the least bit cute, especially since I had Nike Jogging shoes to go with it, but oh well. How was I supposed to know he was going to surface?

When I came out the locker room, he was waiting for me on a bench that sat in a small waiting area.

"It took you long enough," he smiled, showing me the dimple in his left cheek.

"I didn't know you were waiting for me" I blushed.

"Hey, I couldn't let you get away twice. Could I? You know you did a brother wrong the other night; leaving like that without even saying goodbye."

"Well, you seemed a little preoccupied, and I didn't want to cause you any more trouble."

"Please. That was nothing. She was just…"

"You know what, don't even worry about," I said, cutting him off. "How about we start over." I stuck my hand out for him to shake it, and said, "Hello, my name is Jada Ballard, and yours?"

If I'm not mistaken, he appeared to blush a little. I'm glad I took charge of the situation.

"Hello, Ms. Ballard. I'm Michael Riley. It's a pleasure to meet you."

Now we were both blushing from ear to ear like two kids.

"Ms. Ballard, may I have the opportunity to take you out to dinner so we can get better acquainted?" he asked, still holding my hand.

When, when, when? I was thinking.

"I would like that."

I wrote my number down on the back of one of my business cards and my hand shook uncontrollably. It hadn't felt that good giving the digits out in a long time.

****

"I like your car," I softly complimented. "Jags are my favorite, even though you're parked in my space."

He laughed. "That's your car over there isn't it?" he pointed.

"Yeah, how did you know?"

"Well, because I watched you speed away from me Friday night, but you didn't see me. I came outside looking for you after my discussion with that young lady, but you were already driving away."

"Oh, I'm sorry. I didn't know you came after me." *I couldn't believe I was lying.*

39

"Well, you know what? If you have dinner with me tonight, I'll consider forgetting about how you played me?"

"Oh will you?"

"Only if you have dinner with me." he smiled and winked.

If he only knew he was saying exactly what I wanted to hear.

"I would love to."

"Cool, cool" he said, as he clasped his hands together. I'll call you around six. Is that o.k?"

"That's fine."

"See ya later, Ms. Jada," he said, giving me one last wink.

"Bye."

Mara pulled in as he was driving off. I stood and waited for her to park.

"Damn girl, was that 'ole boy from the other night?" she asked.

"YES—IT—WAS! and you aren't going to believe this, but he's Colin's client. You know the one he was begging me to help him with yesterday."

"You're lying."

"NO—I'M—NOT, and he is so nice looking to me. What do you think?"

"Girl, I'm with you, that brother ain't no slouch. Let's just hope he's not gay or something?" Mara laughed.

"Thanks Mara, that was helpful." I said sarcastically. "I hadn't even thought of that."

7

Lunch

*I*t was a beautiful day outside. I could hardly believe Christmas was only seven days away. Houston's weather could be eighty degrees one day, and forty the next. We never know what to wear! You could have on a sweater in the morning and by evening have on a short sleeve blouse. I usually try to dress with the seasons, unlike some Houstonians who find nothing wrong with wearing a white outfit in the middle of January.

Mara and I cruised down Westheimer, one of the busiest streets in the city, while Jill Scott crooned through the system. I love Jill, and so does she. I'm sure we looked like idiots as we sang the lyrics to "Do You Remember?" on our way to meet D.C. for lunch at the Cheesecake Factory.

Surprisingly, D.C. was already there when we arrived.

"What's up, Ladies?" she greeted, standing to give us both hugs like she hadn't seen us two days ago.

I noticed her new hairdo. It was flat ironed with extra highlights shining through. Her nails were freshly done, and she was glowing more than I was.

"I like your do," Mara said as soon as we sat down. "I thought you were sick of the straight look. What made you change your mind?"

"My man, girl," she replied happily. "Honey he paid for me to get my hair done at a salon in Rice Village yesterday. You know over where the ritzy folks go. Anyway, he stayed with me, and told the lady exactly how he wanted it done, and the color he wanted added. Wasn't that nice of him?"

D.C. rambled on, and I sat amazed at what I was hearing. She never let a man dictate anything, especially a decision on her appearance. This was totally out of character for her I thought.

"I can't believe you let him make that call for you," I said, looking at her like she'd lost her mind.

"Well Baby when you got a man as good as mine, and he wants to do nice things for you, you're not supposed to tell him no. Hell, another woman wouldn't turn him down. I ain't stupid now."

"Well, do you like it?" Mara asked.

"It's alright. I've worn my hair like this before, so it's really no big deal. Anyway, enough about me. Jada, tell me why you were sounding so happy on the phone today when I called? What's up?"

"You're not going to believe this, Dee, but Michael, the guy from the other night; you know, the one you introduced me to, Colin is rehabbing him before the season starts."

"Are you serious? What did you do when you saw him?"

"I damn near passed out. I couldn't believe it! Colin had asked me to help him with a client, but by no means did I think it was him."

"Honey, that brother is fine!" Mara said as she sipped on her Margarita.

"He is nice looking," D.C. agreed. "So did he ask you out, or did you scare him away like the last time?"

"Girl, he asked me to go to dinner with him tonight. All day I've been thinking about what to wear, and how to fix my hair. I don't know whether to wear jeans with a blazer, or go for a fitted sweater dress with my knee high Gucci boots.

"Definitely not the jeans" D.C. advised. "That's too many damn clothes girl. He won't be able to see what you got."

Mara looked at the ceiling like she thought D.C.'s comment was ridiculous.

"I'd go for whatever shows a little flesh," D.C. continued.

"And don't we know you would," Mara mumbled with an air of sarcasm.

D.C. put up her middle finger.

"Well, I guess I have to go out into the mall and help you pick something, 'cause' if you don't have anything to wear I'm always in the mood for some shopping girl" D.C. suggested.

"Damn, Dee. You've been doing a lot of shopping lately. Did you get a raise or something?" Mara asked. "Or are you selling crack now instead of pharmaceutical supplies?"

"No, I didn't get a raise, and no I'm not selling crack. I'm just rollin' with a baller," she replied with arrogance.

"Whatever. You better make sure that man ain't married, or got somebody else in another city that he's wining and dining too."

D.C. had a frustrated look on her face. "Mara, you can't ever be happy for nobody. I don't rain on your parade when you're in love. Why are you always dogging me out?"

"For one, I don't fall in love, and for two, I'm not dogging you out. I just want you to keep your eyes and ears open. This man has come in here and started buying you shit and giving you money and you have barely known him a month. You know there's got to be something wrong with him. It may not be something as serious as a wife, but I ain't never met a man without at least a few skeletons in his closet. Especially a black man."

"I don't want to talk about it. If you're gonna hate on me with what I got going on, then I just won't tell you anything else."

"Fine, suit yourself. I'm just trying to have your back. Don't get too exited until you've investigated everything. Ain't no brother that good!"

The waitress came and took our order at the right time because it was getting a little heated. They'd had disagreements before, but this was pretty intense. I was relieved it was interrupted.

****

When I got home I checked my messages to see if Michael had called, and he hadn't, so I went to my closet to pick out something to wear just in case he did. After pondering which outfit to wear, I decided I'd ask him where we were going just to be on the safe side. I selected my brown sweater dress with the V-neck collar that showed a little flesh, like D.C suggested. I had the perfect boots to wear with it.

Just as I was getting out of the shower, the phone rang. It was five fifteen. I checked my caller I.D. to make sure it wasn't Shakeem, or one of my other nuisance friends. The "unavailable" on the screen forced me to answer.

"Hello."

"Hello. Jada, please."

I knew it was Michael. I'd recognize that sexy voice if I were in a tunnel with a hundred other men.

"Speaking."

"I'm glad you answered, Ms. Jada. I was wondering if you were going to play me."

"Why would I do that?" I asked, smiling from ear to ear.

"I don't know, but for some reason, I think you're full of surprises."

"Don't you like surprises?" I responded in my low soft voice.

"Why don't you surprise me and tell me you're still available for dinner tonight?"

"I sure am. What did you have in mind?"

"Well, I'm new here, so I was hoping you'd give me a little assistance with choosing the restaurant. I love seafood, but I've been to Pappadeaux's a million times already. I keep hearing there are loads of other places I need to try, but I don't know where to start."

"Hmmm," I said, stalling, trying to think of a place I liked. "Well, how about I ask what kind of mood you're in. Meaning, are you dressed up or down?"

I was glad I had the opportunity to slip that in.

"Actually, Sweetheart, I'm in jeans. I mean, if you want me to dress up I can."

"No, no. I just didn't know what you wanted to do." I answered, relieved he wasn't in a suit and tie.

"How about you tell me how to get to your house, and we'll figure out the rest once I get there," he laughed.

I gave him directions. His location left me with at least thirty minutes to get ready. After we said our good-byes, I continued to get dressed. I slipped on my dress, took my hair down and started curling each layer so it would fall correctly.

At six thirty, my doorbell rang. I checked myself in the bathroom mirror, and did a quick survey of my house to make sure everything was in place. I am somewhat of a neat freak, so I didn't have to worry about the appearance of my little townhouse. It stayed tidy.

I took one last deep breath before I answered the door. His cologne slapped me in the face once again. I love a man that smells good.

"Hello," I said, feeling my family of butterflies returning.

"How are you?" he said

I stood back to welcome him in. Hummm. I liked what I saw.

"Nice place," he said as he strolled over to my fireplace and looked at the few pictures I had on the mantle.

"Oh, so you're a Delta?" he said, looking at a picture of Mara and me in college after we pledged.

"Yes, I am. Did you pledge?" I asked

"And you know it."

"You're an Omega aren't you?"

"How'd you guess? So what's up soror?" he smiled.

Just great, I thought to myself. Another damn Q dog. I didn't want to think about how many women he'd probably dogged. I checked out his attire, as he rambled a little about getting beat when he was on line. As he talked I glanced him over on the sly. He had on a nice pair of blue jeans, a black fitted sweater and another very classy leather jacket. His boots were nice and polished.

"Those were the good old days, weren't they?" he laughed.

"Yeah, they were," I agreed, knowing I hadn't really heard a word he'd said for being mesmerized by his looks.

I got my jacket and he helped me put it on.

"You have some nice African art in here. Do you collect it?"

"Yeah, just a little. Actually, I like to antique shop, so some of my pieces I found at different shops in town, and some I got through travels. I haven't exactly visited Africa yet to get all those masks and other pieces, but who would know."

"You have really good taste. I like your ethnic touch. Maybe you can help me decorate my place."

"I'd love to."

He opened my door and we walked out. As I tried to lock my deadbolt, my hand shook, as it always did when I was excited or nervous, so I closed my eyes and said a quick prayer.

"Please, God, let this one be normal."

8

Dinner Date

Michael and I talked about our childhood as we drove to P.F. Chang, an elite Chinese restaurant on Westheimer. Since he'd already had seafood and Mexican food at the city's most popular restaurants, I suggested something different.

We talked non-stop about my middle class upbringing and his childhood in the projects of Chicago. Even though he was now a millionaire, he was a very down to earth man. I'd always gotten the impression that athletes were arrogant and egotistical. I was pleased he wasn't. His polite demeanor was unreal, and I reflected on how Mara had warned D.C. about people's skeletons. I wondered what skeletons he could have. Would I get my feelings hurt dealing with him?

I knew on our first date, I shouldn't be thinking that deeply about it, but he had it going on and, I didn't want anything to go wrong.

The valet took Michael's keys to park his blue, five series Mercedes, which might I add was just as **tough** as the Jaguar I'd seen earlier. He extended his hand for me to take his, and I thought "What a romantic gesture for our first date."

Most of my dates in the past didn't have the decency to wait for me to get out the car, let alone valet park.

We entered the restaurant hand in hand, and I felt like a queen. His grip was firm, but gentle, providing me with the security I wanted.

"Yes, may we have a table for two please?" He asked the hostess in a confident commanding voice. **I love a man who knows what he wants.**

We were seated in a cozy corner that blocked the world out. Although we could hear the commotion in the restaurant, we weren't in the mix of everything. Michael helped me with my chair and asked if our seating was o.k. "This is fine, just fine," I responded as I picked up my menu and began reviewing it.

"So, Ms. Jada, what do you usually order when you come here?"

"I love their shrimp fried rice because it's spicy."

"Oh, so you like spicy food?"

"Yes, and I can't help it with both of my parents being from New Orleans. Everything I ate as a child was spiced up with Cajun fixings."

"I bet it was heaven being in a household like that." He said.

When the waiter came to take our order, we were ready. Michael ordered the peppered steak, and I ordered the chicken fried rice.

"So, what made you study physical therapy? He asked, looking in my eyes with half a smile on his face."

I was enjoying his interest.

"I've always been intrigued with the body. My mother says when I was a kid I wanted to be a doctor so I could help sick people. Also, my cousin Stephanie was born with Cerebral Palsy and as a kid I would go to therapy with her. I memorized her exercises and stretches and I loved listening to her therapist talk to my Aunt Mimi about her condition. It's weird how I remembered everything they discussed even when I was in college.

My cousin is a tough cookie though. Her disability doesn't affect her determination. Right now she's working on her Master's Degree. I admire her more than anyone in this world, and actually she was my inspiration for becoming a therapist.

"Do the two of you stay in touch?"

"Maybe once a month. She's pretty busy with school, and I'm busy with work."

"Well I'm glad you took time to go out with little 'ole me" Michael smiled, as he reached across the table and caressed my hand.

A silent moment fell upon us, as we stared into each other's eyes. It was like I had been hypnotized. *He is my dream man,* I thought.

"Be careful, the plates are hot," the waitress announced, interrupting our moment.

"Excuse me, Michael, I need to go to the ladies room."

He stood, and politely dismissed me from the table. As I walked to the bathroom, I knew he was watching me, so I tried to add more flavor to my strut, the way D.C did. It works for her, so it had to work for me.

When I got to the ladies room and looked in the mirror, there was a smile on my face and in my eyes that hadn't been there in a while.

I straightened my clothes, checked my lipstick, and fixed my hair. Everything had to be perfect for my return to Mr. Chocolate. After a few minutes, I inhaled and headed back to our table.

"Do your thing girl," I mumbled to myself.

As I approached the table, I noticed him throwing something into his mouth and drinking water.

"Are you o.k.?" I asked once I got to my seat.

"Oh I'm fine. I just forgot to take my vitamins."

"Well it's good you take them. I'm sure your body needs something extra with all you go through.

"Yeah, we get hit pretty hard out there, but after ten years I'm used to it."

"So tell me more about yourself. How do you like the NFL?"

"What can I say but . . . the NFL is the NFL. I love it, every rough and dirty part of it?

"What do you love about it?" I probed further. "I mean, it seems so cut-throat, the way they get rid of players. I don't understand how it works, but every once in a while I'll hear on the news about somebody being released, or a coach that was fired. What do those guys do when they pull the rug from underneath them without any notice?"

"Well the players already know, that NFL, really stands for "Not For Long," so when shit happens, you do what you got to do. It can end at any moment, either by injury, or just when they don't want you anymore. That's why a lot of us try to invest and open up businesses while we're still in, so we can have something to fall back on when it's over. We try to hold on, even though we know it's a cut throat business."

"Did you have the opportunity to finish college?" I innocently asked.

Michael laughed.

"I like the way you put that, Jada. Most people ask a little more sarcastically than that. Kind of like "I know you've finished school by now with all the time you have had in the off season. Actually, to answer your question, I did finish my degree in Communications."

"That's interesting." I said

"Yeah, I guess. I just finished a year ago. Don't ask me why it took me so long, but when you're making money it's hard to go back. Plus, I went through a divorce while I was in college, and after that I got drafted, so my mind became consumed with making the team. I ate, drank and slept the NFL."

I know he could tell I was surprised by the way I was looking after he mentioned the marriage part. My hopes diminished because I knew if there was an ex-wife, then there probably were some kids too.

"You should see the look on your face, he smiled. "Have I scared you away already?"

"No, no. I'm just shocked you were married before."

"What? I don't look like the marrying type?"

"No, I didn't mean it that way, I'm just surprised."

"Well, if it will ease your mind some, that was a long, long time ago, and we didn't have any children, so there is absolutely no attachment to her.

We got married in college, too young, and after two years we were divorced."

"Michael, I'm sorry. You don't owe me an explanation. I didn't mean to look crazy when you said that. You just caught me off guard."

"That's ok. I understand."

I sat for a moment feeling stupid about my remarks.

We didn't talk about his ex-wife much after that, but we did talk about the NFL. He explained to me that he had no complaints with his position as a defensive back, and as far as he was concerned he wanted to play ball until his body couldn't handle anymore. He also said that he is a "Franchise player," which basically means he is one of the most valuable players on the team. At the end of the season, when other players' contracts end, he will still be valuable. Though I didn't fully understand what he was saying, I pretended to.

He told me he was drafted by the New Orleans Saints from the University of Michigan, and after two years, he was traded to the Cowboys where he stayed for three years. His last four years were spent with the Oakland Raiders. Now he is entering into his tenth season with the Bulls.

"You know, you don't act like I thought most athletes act." I said

"And how is that?"

"I don't know," I continued. "You read and hear about athletes being in trouble in the news, and you can't help but stereotype all of you guys. I mean like the Ray Caruth and Ray Lewis thing. These brothers were involved in serious situations. People actually lost their lives, and I just don't get it—Never mind," I smiled.

"No, no, keep going. What you're saying is what a lot of people want to say. You probably think most of us just want to party at any cost, and make ghetto ass decisions. Seriously, there is a good percentage of us that live right and want to stay out of trouble. Those two brothers just got caught up, that's all. It happens to all of us because—that's the name of the game. Everybody is looking for negative things on us. There's pressure everywhere we go. If we do anything it gets blown out of proportion. Also, the media doesn't ever talk about those of us who are on the right track. The black athlete only gets attention when it involves a murder, rape, or drugs. They forget white boys do just as much dirt, if not more. That's how it's always been, which is why I try to stay to myself."

"That makes sense." I answered, shocked that he'd responded to all of my questions straight to the point.

"So what else were you going to say?" he asked.

"Nothing. That was it."

"Come on tell me. We can't get to know each other if you don't feel comfortable around me. So ask me whatever. I won't be offended."

I racked my brain for kinder words to use when discussing the athletes I'd seen acting ignorant on television, but I couldn't come up with any. Finally, I found the courage to ask more about the attitude of the athletes. I was getting ready to tell him when I was interrupted by Courtney's appearance at our table.

"What's up, man?" Michael greeted as they showed each other love.

I was surprised to see him, especially without D.C. hanging on his arm. I assumed if he were out enjoying himself, she had to have been right behind him considering how much time they'd been spending together.

I said hello, and turned to see if I could spot her, but she wasn't with him. Then out of nowhere, Mara appeared at our table.

"Hey girl," I said, really surprised to see her. "What are you doing here?"

"Hey Jay. I'm supposed to be meeting with Duwayne and Courtney to discuss some business. They said they needed some legal advice."

"Oh, where's Duwayne?" I asked.

"Girl, I don't know, but I'm not going to be here all night with them. I don't even like Chinese food. Plus, I don't know if I can help them anyway. I told them I didn't know much about contracts and all that stuff, but Duwayne insisted on getting my opinion.

"He must be still trying to holla'," I said.

"Shit, I hope not. He is not my type."

Courtney and Michael were busy discussing upcoming requirements for the team, as I checked out Courtney's sagging blue jeans, his Lugz boots *(which I thought he was too damn old to be wearing)* and his sky blue down jacket. The blinking diamonds in his ears, around his neck and on his wrist were doing way too much. *How old is this man*, I wondered? What had D.C. so sprung. It couldn't have been his style.

"Mara," I whispered. "I didn't know you and Duwayne were even staying in touch."

"Girl, he's called me a couple of times since that night, but he's so arrogant, I can't stomach him. You know he's an attorney, so we've been talking because we have that in common. Other than that, he wouldn't get the time of day, and I hope he didn't make up this little advice dinner either, or I'm gone. But I guess since Courtney is here he may be telling the truth."

"Mara, you want to go ahead and get a table while we wait for Duwayne?" Courtney suggested. "That man is always late, and I'm starving."

"Yeah, why not," Mara answered. "I don't do Chinese food, but I'll find something."

"Well, man, I'll check with you later," Courtney said to Michael, showing him love one last time.

"Alright then, Bruh'."

"See ya' later Jada. I'll call you tonight," Mara said as she walked off with Courtney. I smiled as I watched her switch off. She had that same hot momma walk that D.C. had. The walk I was determined to get.

****

Michael drove slowly down Highway 59 en route to my house with Eric Benèt softly playing in the background sounding sexy as I looked ahead at the bright stars

"I really had a nice time Jada" he said, grabbing my hand that was closest to him. "I hope we can hook up again."

"I had a nice time too, Michael."

"Well, tell me what kinds of things you like to do. I can't be messing with you if are into that horseback riding and cowgirl stuff."

I laughed. "Did I tell you I was a cowgirl? No, I did not. Everybody in Texas wasn't raised on the farm you know. That's the ghetto coming out in you. You do know that don't you?"

Michael continued to laugh as I talked. "Awww, now I'm ghetto."

"Yeah, Mr. Chicago."

Silence.

"You have a beautiful smile," Michael threw in.

He threw me for another loop with his words, and I was speechless.

When we entered the gates of my town house complex, I didn't want the date to end. It was only ten o'clock and I was nowhere near sleepy. I wanted him to come in for more conversation, but I didn't want to seem too excited. I was sure he got that from lots of women.

"So," he said, breaking the silence. "What time do you go in tomorrow?"

"Probably around nine. Tuesdays are my easy day. I don't have too many clients."

"I come in tomorrow for my session. What about lunch?"

"Yeah, that'd be cool."

Eric Benèt was making me crazy singing "Come As You Are." His lyrics made me want Michael even more, so I decided to get out the car before I ended up in a position I wasn't ready for.

"Well, I'll see you tomorrow and thanks for everything." I politely said.

"Alright. Thanks for the date, Lady."

"You're Welcome."

I turned to get out the car, and he touched me on my shoulder. We stared in each other's eyes for a second, while my heart fluttered. I thought I was having a heart attack. I knew the kiss I'd cherish for a lifetime was about to happen. Then he leaned toward me. His lips were soft and wet, and at first it was just a gentle kiss, but he opened his mouth just a little and I welcomed his tongue. It lasted what seemed an eternity, sending my hormones haywire. I wanted him in my house, and in my bed, but I knew it wasn't the time, so I finally ended our passion, and gently pulled back.

"He smiled, "Thanks."

"For what?" I asked.

"For giving me that nice kiss, and for taking me out and showing me a little of your city."

My face was fire hot from excitement.

"You're welcome."

We got out of the car and he walked me to the door.

"Sleep tight, Ms. Jada," he said, giving me one last peck on the lips.

"You too."

****

Mara Sampson

We sat quietly at our table and I was desperately looking over the menu trying to find something that halfway sounded appealing to me. I don't particularly care for Chinese food, so it was a struggle to read through the selections. Courtney on the other hand sat with his face in his soup bowl, eating the Won Ton soup he'd just ordered. He'd already told me that P.F. Chang was one of his favorite restaurants. When the waitress came, he ordered his soup and entrée immediately.

"So—have you found anything yet?" He asked.

"No. I think I'm just going to have a drink and call it a night."

"Come on now. I know there's something on that menu you could try."

He re-opened his menu. "Do you like chicken? They have a lot of good shit on here with chicken in it."

I snickered because he sounded like a ghetto man, putting on his best air for someone he was trying to impress.

"What's so funny?"

"Nothing," I smiled. "I'm just trying to find all the good shit on the menu that has chicken in it."

We both smiled.

"Oh you got jokes, huh."

As he smiled, I realized there was something very sexy about him. I mean, I had already given him credit for being fine as hell, but he was so hip-hoppish, I didn't really pay him any mind. He reminded me of a rapper or somebody.

This time, I noticed he had long eyelashes and strange greenish-gray eyes. The dimples in his chin and cheek was so deep, it looked like someone had cut him with a knife and it healed perfectly. His blemish free, light caramel complexion was a real turn on to me. I could see why D.C. was so into him, and of course   playing football gave him extra brownie points in her book.

"On the serious tip, Mara. We can dump this joint if you're hungry and go get something else, because it's almost nine o'clock and we haven't heard from Duwayne's lying ass."

"Thanks Courtney, but I'm alright. I'll just grab me something on my way home."

Silence.

"So can you call him one more time on his cell so we can see what the hell is up with him?"

Courtney dialed Duwayne again "You like him don't you?" he asked with the phone still up to his ear.

"I didn't say that. I'm just here to help you guys with whatever business you needed my advice on."

"Yeah, right."

"Look, Bruh', don't start with me," I rolled my eyes, while smiling too. "Don't you worry about who I'm interested in. You just find your damn friend. I'm about to leave."

It didn't make any sense for Courtney to have that much jewelry on. I mean how rich was the man? The earrings he had in both ears were very clear diamonds, mounted in platinum. The diamond bracelet appeared to be platinum and looked heavy as hell and very expensive, and the ring on his right finger shined so much it blinded me.

Courtney hung up the phone. "He's not answering. I don't know where the fool is?"

"Well, I guess I need to be getting out of here," I said as I reached for my purse.

"Mara, don't leave. I thought you were going to order a drink when the waitress came back with my food?"

"Thanks, Courtney, but I need to go home sober, so I can get some studying in."

"You're not going to make me eat my dinner alone are you?" he asked with a pitiful look on his face.

That's when I knew he was trying to kick game. *I should have gotten up then.*

"What you want me to do, hold your hand?"

"If you want to," he smiled.

I became a little uncomfortable. Was he really trying to flirt, or was I reading the situation wrong?

Our waitress returned with Courtney's hot plate of something that looked like stir fry with chicken.

"Looks good doesn't it?" he asked with a huge smile on his face.

"Yeah if you like chicken shit!"

"That was a good one." He laughed. "So you gonna get a drink and stay to keep me company?"

"What? You can't sit here and eat by yourself? You're a grown ass man."

He showed that sexy smile again.

"Yeah, I can, but I'd much rather sit with a beautiful woman like you."

"Where's D.C.? Call her so she can come and entertain you," I asked in a snappy tone.

He put his fork down and gave me a sly, cute smile. He knew I'd pulled his card.

"I got you, Mara, but the truth of the matter is if I wanted D.C. here right now, I could call her. Obviously, I'm not trying to spend my evening with her because she isn't here. Right?"

"Whatever, Courtney. You and your slick talk."

I admired his perfect white teeth and sexy smile during our conversation.

The waitress came back to see how he was doing with his meal, and that's when he took upon himself to order me a drink.

"Everything is fine Ma'am. Will you please get the lady here a Margarita?"

He was taking charge and I liked that. His arrogance and persistence was turning me on.

"You're used to getting what you want aren't you?" I asked.

"Not all the time, but usually."

"I like the way you eased that drink in. That was some real manipulation right there."

"I didn't manipulate you. I just took charge. Can you blame me for going for what I want?"

Damn he was good.

By then I was blushing, but trying desperately not to.

"So what do you want from me, Mr. Courtney?"

"It's Mr. Vincent," he smiled. "All I want is for you to enjoy your Margarita and sit and have a decent conversation with me. Is that too much to ask?"

"Well, it's not that it's too much; it just doesn't look right for me to be chillin' with my girl's man."

"Hey, hold up, I'm not anybody's man. I'm my own man and I do what the hell I want to do."

"Well excuse me, Brother Man. I was just making a statement."

"That's alright. I'll let you slide today because you're so damn sexy to me."

Why'd he have to lick his full, perfectly shaped lips after saying that?

****

I'm so ashamed to say that after my third Margarita, I was lit!

Courtney drove me home after much debate in the restaurant's parking lot over whether I was able to drive or not. He took my keys and basically forced me into his truck.

I had a very nice buzz, but I was quite aware, I thought, of what was going on. Courtney didn't believe I was sober enough to make it by myself, and I appreciated his concern. But what he really needed to know was I was no dummy. I knew that Mr. Vincent had other thoughts on his mind.

****

When we got to my place, I asked him to tell me how the hell I was going to get my car from the restaurant.

"Don't you worry about a thing," he said. "I'll have your car here first thing in the morning, before you even wake up."

"And how? I smartly questioned.

"Don't worry about it. It'll be taken care of."

We sat quietly for a moment and I hated what I was feeling inside. It was that feeling you get when you're turned on by someone. A feeling I shouldn't have been having.

"Well, thanks for the nice evening" I said before preparing to get out of the truck.

Then what I feared would happen, happened.

Courtney leaned toward me, and within seconds we were kissing. This wasn't a gentle smack on the lips either. This was a kiss that lasted a good while.

"Can I spend the night with you?" he asked with those slick eyes of his.

I hesitated, because I knew damn well the whole thing was wrong, but he was so fine and I'd gotten so heated I couldn't stop.

****

Courtney Vincent really put it on me. He was the best I had ever had. The man was gentle and so unbelievably affectionate that we made love not once, but twice.

60

Notice I said made love. I say that because there was such an instant connection between us, in and out the bed, that it had to be the beginning steps of love. I know that sounds shallow, but that's what I was feeling.

When I woke up the next morning, he was gone. He left me a note on my nightstand saying that he really enjoyed my company, and we most definitely had to hook up again. He also said my car was parked outside, and for me to have a good day.

The funny feeling I had while I was sitting in his car returned and made me smile. That smile stayed on my face the rest of the day.

9

The Phone Call

"*G*ood Morning, Rotsworth Rehabilitation. This is Jada Ballard speaking."

"Well damn, Jay, you could have called a sister and told me the details of the date last night," D.C. said.

"Oh hey, Dee. What's going on girl?"

"What happened last night?"

"Aren't we a little on edge," I laughed.

"Quit playing, Jay. Tell me what happened."

"All I can say is he's cool, fine as hell and seems to know how to treat a lady."

"Girl, I know how you feel. That's how I feel about Courtney; that man swept me clean off my feet the first encounter."

"Speaking of Courtney, why didn't you come with him last night?"

"Come with him where? Where did you see him?" D.C. asked suspiciously.

"Oh, he was at P.F. Chang last night with Mara. They were waiting for Duwayne so they could discuss some business of some sort."

D.C. got quiet.

"That's strange, he didn't call me at all last night, nor did he ever mention a meeting with Mara."

"Well, maybe he didn't know he was meeting with her until yesterday. Damn, do you have to know his every move?" I teased.

"No I don't have to know his every move," she snapped, but when he goes all night without calling me, it makes me wonder just what he did after the meeting, or who he was with."

"He was just with Mara and Dwayne discussing business. Don't start getting all paranoid," I added. "Anything could have happened to explain why he didn't call. He could have fallen asleep as soon as he got home, or maybe just got in too late from the restaurant and didn't want to call."

I tried to make D.C. feel better about the situation, but it was obvious she was very suspicious.

It was almost eight forty five when I got off the phone, and the clinic was still quiet. Dr. Rotsworth wasn't there, and neither were Colin, Mara, or any of the other therapists. I sat at my desk and reviewed my schedule of clients—Ms.Tami, an elderly lady that suffered a stroke. Mr. Wallace was rehabbing his knee after a knee replacement surgery and my sweet Cierra, a six year old angel, with MS.

My day wasn't full at all and the best thing was that all those clients were to be seen before twelve thirty, so I would be free for my lunch date with Michael.

I heard the clinic alarm ding, so I knew that someone was entering and I assumed it was the Doc. I pulled out some files from the cabinet and began reviewing them but when I turned around, standing in the door was Shakeem. I jumped because he was the last person I expected to see.

"H—Hey, Shak," I mumbled. "What are you doing?"

He didn't respond. He just stared.

Shakeem was starting to scare me with his persistence. He just wouldn't accept the fact that I was moving on, and didn't want anything to do with him. I got fed up with him, his women, the drugs and his sneaking around, so I called it quits. I was also tired of hiding our relationship from my mother, who might I add, despised him for playing in a band. She thought he wasn't good enough for me, and she had no problem sharing her opinion with me daily. She was a trip like that.

I could see the disappointment in his eyes, and I knew instantly what his visit was about.

"Jada, why haven't you called me?" he asked as he stood with his hands in his pockets, leaning against the door for support.

"Shakeem, we aren't together anymore remember," I said nice but nasty. "I don't have to check in with you before I do anything, and neither do you."

I shouldn't have been talking crazy to him because he was looking a little off. He was dressed in a pair of ragged jeans, and a sweater, which was totally out of his dress code. Today his clothes were filthy, eyes were glossy, and he hadn't shaved.

"Jada, I don't want it to be like this. I want you back." He pleaded. "I swear I'll stop doing gigs and stop the women from calling me. I'll do whatever it takes to get you to come back to me."

Everything he was saying was sweet, and I had never had a man plead as much as he had, but the truth of the matter was my feelings were gone. I had put a lot into the year we spent together, but he didn't appreciate me. Everything centered around his band and his dream, not to mention all the other bull.

"Shakeem it's time you move on, because I have. We aren't made for each other, and I've accepted that, why can't you?"

He walked closer to me, and the look in his eyes was frightening. I got nervous and began to back up.

"Shakeem, please leave. This is not the time or the place for this. Please go before I call the police!"

"You wouldn't do that, Baby," he smiled. "You wouldn't do that to the man you used to make love to all night long. Now would you?"

Finally he had me cornered against one of the file cabinets.

"Shakeem, the others will be here soon. Please Go!"

"I'm not going anywhere until you tell me this is still my stuff," he whispered in my ear, as he ran his finger slowly down the front of my pants.

I was too afraid to cry or scream.

"Shakeem, please don't hurt me," I whispered. "I never meant to hurt you. I just thought we were…

"Jada, I'm sorry!" he said immediately as if a timer had gone off inside his head and told him to stop acting crazy.

"I'm so, so sorry for scaring you. That won't ever happen again."

He started backing away from me, but I was still trembling. I just knew he was going to rape me.

"I'll always love you, Jada." He said from the door.

I heard the pleasant sound of the alarm ding again. Someone had finally made it to work.

"I'm not going to let you go. I'm not." He whispered as he turned and walked away.

I could hear Colin saying hello to Shakeem as he left. I inhaled and sat back at my desk when I heard him leave. I didn't want any tears to come down, but they did.

They weren't tears of love and hurt, but tears of fear. Something was different about him, and I'd never seen him act that way. "Would he really try to hurt me?" I asked myself as I came to the realization that he was possibly dangerous, and I needed to file a restraining order against him.

"Jada are you ok?" Colin asked as he peeped into my office. "Wasn't that your old boyfriend?"

"Yes." I answered nervously.

"He didn't do anything to you, because he looked a little crazy to me."

"No he didn't, but I'm scared of him. Should I go to the police?"

"Yes, because he may not have hurt you this time, but who's to say he won't. I mean, I'm not trying to frighten you, but you need to realize that if this guy has been stalking you this long, he could try anything."

"I know. I'm going to call today."

The phone rang, interrupting our conversation.

I answered, doing my usual salutation, trying to sound clear and as sane as possible considering what had just taken place.

"Yes, may I speak with Mara Sampson please?"

"She's not in right now. May I take a message for her please?"

"Yes, please tell her Duwayne Anderson called."

"Hey Duwayne. This is Jada. You met me last Friday with D.C."

"Oh, yeah. Hello, Jada. How are you?"

"Fine and you?"

"I'm doing pretty good. I'm just calling to talk to Mara. I didn't get to make it for dinner last night."

"Oh, I didn't know you weren't there."

"No, I had some other things I had to attend to, so I couldn't get there in time. I tried calling her, but I guess she didn't have her phone on. Matter of fact, I called her up until one o'clock this morning. I know she's calling me all kinds of trifling names."

"She's probably not mad, but you know what, I'll give her the message and I'll have her call you as soon as she gets here."

"Thank you, Jada. Talk to you later."

I had a funny feeling about the dinner between Mara and Courtney. I know they couldn't have talked to each other until one in the morning.

****

Michael and I decided to eat at Jason's Deli. I had to be back at work and Michael had to meet with his agent who was flying in from Chicago at three o'clock.

We sat at a small booth as I ate my baked potato and salad, and I watched Michael fix his food. I desperately wanted to get to know him. His conversation was on my level. He was a nice man, and at my age it's difficult to find a man with goals and conversation, and no drama. Normally when you find all of that, the guy has a lot of baggage. You know, a bunch of kids, an ex-wife, or a fatal attraction ex-girlfriend.

"I don't think my salad is as healthy as yours," Michael smiled as we both looked at the Ranch dressing dripping from the side of his plate.

"I don't know. You may be right."

We both laughed.

"So, Ms. Jada, do you have a man?"

"No, I don't."

"Well, not that I really care. I just asked so I can know how much pressure to put on you."

"Oh, so you're going to pressure me into seeing you."

"In a way," he smiled. "Let's just say I'm going to *spit so much game,* you will feel the pressure."

I shook my head. "You're very confident, Mr. Riley."

"Yeah, I guess. But really, I just know what I want."

He stared at me for a moment. "Do you know what you want?" he asked.

I nodded my head yes. "Pretty much."

"Well tell me. What kind of man do you want?"

"What's with all the questions?" I asked.

"I don't know. I'm just curious. Come on now. This is just part of our get-to-know-each other process."

"So, what do you want to know?" I asked.

"Just what I said. What kind of man do you like?"

I smiled again and took a sip of my tea.

"Let me see... I like a man that's patient, generous, romantic, kind, sensual, smart and of course honest."

Michael smiled, "That sounds like a punk to me."

"Smart ass," I chuckled.

"No, I'm just joking with you. Seriously, don't worry. I have all you're looking for in a man and some."

"You have everything under control I take it?"

"Don't you worry about a thing, Baby. Just enjoy the ride."

I couldn't believe I was starting to feel comfortable with him so soon. Little did he know I could barely wait for the ride to begin.

10
An NFL Affair

*T*hings had been going really well for Michael and me. We'd been talking on the phone everyday for hours at a time, just like we were in high school. We talked about our families, college days, and our careers. You name it, we discussed it.

Michael made a point of seeing me at least three to four times a week. Whether we went to lunch, dinner or the movies, I could count on seeing his wonderful face, or hearing his masculine voice. We were thoroughly enjoying each other's company and I was gradually falling under his spell. Matter of fact, I knew he possessed all the qualities to make me fall in love with him.

****

I felt like Cinderella going to the ball when Michael asked me to be his date for the defensive back coaches Christmas party. It was just like a man to ask the day before the occasion, but according to him he hadn't intended on going, but after hearing the other guys discuss it during workout, he changed his mind. After all, there were still more players signing with the team everyday, and Michael knew he needed to show his face if he wanted to stay around. It wasn't like he was fresh out of college. He had to play the game on and off the field too. I huffed a little after he propositioned me with the idea, but deep down I was elated!

****

Momma came by before I went to the party. She thought I should wear her two-carat diamond earrings since I was wearing my hair in a bun with Chinese hair pins holding it in place. I knew she just wanted to meet Michael. Momma needed to see who I'd been spending my spare time with.

When I called to tell her I'd been invited to an NFL affair, she became a little excited and asked me what I was going to wear. Of course I had no clue since I'd never dated an athlete or attended a function with one before.

"Jada, I really like this dress," Momma said as I slipped the maroon, satin t-length over my head.

"Where did you get it?"

"Momma, you remember this dress. I wore it last Christmas to the party D.C's mother gave. Remember?"

"Child, I can't remember nothing from last Christmas. I can barely remember my own name, let alone a dress. Anyway, I'm sure you looked just as gorgeous then as you do now."

"Thank you Momma."

"I hope this young man knows what he has."

"Momma, he's a real nice guy. I think you'll like him."

The doorbell rang at seven on the nose. He was always on time.

"Mom, will you get that for me please?'

While Momma was getting the door, I looked for my black evening purse. I found it and I put my lipstick and a few other items inside. I could hear Momma and Michael getting acquainted.

"What if she doesn't like him?" I mumbled to myself. Then I'll be going through the drama I went through with Shakeem.

With that in my mind, I decided to get on out there, because Momma could be very snooty, especially when it came to me. She was very possessive, and that drove me crazy as a kid. I could never spend the night with other children, and every time a parent offered to take a group of us someplace, Momma had to drive me herself. I never understood why, until Daddy explained to me that they lost two daughters before I was born, and one lived for three months before she passed. Since that day, I've looked at her in an entirely different light.

****

Michael was handsome in his tailored black suit with a charcoal gray shirt and black silk tie. His black leather suave shoes looked like they had just been shined. There was no doubt we looked good together.

"You look nice." He said with a smile on his face when I came out of my room.

"Thank you, so do you."

He walked over to me and kissed me on the cheek, and I slightly closed my eyes as I welcomed his soft lips against my face.

"Are you ready?" he asked gently, still not taking his eyes off of me.

"Whenever you are?"

"Oh, did you meet my mother?" I nervously asked. I was so intoxicated by how handsome he was, I'd totally forgotten about Momma standing in the corner spying our every move.

"Of course he did," she gladly added. "You know I introduced myself, Missy."

"I know, Momma."

"It was nice meeting you, Ms. Ballard," Michael said as he walked over and shook her hand.

"Same here, Mr. Riley. Maybe I'll have to invite you over for Sunday dinner one day."

"That would be nice, Ma'am."

"Momma will you lock up for me," I said as I gave her a kiss on the cheek.

"Sure baby. You just get on out of here."

When Momma shut the door, he stopped me. "What happened? Did you forget something?"

"No, I just think you look beautiful. May I please have a kiss?" he asked with a huge smile on his face. Before I could respond, he had pressed his lips against mine, melting me on the inside. His touch against my bare back had me tingling. I touched his face as we kissed to let him know I was feeling him, really feeling him.

****

Michael had no clue how to get to Greatwood, an exquisite neighborhood in Sugarland, where a lot of athletes and other well to do people live. I had only visited that area a few times, and each time, I fell in love with it even more.

The homes ranged from a quarter of a million to well past a million. I loved to let my imagination run wild when I'd look through the newspaper at the homes that were for sale in the area. Since one of my mother's favorite pastimes is looking at model homes, I'd been inside a lot of outstanding houses.

When we arrived at the guarded gated community. Michael told the guard he was attending a Christmas Party at the Johnson's, and without any further ado, the polite man let us in.

It was dark outside, but the area was lit enough for me to admire the well manicured landscaping. The flowers were in full bloom, showing off their bright colors. The grass was plush and green, especially on the golf course we passed as we entered.

"This is really nice," I said as we made our way to their home.

"Jada, Babe help me find 8808 Sunshine Road."

We drove into a couple of cul de sacs and a few dead end roads before we finally saw a group of parked cars that lead us directly to the Mediterranean-style, stucco two story home.

The house was fabulous! I tried to keep my composure as Michael luckily found a parking space in front of the house. In my mind, I was thinking, 'this sucka is PHAT!' but I couldn't verbalize that for fear he'd think I'd never been exposed to the finer things in life.

"This is a Phat ass crib!" he announced as he turned his car off. I smiled.

"It is beautiful isn't it?" I agreed, glad he'd said what I was thinking.

Michael walked around to my side to help me get out of the car. "Did I tell you that you are wearing the hell out of that dress?"

"No you didn't" I smiled.

"Well, Jada, Sweetheart, you are doing something really special with that dress. I really like it."

"Thank you," I responded shyly, as I leaned forward and gave him another kiss.

What was he doing to me?

We walked up the tan brick sidewalk, like we were walking up the yellow brick road in the Wizard of Oz and I admired the shrubbery, and the variety of perennials that were spread throughout.

Lights shined against the home adding another elegant touch to the mini mansion.

Michael rang the doorbell, and a Hispanic woman in a black and white uniform answered.

"Welcome," she said as she stepped to the side to let us in. When I entered the door, the chandelier and the sparkling crystals on it, hit me in the face. It was centered in the foyer to welcome everyone to the home, and also to provide an extra glare to the crème colored marble pieces that were delicately placed on the floor.

"Hey, Michael," an older black man with salt and pepper hair welcomed. "I'm glad you could make it."

"Hey coach," Michael replied as he shook the stout man's hand. "Thanks for inviting me. Hey this is Jada Ballard, a very dear friend of mine. Jada this is Coach Johnson, our defensive back coach."

I wondered how many dear friends Michael had.

"It's nice to meet you," I said.

"Same here." You didn't have any trouble finding the place did you?"

"No, actually, we came right to it. Jada is from here, so she was a little familiar with the area."

"You have a beautiful home," I added as I glanced up at the two sets of stairs that had wrought iron spindles.

"Why thank you. We are pretty pleased with it thus far. I'm glad you like it. Well, you guys help yourselves to all the food and drinks you like, and I hope you have a good time."

"Thanks," we both replied.

"He was nice." I said.

"Yeah, he is a pretty cool cat so far. You know they change after the season starts. I just hope he isn't a sell out like most of the brothers become when they get these positions. They say he was a bad boy back in the day when he played pro. I have much respect for his game. I hope I'll feel the same about his coaching."

Michael slipped his hands around my waist, and we strolled toward the sunken den, where most of the people were mingling. There were all colors of the rainbow laughing, talking and drinking, but I wasn't paying them too much attention because I was busy trying to check out the house.

The house had all the amenities I wanted in my dream home. Vaulted ceilings, marble floors, elongated windows, crown molding accents, just to name a few. It was sharp!

It was decorated in a southwestern way, just how I liked, with a lot of browns and oranges. Big clay pots with a variety of Bamboo sticks. The bulky dark brown leather couches were just what I wanted too, but couldn't afford, and here they sat, in all different shapes and sizes.

The traditionally decorated Christmas tree sat in the dining room standing firm and tall. There were doves hanging from it, and beautifully designed ribbon weaving in and out. The lights were all white, blinking alternately to add finishing touches, and it was packed underneath with perfectly wrapped presents.

"What's up, Man," a big chocolate brother said to Michael, interrupting my thoughts of what could be inside the presents.

They chatted and I continued to admire the house. I casually eased my way into the kitchen while Michael was being entertained by Big Poppa.

The kitchen was in my décor too. First of all it was as big as my entire town home, and it had all the stainless steel appliances that everybody was starting to purchase. The reddish brown cabinetry and the granite countertops were the bomb! Not to mention the island that had a six burner cook top. After admiring the kitchen, my mind was trying to get me to wander off on my own to see the rest of the house, but I knew that would be tacky so I slowly headed back toward Michael. The house had to be at least seven thousand square feet, and I was barely seeing two thousand of it.

"Jada, Babe, this is Kevin Mosley," Michael said when I eased back by his side. "He plays with me."

I shook Kevin's big hand, and smiled. I wasn't thinking about the blonde he was with, who stood looking too confident to be with the big sloppy brother.

"Natalie, this is Michael and Jada," he said.

"Hi," she answered, almost as cool and nonchalant as a sister would respond.

We gave each other fake smiles, and then they were on their way.

"That brother is wild!" Michael said when they left. "He might be one of the wildest brothers I've met in all my years in the league. From what I've heard, he's been married three times, and they were all white girls. He has about ten children and still hasn't learned his lesson. I suppose he thinks he doesn't have to learn anything as long as he keeps signing fat ass contracts".

I cut my eyes over at the Natalie chick one last time before we walked around, and she was looking dead at me. She gave me another one of those fake half smiles and I gave her nothing in return. It pissed me off that she was hanging on him, pretending to care, when I knew damn well she was all about the money. I clutched Michael's arm and turned my head.

When we got outside by the pool, there were people out there dancing, talking and drinking. It was a pretty warm evening for December so everyone stood outside enjoying the band. Some danced while others snuggled to each other. The candles and Poinsettias that decorated the area really set the mood.

"Would you like to dance?" Michael whispered in my ear.

"Yes."

We danced to one of my favorite songs, "A House is Not a Home," by Luther Vandross.

"I'm really glad you invited me." I whispered in his ear.

"I'm really glad you came," he smiled and gave me a kiss on the cheek.

We danced in silence and he held me close to his body, caressing my back and arms to keep the chill away. I wondered what he was thinking as we swayed to the music.

"Will you stay with me tonight?" he asked, looking me in the eyes.

We both stopped dancing. I felt warm all over again, as I nodded, yes.

Michael's smile made me feel good about the decision I'd just made. I wasn't sure what was going to take place, but I did know I felt safe with him and I wanted more than anything to show him.

****

Michael was finally ready to leave around eleven. We said our good-byes, and thanked the host and hostess for their hospitality.

"Jada," Mrs. Johnson said, "Please be sure to grab a gift from underneath the tree. The ones with the gold bows are for the guests."

I was surprised. "Why, thank you, Mrs. Johnson. Thanks for everything."

"Kenyetta. Please call me Kenyetta," she answered.

I walked over to the tree and picked up one of the elegantly wrapped presents. I was so anxious to open it, but I tried desperately to appear nonchalant especially as I walked toward Michael.

"What you got there?" he asked.

"I don't know. I'll open it in the car."

There were people still coming when we were leaving, parking their luxury cars up and down the driveway. We walked arm in arm toward his vehicle, recapping the party when I noticed Courtney and Mara strolling toward us. I was hoping my eyes were deceiving me, but when we got closer to them, it was definitely Mara, my best friend.

"Hey, Jay." She said happily.

I gently tugged her arm, and we walked off to the side. "What are you doing?" I asked.

"I'm not doing anything," she said calmly. "He asked me to come to the party with him, so I said yes. "What's the big deal?"

"Mara, you know that's D.C.'s man."

"No, D.C. thinks he's her man, but according to him, he's free as a bird. He says he doesn't have a woman, and he and D.C. aren't messing around anymore. Plus, what's the big deal, Jay? I'm taking an opportunity that any woman would take."

"I can't believe you. Since when have we ever taken opportunities at the risk of losing our friendship?" You know that's not right, Mara."

"It's not that serious, Jada, so quit tripping!"

Michael and Courtney were finished talking, and by the expression on Courtney's face, when I looked at him, he knew Mara and I were talking about him.

I was PISSED!

"I'll check you later, Man," Courtney said.

They walked off, and Michael and I went to his car.

"Are you alright, Babe?" Michael asked.

"Yeah, I'll be ok. I'm just aggravated."

When I got in the car and fastened my seatbelt, I began unwrapping my gift. It was so delicately wrapped, that I almost didn't want to tamper with it. On the inside was a beautiful crystal snowflake ornament, by Swarovski.

I held it up so Michael could see it. "That's nice," he said.

"Yeah it is. Very nice."

I sat quietly, fidgeting with my gift as I thought about Mara. How could she go on a real date with Courtney knowing one of her best friends was in love with him?

"What's on your mind, Sweetheart?" Michael asked, breaking my thoughts.

"Nothing."

"Come on now, Babe. I can tell something is bothering you. It's written all over your face. Is it Mara and Courtney?"

I hesitated before responding because I didn't want to sound childish about the situation.

"Well, yeah it is. I just don't know what's gotten into Mara. Why in the world would she even consider going out with a man like Courtney? I mean he's not worth a damn dime."

"Hey, hey now," Michael interjected, "Courtney is a nice brother and intelligent, too. I think if you give him a chance you'll see that he's not at all what you're thinking. Did you know he graduated at the top of his class with a business degree from UCLA?"

I rolled my eyes. "Michael, I don't care about his grades, nor do I give a damn what school he went to. All I care about is how he's playin' my two girlfriends."

"Come on now, Jada, maybe it was just a fun little date, and nothing else is happening between them. Don't blow it out of proportion just yet. Plus you have other things you need to be worrying about, Sweetheart."

"Like what?" I said, looking at him like he was crazy.

Michael pulled into a grocery store parking lot.

"What are you doing?"

"I'm pulling over. What does it look like?"

"May I ask for what?"

He put the car in park and turned to look at me with a beaming smile.

"So, you need to know why you need to mind your own business, huh?' he asked leaning closer to me.

"Tell me, Mr. Riley, why do I need to mind my own business?"

"Well, Babe, the way I see it, you need to keep your mind focused on me, and how I'm going to blow it?"

"Oh really," I smiled.

"Really," he answered as he planted another one of his soft gentle kisses on my lips.

Our eyes were locked for a moment, and then we kissed again.

"Can you handle me?" he whispered.

I looked deep into his beautiful eyes, "Of course, I can."

Michael and I kissed one last time before we both finally agreed that we needed to take our heated session to his place. I didn't want the moment to stop. I wanted him to be all over me right then and there.

11
The Truth

Mara Sampson

I was constantly racking my brain trying to figure out what my issue really was with D.C. For me to want to date a guy she was seeing was totally out of my character and I despised women who ruined relationships because of a man. Now, I'm thirty-two years old, and I decide to slip. Not only have I had sex with my best friend's man, I have the nerve to go and fall in love with him.

I finally admit that it's D.C. Though I love her, I really don't like her. It's her whole "I'm the shit attitude." Ever since we were kids, people have always given her attention because of her looks. I can remember our elementary school teachers saying hello to all three of us, but always stopping to say a little extra to Deidre. "Oh Deidre, your hair is so pretty today", or "Oh Deidre, I love your dress." That crap would piss me off!

I don't think it phased Jada too much, but it frustrated me. Hell, it wasn't like Jada and I were coming to school looking like hood rats everyday. Why couldn't they compliment us like that as well?

I do admit D.C. is a pretty woman, but damn is she prettier than me or Jada just because she isn't one hundred percent black. Her hair is silky straight, without the assistance of a chemical, and Jada and I have to visit the beautician faithfully but does that make her the flawless woman?

Actually there are some things I never settled with D.C., which is why I'm not feeling as compassionate about the situation like I would if it were Jada.

First of all I'm still pissed about the incident I had with her back in 1990. I know that happened a long time ago, but she betrayed me. She knew I was digging Eric Mathews, but she did her little prancing and slinging of the hair act every time we were all together, like any brother with eyes wouldn't look. When she first started doing it, I didn't pick up on it, but as I observed Eric's nervous, somewhat giggly behavior when she came around, I discovered that he had a thing for her. The only problem was I didn't think D.C. was doing it on purpose. I think she was just being her natural flirtatious self.

Of course, I confronted Eric's bitchy behind, and quite naturally he denied my allegations, but when I saw them together at a club, that confirmed everything.

I'll never forget that day. Never had I felt so embarrassed and deceived my entire life. Here I had been bragging to my girls about how sprung Eric was and how I thought we might have something going, and in walks this idiot with my best friend.

Of course I got up and left before either of them noticed me. *(Hey, momma told me to never make myself look bad, and that was a situation that would definitely make me look stupid.)*

D.C. never saw me, and to this day, I haven't brought it up. But I think she knows. I know that punk ass Eric told her everything I said after I cursed him out, but she still hasn't mentioned it. I'm not for sure if she brushed it off or she really didn't know.

I never brought it up to D.C. because I continued to give her the benefit of the doubt by thinking maybe, just maybe, she didn't know how much I really liked Eric. I never really liked telling who I was interested in, just in case I got my feelings hurt. I could have sworn I told her I adored him but maybe I only mentioned that I liked him.

I don't really know, but I do know she has this attitude like she's the finest thing that walks the earth, and it irritates the hell out of me.

Another problem I have with her is how she is always so quick to assume that no big time men will want a full-bodied woman. She's even slipped and said, "Ya'll know I can't eat out with you guys because I have to watch my figure. Rich men enjoy slender, fit women."

My question is, how the hell does she know what every man on this earth likes?

White America has black women thinking that their physical appearance needs to be similar to theirs to be accepted, which is a small waist, big boobs, and no booty.

Not all men are interested in the light skin, size five woman. Some brothers like a little meat to hold on to, and I'm flattered that obviously, Courtney is one of them.

12
Tempted

Maxwell's song "A Woman's Work" had me in the lovemaking mood, as I stood nude in front of Michael with chills covering my body. My breasts were at attention as I anxiously awaited what was about to happen to me. The anticipation of what he was going to do to me was killing me.

Candles flickered around his bedroom, giving him just enough light to see my brown body. I was as nervous as the night I lost my virginity. I couldn't believe I was standing in front of him upon his request, showing it all.

"You're so beautiful, Jada," he said as he began kissing my neck. His skin pressed against mine was comforting as he held me closely and his hands roamed freely about my body. We stood caressing each other, teasing each other as I ran my hands over his firm chocolate chest and strong arms. His body was lean and his muscles were cut to perfection. He by far had the best physique I'd ever laid my eyes on.

"Are you sure you want to do this?" he whispered in my ear.

"Positive."

Michael led me to his king sized bed. As I lay on his firm mattress and he climbed in and slid on top of me.

"I want you to feel comfortable with me," he said as he lightly stroked my face.

"I do."

I want to please you Jada. Is that ok?"

I couldn't believe he was talking to me before we made love. Michael kissed and caressed me. His foreplay alone had my mind so far gone that when it was time for the real thing I was mentally drained. I'd forgotten about the places he kissed me, since it had been so long since I'd been touched. He definitely had a serious sensual side, and I loved it.

"Hold on, Babe," he said as he reached for a condom. I was relieved he had sense enough to grab one, because I definitely was about to stop him if he hadn't.

When he came back to me, he gently kissed me on the lips. "Let me know how you feel, ok?"

I nodded my head yes, as I felt him enter me.

He stroked my face as he made love to me, telling me how soft my skin was and how beautiful my eyes were. He looked at me the entire time, showing expressions of pleasure here and there. By looking at his face I could tell he was pleased, and I knew he could tell I was pleased, as well.

After we made love, I closed my eyes and snuggled closely under Michael as I reflected on the entire evening. It had been wonderful; like a dream come true. I couldn't believe I had sex with him after such a short time dating; never had this happened before.

****

It was three o'clock in the morning when Michael eased from my tight grasp. He slipped his boxers on and went downstairs. I figured he was getting something to drink since the only rooms that were on the lower level of his place were the den, kitchen and a bathroom. His townhouse wasn't too big, but the perfect size for him.

85

His home was a two story with three bedrooms and two and a half baths. The décor was contemporary with expensive marble pieces and black metal statues perched throughout. I couldn't help but wonder who had helped him decorate and get situated since his place was so immaculate.

Michael had only been living in Houston since the beginning of November, when the bulls signed him. As far as I was concerned he'd performed a miracle in a short amount of time with his home.

The art on the walls was very eclectic, letting me know he liked the unusual. I tried to figure out why he wanted help decorating when it appeared to me he had everything under control.

I was awake and, and when I felt for him, I realized he was gone. I wondered where he'd gone, so I slipped on his silk robe that was lying in a chair next to his bed, and decided to go looking for him. His robe felt really good up against my skin.

I crept downstairs to where he was. I had to go down about eleven stairs to get to the downstairs living area. On my way I could hear cabinets opening and water running, so I knew he was in the kitchen. He couldn't see me nearing, so I decided to sneak up on him. He was standing over the sink with a glass of water and I noticed a medicine bottle on the counter.

"Boo" I said, touching his back.

Michael jumped, dropping whatever it was in his hand down the drain.

"Fuck!" he said under his breath.

"I'm sorry, Babe," I said as I wrapped my arms around his waist.

"Are you ok?"

He didn't acknowledge me or my apology. He was too busy digging around in the drain trying to find what he'd lost. His actions were strange and jumpy to me, but I was trying not to read to heavily into it.

I turned to walk away when I realized I'd aggravated the situation by coming downstairs and he grabbed my arm.

"I'm sorry, Jada. It's not a big deal, Babe. It was just some medicine I needed to take."

"Did I wake you?" he asked in a concerned tone, obviously trying to fix the situation.

"No, I was just wondering where you were."

"Oh really," he responded surprised.

He wrapped his arms around me, trying to smooth the situation, but my feelings were hurt. At that moment I had a gut instinct that something wasn't right with him.

We went silently back upstairs hand in hand, and I stopped on the stairs and looked at him.

"Michael, are you ok.?" I asked politely.

"What do you mean, Babe?"

"Is everything ok with you?"

"Yeah," he answered, looking at me strangely. "Everything is cool."

****

The next morning, I was determined to find out what Michael was hiding. The last time I was with him at the restaurant, he was taking vitamins, and I didn't think anything of it, but for me to see him taking Sinus medicine at three o'clock in the morning, drew suspicion.

I tiptoed downstairs before he awoke and I looked for any sign that would help me understand what was going on.

Maybe it was nothing. Maybe I was overreacting. Whatever the case, I was determined to find out something before we went any further into the relationship.

Was the man sick? Did he have an illness he was embarrassed about? I hoped like hell he didn't have something fatal I could catch?

The bottle wasn't on the counter when I got to the kitchen, which meant I had to go through his cabinets. I hated to search the man's cabinets, but I had to know what I was getting myself into.

Obviously, he'd put it away, or taken it back upstairs with him.

I opened the cabinet where the seasonings were supposed to be, and I was shocked to find it full of medicine bottles.

I picked up one bottle, and it said Indocin, an anti-inflammatory drug. The next one was Vicodin, a very popular pain-killer. The third, fourth, and fifth bottles in the cabinet were Vicodin also. There were even a couple of bottles of Tylenol with Codeine.

Michael was in pain from either his neck, back or his knees. He'd endured so many injuries throughout his career that it would've been impossible for me to pinpoint which one was causing him the most trouble. Hopefully he was only taking the Vicodin on a temporary basis, because I'd heard of patients that had gotten hooked on it. It was a very addictive drug.

"Jada, are you down there?" he called out, scaring me to death.

"Yes, I'm in the bathroom."

I quickly put the pill bottle back and ran into the bathroom. I flushed the stool so he'd think I was using it. What was going to be my explanation for being downstairs using this bathroom, especially when there were two others I passed.

I stayed in the restroom for two to three more minutes before opening the door, and when I did, he was right there.

"Hey—Why'd you come down here to use the restroom? There are two upstairs."

"I know, but I didn't want to disturb you. You looked like you were in such a deep sleep."

"Well, thank you for being considerate, but next time, feel free to use the bathroom that is in my bedroom."

"Oh, so I'm welcome to come back," I asked, sliding my arms around his waist.

"Hell, yeah. Don't think you can come in here and do what you did to me last night and not return. That can't happen."

13
Feelings

$\mathcal{D}.\mathcal{C}.$ had been out of town on business for a couple of days, and Mara and I hadn't had a deep conversation since I'd seen her at the Christmas party with Courtney. We never had the opportunity to discuss her reason for going out with him other than her weak excuse that he was *"fair game"*. We tried talking about it at work, but Colin or someone else would come and interrupt every time we got deep into the conversation.

I'd been busy with Michael, spending most of my nights at his house. I missed a lot of my messages from D.C. and Mara, so D.C. came to the clinic when she returned from San Antonio and demanded we hook up for happy hour. We scheduled it for the same time and place, but to be honest, I wasn't looking forward to it.

Mara came to my house after work to pick me up, and so we could finish our discussion before meeting D.C at Pappadeaux's. I knew the whole thing was bothering her, no matter how hard she tried to play it off. The bottom line is Mara isn't a cold-blooded person, and for her to mess around with a man she knows one of us has feelings for was totally out of character. True enough she had a negative outlook on marriage and relationships since her father wasn't worth a dime and had cheated on Mrs. Sampson, repeatedly. I just didn't think she'd let any of that influence her into becoming scandalous.

"Jada, I have always been the one in the sorry relationships," Mara said shortly after she'd entered my house.

"That's not true."

"Yes, it is, and you know it. I'm *always* the one with the worthless man! I haven't been in a good relationship since Craig, and that was obviously a waste of my time. If I had known he was screwing half of Houston while we were dating, I would've let him go a long time ago."

Mara's voice started to quiver. "Sometimes Jay it hurts when men can't look past my weight. I know I'm not a huge woman, but nowadays with the taste in men I have, a size sixteen is not what they're looking for. I want a man that has it going on just like everybody else. I know you guys think I don't trip off men, and all I think about is sex, but you're wrong. I want someone that will love me for me and not for how I make him feel."

I was stunned at Mara's confession because she was always so confident. I never thought her weight played a part in anything.

"Mara, I didn't know you felt like this. You have always been so nonchalant when it came to men and relationships, plus you said you didn't have time for a man until after you passed the bar."

"I know what I said Jay, but it's just a front most of the time. I would love to be in a relationship like you guys. Shit, I'm tired of screwing, and knowing that it's going nowhere. Take Colin's gay ass for example. He can't even decide if he wants to be in a serious relationship or not, but he can call me late at night, for a booty call. I finally told him to kiss my ass the other day, and I haven't been to his house since. Now Courtney on the other hand, he really knows how to treat a woman."

I turned my lip up when she said his name.

"Don't frown Jada. Courtney doesn't have anything to do with this. I made the decision, he didn't. I enjoy his company. He makes me laugh, he's very complimentary, and he's a gentleman. Being with him at that Christmas party made me realize what I'd been missing in a man."

I couldn't help but reflect back to D.C.'s comments about Courtney making her feel the same way. Obviously, the man was a playa', couldn't she see that?

"There are a lot of brothers out there that want to wine and dine their woman. I just haven't been looking in the right places." Mara finished.

"But what about D.C.?" I asked

"Damn, Jay. I didn't say I was in love with the man. I just said he is very good company. As far as I'm concerned D.C. doesn't ever have to know, unless of course you tell her."

I looked at Mara like she'd lost her mind. I couldn't believe she wanted to keep this a secret.

"Can you handle that? Can you keep this between you and me?"

I had nothing to say.

"But what about....?"

"But nothing, Jada," she said as she stood and looked at me with her hands on her hips. "Either you can keep it between us, or we can tell D.C. and get a whole lot of shit started. Like I said, it's not like I love the man."

"How could you say some shit like that Mara. Here you have been creeping around town with your best friend's man, and you don't see why I'm making it a big issue. This could ruin our friendship. This could make D.C. not trust either one of us ever again, and to me, Courtney and his money is not worth it. We have too many years and memories to let some cocky ass football player tear us apart."

I left her in the den and went to my bedroom to get my purse. When I came back she was sitting with her head in her hands, apparently in deep thought.

"You didn't bone him did you?" I asked.

Mara turned and looked at me with one eyebrow raised and her lips puckered. It was an expression I knew all too well. It was the face she gave us when we asked or said something she thought was stupid.

"Mara, you didn't. How could you?"

"Jay, I already explained it to you once, and I feel horrible enough. Please don't ask me to go through it again."

What Mara had done was totally inexcusable. She had let her weakness for sex jeopardize a lifelong friendship, and in all the twenty-seven years we'd been together, we had never deceived one another. Matter of fact, we always talked about women who ended their friendships over men. Now the same thing was happening to us.

****

D.C. was already seated when we arrived at the restaurant. She had a Swamp Thing, one of Pappadeaux's popular drinks in one hand and her cell phone in the other.

"Let me call you later," she said once we got to the table.

"H-e-yyy, girls. What's been up?"

Mara and I hugged D.C. and sat down. Even though Mara had lectured me about keeping my mouth shut, the expression on her face read "guilty, and I knew if she continued to look like that, it was only a matter of time before D.C. figured something out. I felt like I'd betrayed her too as I gave her a hug.

"Long time no see, Ladies. Ya'll lookin' good. Not as good as me, but ya'll lookin' good." She laughed.

"Whatever D.C.," I smiled, glad to see her face.

"Talk to me Ladies. What's been happening in the big H since I've been in San Antonio?"

"Dee, you were only gone for three days. You're acting like you were gone a month," I laughed trying to change the subject and not sound suspicious.

"Whatever, Girl. I was just trying to show ya'll some love, but since you don't want any, I can gladly fill you in on what's been happening with me."

I looked at Mara, and she rolled her eyes to the ceiling like she wasn't trying to hear it.

"You know I was dying not seeing my baby Courtney while I was gone. We talked everyday until I got back. I'm telling ya'll, I think I'm falling for that man. He's so fine, it doesn't make any sense! I'm here to tell you it ain't nothing like a fine ass rich man."

My heart almost stopped beating. I looked at Mara shortly after the statement and she looked the other way.

"He's always telling me how beautiful I am, and how I have all the characteristics of a good woman. Not to mention the man really knows how to lay it down in the bed. Girl, I swear I haven't had nothing that good in a long, long time."

Before D.C. could finish her sentence, Mara excused herself from the table to go to the ladies room. D.C. didn't think anything of it because she was too busy giving me details of how freaky Courtney was in the bed. I watched Mara walk away, and I knew she was hurting.

"Hello, Ladies, how are you this evening?" the waiter asked as he sat three tall glasses of water on the table. "Before I take your order, I'd like to say that the gentlemen over at the bar asked me to inform you that a round of drinks is on him. He's sitting right over there in the brown turtleneck," he pointed.

D.C. and I turned around and there looking sexier than ever was Michael.

"Ah shit," D.C. laughed. "I thought it was somebody important."

Michael held his drink up to me as if we were toasting something and smiled. A smile spread across my face bigger than a double laned highway.

"Go over there and say hello to him, Girl. What you waiting for?" D.C. asked

"I'm going, but not right now. I can't act too excited. You know the game."

"Whatever, Child. This isn't the sixties. You better stop playing that game, because, Baby, if you don't show the interest, somebody else will."

Mara came back to the table, half smiling. I could tell she wasn't really into the outing.

"What happened to you girl?" D.C. asked "You been in that bathroom for a minute. What, you pregnant?"

Neither one of us laughed at D.C.'s comment.

"No, I am not pregnant." She rolled her eyes. "There was a line in there, Smart Ass."

"So what's up with you, Mara? You still after that yellow brother at the clinic or have you fired him?" D.C. asked.

"Girl, he's sick like all the rest, and I don't have time to heal his tired ass."

"I know that's right, Girl," D.C. blurted as she reached over the table and gave Mara a high five. "I'm feeling you, Sista', but I have to get me some on a regular basis, and that hard role you playing will keep a sista' on drought."

D.C. you're out of control," I laughed.

We ate our food and chatted like we always did. I could see the line out the window. I knew the people on the outside wanted to curse us for not getting up, but we didn't care. We were in our own little world.

Every once in a while I would turn to see where Michael was, and my heart was relieved to see that he wasn't moving, nor were there any women in his face. He appeared to be just chillin' with a few other guys, talking and drinking, and that was fine with me.

"I'm telling ya'll" D.C. started, "I was scared shitless on that plane. With Bin Laden still on the loose, I almost had a damn heart attack."

Mara and I started laughing.

"Ya'll laughing but I'm, serious. America is in trouble for real, and I'm in even more trouble because I have to fly everywhere with my job."

"Whose cell is that?" I asked, interrupting her when I heard the ringing.

"Oh, that's mine," D.C. responded as she jumped and began digging through her purse to answer it.

"Oh hey, Baby," she said with a smile on her face "Yeah, I can come over. Make sure you're ready when I get there," she blushed. "See you in a minute."

D.C. hung up the phone, and by the look on her face Mara and I instantly knew who it was.

You would've thought Mara had seen a ghost, as pale as her face turned.

"You ladies don't mind if I cut this short, do you?" D.C. asked.

I looked at Mara, as she pretended to be reading over our ticket.

"No girl, you go and have fun." I said.

"I know I'm going to have a WONDERFUL time," she winked. "I'll call you ladies tomorrow." D.C. said and excused herself from our table.

"You know what, Jada," Mara began after D.C. was gone. "I feel bad for what I did, but I feel worse because I think I do have feelings for him."

"But I thought you said earlier that you didn't" I reminded her.

She shook her head. "I lied Jay, I do."

****

Michael had been winking at me the entire time I sat with Mara at Pappadeaux's. I tried to focus on our conversation, but it was difficult trying to listen to her, while my mind was constantly going back to our last sexual encounter.

After about an hour of Mara and me trying to evaluate why she did what she did, and reflecting back to her past unhealthy relationships, she decided to say forget it because she realized she was wrong. She also admitted she enjoyed the attention Courtney had given her, and that they had been together more than I wanted to know.

The waiter brought over our ticket, and I noticed Michael had turned his back to us and was talking on his cell.

Naturally, I wondered who he was talking to, yet I felt silly for letting the thoughts of other women run through my mind. After all, it was still very early in our relationship, even though we'd been acting like we'd been together for months.

"We need to go because I got a lot of studying to do tomorrow," Mara interrupted.

"Mara, everything will work out," I said as I patted her on the hand. Courtney isn't worthy of you or D.C. as far as I'm concerned. If any man is dog enough to knowingly mess around with two friends, he can't be worth a damn!"

Mara closed her eyes, and shook her head.

"I know Jada, there's just something about him that makes me crazy."

She paused again

"Anyway, thanks, Jay, for being there. Girl, I know I put you in a bad position."

We hugged, and as we were finishing, Michael appeared.

"Hey, hey, what's up with the hugging?"

"Hey Michael," Mara said, giving him a hug too. "I know you've been sitting over there waiting for me to get the hell away from this table, so I purposely kept Jay tied up so I could watch you squirm."

"Oh, **Really**. You know what they say about payback don't you?"

"Yeah, Man, I know, but I'm not worried."

"So — Miss Jada, do you have plans with your girlfriend after this, or can I kidnap you?"

I looked at Mara.

"Don't look at me." Mara rolled her eyes, "I'm outta' here, and you know my feelings aren't going to be hurt."

"Thanks, Mara." I said, giving her a tight hug. "I'll call you tomorrow."

Mara left and Michael and I sat for a moment.

"So what would you like to do now?" He asked, holding on to both of my hands.

"I don't know, maybe take you to a quiet spot. What do you think?"

"Ooh, I'd like that," he said, licking his sexy lips, and winking at me.

Here he was again looking fine as hell. He was never over dressed, or flashy like Courtney, but always just right. He looked extra fine with that dark brown turtleneck choking his thick neck and muscular chest, and his light blue jeans accompanied by a dark brown leather jacket.

"May I have your keys please?" I asked in an innocent, yet sexy tone.

"Oh you want full control, huh?"

"Yes I do. Do you mind?"

"You know I don't let just anyone drive my Jag."

"Well, I'm not just *anyone*, am I?" I winked.

I took him by the hand and led him out the door, and that's when I got a quick look at the diamond faced, stainless steel Rolex he was wearing. We were both grinning from ear to ear as we headed out the door. I noticed a few women, whispering as we walked out.

He pointed me in the direction of his car. I located it immediately. There it sat backed in, shining like it was on the showroom floor. It felt good sitting behind that leather wheel. When I started it, I could barely tell it was on because the engine was that smooth. I adjusted my seat, and put on my seat belt.

"You ready?" I asked, smiling at him.

"Whenever you are, Baby?"

I started the car and was preparing to leave when I heard Michael's phone vibrate.

My eyes immediately focused back to the clock in his car which read 10:30.

Michael looked at his phone, and then at me.

"Well, are we going to leave?" he smiled.

"Well, are you going to answer your phone?" I returned.

"See, Woman, now you're in my business," he laughed. "Let's go to your quiet spot. I'm not worried about nothing else."

****

I led Michael into my spot, my bedroom, and I lit a Mulberry candle. The CD player was loaded with Musiq's CD 'I just want to sing.'

"Will you take your clothes off, please?" I asked politely.

"Why, Jada, are you trying to seduce me?"

"Maybe," I blushed.

"What if I'm scared?"

"Don't be, I'll take good care of you."

Michael removed his jacket, shirt and undershirt. He stood for a moment with a serious look on his face; then came the pants and boxers. I couldn't believe what I was doing, as I watched him stand ready and willing for whatever.

"I think you're a freak," he said with a sexy smile on his face. *If he only knew, he was the first to get this treatment.*

"I didn't say that when you asked me to stand in front of you naked did I?"

I walked over to him and ran my fingers over his chest, caressing his soft butt. His skin was baby smooth and as usual his cologne smelled heavenly. I was about to touch the special part on his body I was so yearning to feel when he picked me up and carried me to my bed.

I smoothly switched our position to be on top, taking control of the situation as I kissed his chest. I slowly ran my tongue down his stomach, paying close attention to his navel, and nipples. His groans were turning me on.

"Come on, Babe, make love to me" he panted.

That's when I began gently stroking his private, driving him crazier.

"I know you're ready, Baby, but I'm not finished yet," I whispered.

I guess Michael couldn't take it anymore, because before I knew it, he had flipped me over and was kissing my breasts.

"You're so damn fine," he panted in my ear while sliding inside of me once again. He began to satisfy me in a way words could never explain.

14

Moving On

Deidre Carol Thompson (D.C.)

I hated to lie to Mara and Jada and leave Pappadeaux's early, but I couldn't let them know I was going on a date with another guy that played for the Bulls. If they knew, they would think I am going crazy trying to date two brothers on the same team. Especially that damn Mara, who had already accused me of being a groupie in the past. I knew what she would say.

The fact of the matter is I'm not a groupie at all. I just happened to attract athletes and men with a lot of money. It isn't my fault they draw to me like magnets. I mean what am I supposed to do, tell the men with money to leave me alone, so I can date the damn truck drivers? I don't think so! My mother dated athletes and men with money, and she was always very well taken care of. As the child of an ex-ball player, I'm for damn sure trying to have the life I'm accustomed to living.

My father played thirteen years, and was paid from what Momma tells me. Unfortunately, he was an asshole and refused to marry her, which is why he was hit with child support. That check assisted Momma and me in having easy living. I still have over a hundred thousand dollars from a trust fund that I haven't touched. The judge forced him to set that up when I was a kid.

****

Mario was a guy I met about two weeks after I met Courtney. He's a youngster, but a paid youngster. We met at T. Sylva's Customs on Richmond Avenue, which is where I go to get my custom made suits and to have things altered. I figured he was getting something made, too, because Robyn, the manager was taking his measurements when I walked in.

Since the store isn't big enough to browse around, I took a seat and started searching through the fabric books while she measured him. I was hoping to find a different material for the slamming suit I was going to have Tyrone design for me. As I searched, I overheard the conversation Robyn was having with him. They discussed everything from new music to hot tabloid gossip. When he said he flies frequently to L.A. to visit his boys, I knew instantly he played ball.

I should mention the profiling he was doing with the two diamonds in his ear, the two toned Tag Heuer watch, and the platinum chain with the number forty that was dangling around his neck. He was gaudy, but he was an attractive gaudy. He was a brown man over six feet tall, and appeared to be about two hundred and sixty pounds. I assumed he was probably a linebacker because of his size.

His black and white Nike jogging suit hung loosely on his body, with his matching spotless Nike sneakers. I figured he probably had a Nike contract.

He was in the right damn place to be getting some clothes, because I hated a man to wear sneakers all the time. His hair was in one of those neat little afros which most of the brothers are trying to play nowadays, but like I said, *his was NEAT!* Obviously he was somewhat meticulous about his hair because not one strand of it was out of place. His beard blended perfectly into his goatee. *That whole facial hair thing is very sexy to me.*

"Hey, Baby Girl."

I turned to look at him.

"Do you like this suit right here?" he asked me, holding up a red, double breasted suit, that was doing way too much.

I smiled at his innocence and rough neck demeanor.

"No, not really."

"Why not?" he shot back like he was offended.

Robyn laughed, because she knew as well as I did he was trying to holler.

"Well, do you want the truth?"

"Yeah," he said as he held the loud thing up once again for me to get a better look.

"Baby, that's just too ghetto to me," I smiled.

"Ghetto. Naw, naw," he laughed, "This suit is tight!"

"Naw Bruh', it ain't tight. It's ghetto!"

We all laughed.

"What's your name, Sweetheart?" he asked in a hard, but innocent manner.

"What's yours?"

"My name is Mario. Mario Jackson," he said as he walked toward me with his hand extended.

"Well, it's a pleasure to meet you Mr. Jackson. My name is Deidre. Deidre Thompson."

He shook my hand, and his large hand swallowed mine.

"So are you from here?" he asked.

"Yeah, I'm afraid so. What about yourself?"

"I'm from Detroit, Detroit Michigan."

I couldn't help but smile at his need to tell me that Detroit was in Michigan, as if I didn't already know. *The man was harmless and I knew I could do a lot of molding with him.*

"Motown, huh? It's freezing there." I said.

"Yeah, the weather there is serious. You can definitely freeze your ass off. I mean butt off."

His nervousness and innocence was making him cuter to me. No doubt he wasn't anywhere near as fine as Courtney, but he was definitely someone I could invest a little time into, especially since Courtney had been trying to pull the disappearing act on me. He just didn't know who he was messing with. I wasn't the one to wait around, or the one to be played. A sista' like me always kept a stash of brothers just in case of an emergency.

"I've been there before on business," I explained, "and I got a taste of your city's cold weather. I flew in there in this cute little leather jacket, and when I stepped foot outside that airport, I swear the jacket froze up immediately."

Mario laughed, "I know you ain't lying because it's cold as hell there. Folks don't even like to go outside in the winter unless they have to."

It got quiet. I continued looking through the fabric books.

"So is your husband buying you a suit?"

I thought that was cute.

"No, my husband isn't buying me anything. I'm buying it myself."

"So, why you don't have him do it for you? You seem like a woman that gets what she wants."

"No, I don't always get what I want, and for your information Mr. Jackson, I don't have a husband."

"Oh really, he said with a smile on his face "Well you can call me M.J. since you don't have a man and all."

"Why thank you M.J. I guess you can call me D.C. I mean if you don't have a wife and all."

Mario's smile lit up the store which showed me his beautiful white teeth and unfortunately, the gold tooth he had lodged in the upper left corner of his mouth.

He was a big man, but that Gerald Levert kind of big man. You know, fine in the face, but carrying around a little too much extra meat.

"Since you're free, maybe I can come scoop you one day and you can show me around. What do you think?"

"That could be a possibility. Why don't you give me your business card?"

I knew damn well he didn't have any business cards; that was just my way of getting him to admit to being an athlete.

"You know, I don't have a business card. What about you? Do you have one?"

I reached down in my bag, and pulled out my cardholder. "Here you go."

"Deidre Carol Thompson. Tylenol-Pharmaceutical Representative," he read aloud.

"You know, Ms. D.C., I'm going to give you a call so you can help me get my wardrobe together. What you think?"

"That'll be cool."

Mario walked back over to finish his business with Robyn, and I tried to focus on the fabric swatches and my suit.

"D.C. I'll catch you later." He winked.

"Alright."

I watched Mr. Mario get into his white 740 BMW with shining rims.

"What's up with him?" I asked Robyn.

"Girl, all I know is he'll be playing for the Bulls, and he spends a lot of money on his clothes."

Jackpot!

Mario had been calling everyday since we'd met, and strangely I enjoyed his company. I hadn't screwed him yet, because of my fixation on Courtney, but I was determined not to let him go. I had to have a back up plan, and Mario was the number one candidate because he was young, country, and like I said before, harmless. I knew I could have him wrapped in a small amount of time.

15
Off Track

Jada

*I*t was always a pleasure to wake up at home in my old bed, especially on Christmas day. Christmas is my favorite holiday and I could remember thinking I had the best Santa in the world. because he never made errors when it came to my list.

I always got exactly what I wanted and then some. However, now that those days were over and I didn't have Momma or Daddy to grant my many wishes, this particular Christmas all I wanted was a truthful man and I was hoping that man was Michael.

Momma was up early cooking her traditional breakfast, complete with bacon, eggs, hash browns, grits and biscuits. Every year, she'd fix so much breakfast I could barely handle the dinner she and my aunt would prepare.

"So when is Mr. Michael coming over?" she asked as I sat down with a hot plate.

"He said he's coming around noon. He doesn't have anyone visiting him so he's going to Chicago tomorrow to see his mother."

"Well that's backwards. Why wouldn't he go visit her for Christmas day?"

I didn't have the answer for her, and I surely didn't want to stroke my own ego and say he wanted to stay with me on Christmas Day because Momma would have loved to eat me alive with that one. Even though she thought Michael was nice looking, she wasn't about to let me see she was excited that I'd met someone.

She was so contradictory. One minute she was hinting about grandkids, yet the next, she was reminding me that the men nowadays weren't worth a dime.

"I don't know, Momma," I answered, making sure we had no eye contact because that would be her sign to pick me for more information.

"I hope you're not too serious with this Michael. I think he's a nice young man from what you've told me and from what I could see the other night, but the bottom line is he's an NFL player, and I've heard about how they treat women. They run around here having three and four girlfriends at a time, and on top of that they're always having babies with different women."

"How do you know?" I asked, not wanting to hear her negativity.

"Dr. Hunter, over at the school has a niece that dated a guy who played for the Dallas Cowboys, and he was so in love with her for a few months, wining and dining her, buying her expensive gifts, and then he dropped her like a hot potato. Her time was up in his book, so he replaced her. Rhonda tells me that man dogged that poor child to the ground; said she was finding out about women and babies the entire time they were together. After they were finished she found out even more."

"I've heard all of those speeches about athletes being no good, but I think everybody is different. Just because that man did that to her, doesn't mean Michael will do that to me."

Momma could tell I was getting defensive so she changed the subject.

"So—when are we going to open our presents?"

I was glad she dropped it because I sure didn't want to fight on Christmas day.

"I'm ready when you are."

After I finished my breakfast, she and I went to the tree and got our gifts. Momma handed me a small box wrapped in gold wrapping paper with a beautiful red ribbon around it, and I handed her my box. Her box looked like a box from Tiffany's or one of her other expensive jewelry favorites. I knew it was jewelry because she was a jewelry fanatic.

We both unwrapped our presents carefully like we needed to reuse the paper. When I got the paper off, I saw Saks on the outside, so I assumed it was the silver bangles I wanted.

When I opened it I found a key. A Lexus key!

"Momma what is this?" I asked with a confused look on my face.

"It's a key girl."

"But who has a Lexus?" I questioned in a confused tone.

"Oh my goodness, Jada. You're taking the fun out of this. It's your Lexus!"

I sat still for a moment trying to process what she was saying. I put the box and the key down and ran to the back where momma parked her cars, but I didn't see anything.

"It's in the garage, Silly."

"Oh my God, Momma! Are you serious?" I screamed as I ran to hug her.

"Go on and push the garage button."

My heart fluttered as I pushed the genie button, and watched intently as the garage slowly came up. As it rolled, I could see the back of a black Lexus jeep. It was beautiful!

I ran out the door and over to the garage. I couldn't believe it! It was actually a brand new Lexus truck, the one I said I'd get if I had my own practice.

"Momma, I can't believe you did this?"

She stood back and laughed as I bounced around like a little kid.

"I figured your father had saved up so much money for our vacation home, and other things, things I no longer want now that he's gone. I knew he'd be pleased to know I was spending his hard earned money on his baby. You know how crazy he was about you."

Now I was crying. She had made me reflect back on Daddy and I realized how much I missed him.

"Baby, don't cry. I didn't buy you this to make you sad. I want you to be happy."

I hugged her and told her I loved her, and she did the same.

"You're my baby and I'm proud of you. If I can give you the best, I will."

****

It was noon and Michael still had not arrived. I didn't want to call him and harass him since we had already spoken earlier and he stated what time he'd be coming. He had clear directions, so I didn't anticipate any problems. I was hoping he'd arrive before my other family members came so he wouldn't be placed under a fine microscope.

My rude, put-you-on-the-spot Uncle Bert came with his wife Aunt Loni, at twelve on the nose, and the others were soon to follow. My mother came from a family of eight, and half of them lived right in Houston. Whenever a holiday came around, we always got together until the wee hours of the morning laughing, talking and gossiping about the other half of the family that was back in New Orleans.

"So, Jada, I hear you been running around town with one of the Houston Bulls," Uncle Bert said loudly in front of everybody.

I looked at Momma because I knew she was the only person who could have told him.

"I'm sorry, Baby."

I turned to Uncle Bert, "I do have a friend that plays, but it's nothing serious."

"Yeah, right," my cousin Tonya butted in. "You just don't want us to know what's going on."

Tonya got on my nerves. We were the same age, and used to be close when we were younger, but the older we got, the worse she became. She was so competitive with me. She was happy to be the first one to get married. I didn't care because she married a salesman for Footlocker. He was fine but, like I said, he was a regular salesman, not even a manager. Was I supposed to be jealous of that!

Tonya was always complaining about how he was never at home and how she was tired of dealing with their two year old daughter alone.

She also had a hang up with my size after she had Sydni. Every time we'd get together she'd remind me that once I had a child I wasn't going to be able to wear my cute little outfits anymore. According to her, I was going to spread just like she did because it was in our genes.

The doorbell rang just as Tonya was starting to interrogate me about Michael. I was relieved to be interrupted, but nervous because I knew he'd finally arrived.

"Merry Christmas, Baby," he said as he leaned forward and kissed me gently on my lips.

"You look nice," he said as he checked me out.

"I only have on jeans and a blouse, Michael," I blushed.

"I know, but you still look good."

"Thank you, and so do you."

I grabbed his hand and led him around the back of the house to show him my new truck. I was also stalling before taking him to meet my family.

"Oh snap!" Your mother did not buy you that!" he said in amazement.

"Yes, she did."

"You're a brat, Jay! I can't believe you got a Lexus truck for Christmas."

He walked in the garage and opened it to get a look at the inside. "This is nice, Babe. Really nice. You know we got to hook you up with some nice rims. Right?"

"Yeah, I know."

As we stood talking about the rims and the tint I needed to get, out came Uncle Bert and Tonya.

"So, hello there," Tonya said with one of her fake smiles spread across her face.

"Oh, Michael, this is my cousin Tonya and my Uncle Bert."

"How are you?" Michael greeted, shaking both of their hands.

My stomach rumbled because I knew it was only a matter of time before one of them would say something stupid, and sure enough Tonya kicked it off.

"So I hear you play ball for the Houston Bulls?" she blurted.

You could tell Michael was caught off guard by the way she came right out with it.

"Yeah, I try," he answered, trying to downplay his profession.

Oooh, I was pissed at her. She said it like I'd been bragging about him and she needed to verify the information.

"Ummph," she grunted under her breath, looking him up and down.

I swear I wanted to kick her in the ass. How dare her come and inspect my man, and then be rude on top of that. Then Uncle Bert started in with his twenty-one questions. "So do you know them Sharpe Brothers? Those are some bad cats aren't they?"

I desperately wanted to crawl under a rock. Before Michael could answer, I politely grabbed his hand and led him into the kitchen so he could meet everybody else.

"Merry Christmas, Mrs. Ballard," Michael said to my mother as he gave her a hug.

"That's a nice truck you got for Jada."

"Thank you, Michael," she answered, looking surprised to see him.

"And Merry Christmas to you." Momma continued. "I'm sure glad you could make it."

"I wouldn't have missed it for the world," he smiled. "Oh, and before I forget, I brought you a little something," he said as he reached into his jacket pocket.

I was very impressed. My aunts gathered around, and I introduced them one at a time. "What you got there, Linda?" Aunt Karla asked.

"Oh look, it's a gift certificate to the Taste of Texas restaurant. I've never been there, but I've heard a lot about it. Thank you, Michael. How thoughtful of you." Momma hugged Michael and I had the feeling they would be doing a lot of that in the future; at least that's what I was hoping.

After we'd eaten dinner, and played a few games I was ready to be alone with him, so while everyone else played cards, I asked Michael to go for a spin with me.

"Thanks for letting my family talk your head off. I know you get sick of all the football questions."

"Actually it wasn't bad at all. At least they were nice to me. Sometimes I get folks telling me I'm not as good as such and such and they don't know how I've made it this long in the league."

"You're lying!"

"All the time, and the bad part of it is a lot of the times it's from my own family and friends."

"That's got to be hard to have your family slam on you like that," I said as I pulled into my Mom's neighborhood park.

"I'm used to it now," he said as he rubbed his hand through my hair. "Hey, let's open our presents. I've been waiting all day." He handed me mine and I gave him his.

"You didn't have to buy me anything Michael. I mean we just met," I explained.

"And neither did you," he answered with a smile, "But you did."

I slowly opened the elegantly wrapped box.

"Oh my goodness, this is so nice." I said as I checked out the black Gucci handbag he'd gotten me. "How did you know I wanted this?"

"I didn't. You just look like a Gucci kind of woman, and I haven't seen you carry any big purses, so I thought this would be perfect for you."

"Oh thank you, Michael."

We kissed again, but this time it was longer and more intimate. His tongue gently swayed inside of my mouth and I wanted him right there in the park.

"Ok, let's stop this before we get out of control. Now you finish opening yours."

Finally, Michael unwrapped his small box. It took him forever to get inside it.

His cell phone vibrated as he unwrapped it, and I was able to get a quick glimpse of the name "Angela" blinking on his screen.

I felt uncomfortable, but I knew better than to ask about the call.

"This is nice, Babe," he said as he admired the bracelet.

"I've never seen one like this before. It's very different."

"It's a David Yurman. I thought you'd like it, but if you don't, I have the receipt and you can exchange it for something else."

I noticed as I rambled on about the bracelet, Michael hadn't said a word, and he was sweating.

"Babe, we can step outside if you're hot."

He took off his leather jacket. "I don't know, Jada, but all of a sudden I'm not feeling too good."

"What's the matter, Michael?" I asked as I grabbed his hands.

"I think I need to get home," he said as he got out the truck. I don't feel right."

Michael kneeled down next to the truck.

"Michael, let's go. Get in the car, Baby, and we can get you home so you can lie down!"

Michael started shaking and shivering like he was having a seizure, and I panicked!

"Oh my God!" I yelled "Somebody help me!"

I grabbed his head and turned him on his side.

He shook uncontrollably and I tried to keep his head steady so he wouldn't hit it on the concrete. His grasp on my arm was tight, so tight, it felt like my circulation was being cut off. His eyes were slightly rolled in the back of his head, and he was foaming at the mouth.

I was scared to death. We were in the middle of the park on Christmas evening, and there were no cars passing. I sat on the ground, frightened, with Michael's head in my lap.

I wanted to grab my cell phone and call home or 911, but it was in the truck and I didn't want to leave him alone.

After about three minutes Michael calmed down, and I assured him everything was going to be ok. "I'm here baby. I'm here," I said.

We sat completely still for almost twenty minutes before I finally got Michael back in the truck, and we quietly rode back to Momma's house.

"Jada, I'm going to head on to my house," he said in a shaky voice as we pulled into Momma's driveway.

"But, Michael, I don't think you should drive alone. Let me take you."

"No, that's alright. You go ahead and enjoy your family. Don't let me ruin it like I already have. I'm so sorry you had to see that."

Michael got out of the truck and headed toward his car. I jumped out and followed him.

"Michael, please let me go with you, Babe. I'll be too worried if you go alone."

"No, Jada! Damn, just leave me alone!"

His phone vibrated as he walked away. He answered and explained that he was busy, while wiping sweat from his forehead.

When he ended the call, he turned back around and looked at me for a moment but he didn't say a word.

"Will you let me help you, Michael?" I asked in a soft tone.

Instead of responding he got in his car and left me standing looking and feeling stupid.

Tears formed in my eyes as he slowly backed out of Momma's driveway. Why was he closing me out? What had happened? Was he going to be with someone else? Maybe, it was the woman who kept calling?

I knew I couldn't just let him go, so I ran to my truck and followed him.

I called him on his cell to tell him I was behind him, but he didn't answer. What in the world is wrong with him? I wondered. Did those pills have anything to do with it?

I trailed him to his exit and then turned around to head back to Momma's. I drove and I cried because I hated he was closing me out, especially after I'd shown him I cared.

I wiped my tears and called his home number one last time. After all D.C. did say I needed to fight for what I wanted a little harder.

The phone rang and rang, but he never answered.

"Michael, why are you doing this? I mumbled aloud."

I was a nervous wreck when I got back to Momma's house. Just as I was getting out of my car, my phone rang and he charged right in, "Jada, look. I'm sorry for today, and the way I handled the situation, but I'm not good for you right now. Alright!"

We both sat quietly.

I couldn't believe he was saying this to me.

"What do you mean, Michael, I . . . "

He cut me off.

"Maybe it's just not time for you and me yet. So you take care of yourself."

Click

I leaned against my car, holding the phone in disbelief. What the hell had just happened? Was it over that fast?

16
Heart Ache

*T*wo days had passed and still no word from Michael. It was killing me not knowing what was going on with him. Was he embarrassed about what had happened? Did I not handle the situation correctly in his eyes? I tried to be as gentle with him as I could because I had no clue what else to do. Maybe I was supposed to leave him and call 911. Replaying the scene in my head made me crazy.

****

I was in no mood to be at work and I'm sure everybody could tell by the expression on my face. Mara was the only person who knew what had happened, and she was trying to cheer me up, with her confusing speeches. One minute she would tell me to be patient and understanding with Michael, and the next minute she was telling me to forget about him.

The one thing I couldn't do was forget about him. That was definitely out the question. I had fallen in love with the man. It had been a little less than a month and I was crazy about Michael Riley. Not only did he make me feel like a queen, he respected me as person. Never in all my years of dating had I met a man as sensual as he was. I couldn't let it go, not that easy.

****

Mrs. Stephens, my client arrived to the clinic at eleven o'clock sharp. I was in a foul mood. I was hoping she'd be running a little late, or call and cancel like she had done a couple of times before when her arthritis was acting up. Unfortunately, she didn't. I felt really bad for not wanting to be bothered, but my mind just wasn't into it.

"Hey, Mrs. Stephens" I greeted as I helped her to the back area where we always did her sessions.

"Hello, Jada. How are you this morning?" she asked in her soft voice.

"I'm ok. Just a little tired."

Mrs. Stephens stopped and looked at me. "Why Jada, I see worry in your eyes, and I haven't ever seen you look like that. Lord knows you ain't never tired when I come in here. You're always happy and full of energy. Tell me what happened to you Sweetheart?"

Mrs. Stephens was funny. She always hit everything right on the nose. She was seventy years old and full of wisdom. Each time I was with her she taught me a little black history, or quoted a Bible scripture for the day. It was a strange thing, but after my moments with her I'd start thinking more about my relationship with God and the things I needed to do to get back on track.

"Nothing is wrong. I'm just having a little trouble with a guy friend of mine." I said trying to sound like it was no big deal. I'm sure we'll work it out sooner or later."

Baby, you are going to have plenty of trouble with these young men, especially the way they are nowadays. I swear I ain't never seen nothing like 'em'. They just don't seem to have any respect for women like they used to. I don't ever see anybody holding doors, or helping us get in and out of cars. Oh Lord, it just burns me up to see how these black boys are treating you girls. But I tell you Child, I wouldn't be dealing with that at all. I would demand respect, and if a man couldn't give me the respect I deserve, he could take the highway."

"You're right, Mrs. Stephens," I smiled. "If he can't show me respect, then he does need to get to stepping."

When I finished her session I reflected on the dates with Michael, and him showing me respect was definitely not the issue. He did open and close doors, plus other things.

There was something else wrong with him, and I knew it had something to do with all the damn pills he'd been taking. I'd done my research on the Vicodin, and just as I already knew, it was extremely addictive.

I learned that Vicodin is not to be taken with alcohol and I'd seen Michael drinking plenty of times. It's a depressant just as alcohol is, so the two weren't to ever be mixed. There are numerous side effects like breathing difficulties, stomach pain, nausea, slow heartbeats, and hallucinations, and the list goes on. The question I needed answered was how long had he been taking it, and did he need it to make it through the day? Maybe that's what caused the seizure?

I had so many questions for him and I'd made up my mind that I wasn't gong to sugar coat anything else with him. The next time we spoke, if we spoke again, I was going to hit everything on the spot. No more bullshitting!"

****

The phones in the clinic had been ringing off the hook, and it was making me crazy because every call, I hoped it was him.

"Hey girl, you feeling any better?" Mara asked as she patted me on my back.

"Not really. I just want him to call. I thought we had something special going and for him to just leave town and not say anything is getting to me." My eyes started to fill up, as I held my head back to try and prevent the tears from falling. "I think I'm in love with him, Mara. I know that sounds dumb as hell, because it's been such a short time, but I feel something for him that I haven't felt for anyone else."

"Well, Jada, it's not over yet. He's only gone for a minute. The brother still has to come back. After all, his job is here. It's not like he was here visiting. He has a place, cars and everything else here, so he has to come back. You just need to keep on calling all his numbers until he decides to answer. I know that's not your style, but if he means that much to you, you'll go off the deep end to get to the bottom of this."

"I don't know, Mara, that's going to be hard. I don't handle rejection very well, and what if he rejects me? What if I tell him how I feel and he cracks my face?"

"Well, it seems to me that that's a chance you're going to have to take. You've been disappointed before, so what's one more time going to do, I mean if that happens.

The man may just be clearing his head. He may actually be a little embarrassed that you had to see that."

"But I…"

Just then we were interrupted by another phone call

"Rotsworth Rehabilitation," Mara answered professionally.

While she handled the call, I started wondering if I could really go out like that. Could I fall over a brother and tell him how I felt before he told me? That was going to be hard.

Plus, I didn't want to jock him like all the other women in town. Hell, I'd already been sleeping with the man without making him wait first.

"Come on, Jay, we have to go outside and meet D.C.," Mara said quickly. "She's out in her car crying."

D.C. unlocked the doors and we got in. Mara in the front and I in the back.

"What's going on girl?' Mara said.

I scooted to the middle of the backseat so I could be closer to them.

"This is so fucked up!" she yelled.

"What happened?" I asked, stroking the back of her hair. "Did somebody die?"

"No, no" she sniffled. It's no death or anything. Hell it might be worse."

"Well what is it, Dee?" Mara asked. "You're scaring us."

D.C. turned to look at us, and her eyes were red and puffy. It looked like she'd been crying for days. Her hair was tangled and the clothes she had on looked like she'd had them on forever. I had never seen her look like that.

She wiped her nose and blotted her eyes, but she wouldn't hold her head up long enough to look at us.

"Come on, Dee, tell us," I pleaded softly.

She fidgeted with her Kleenex for awhile, and then she took a deep breath.

"Ya'll he's mar—rr-ried!."

I didn't fully catch it the first time. "What? I asked trying to scoot closer in so I could hear her.

"C-Court—nney is married," she stuttered.

My eyes got big and my mouth dropped. I looked at Mara and she was looking just as dumbfounded.

"You're lying," Mara said faintly.

D.C shook her head, no. "I wish I were, but I just met her."

"What? You met her?" I asked.

"Ya'll it was horrible. I went over to his place after lunch today to surprise him because he'd been saying it was over between us because of some bullshit I care not to go into detail on. I went and bought some wine, ran by my house and took off my clothes. I put on this floor length leather coat and my black heels and I was ready to turn him out.

"Well, I didn't call him before going over because it wouldn't have been a surprise if I had, right?"

Mara and I shook our heads in agreement. "Anyway, I pulled into his driveway, got all my little things out and rang the doorbell. I rang it at least four or five times. His car was there, so I thought he was trying to avoid me, or was gone with someone else. I was about to turn and go to my car when she answered the door."

"Are you serious?" I asked with my hands over my mouth.

"She had a smile on her face, and she was in his robe, the one I've worn so many times." D.C. started to cry again.

"It's ok. Dee," Mara said as she rubbed her back. "It's ok."

"She asked me if she could help me. I was getting ready to say yes, I'm looking for Courtney, when he appeared and cut me off."

"Oh, Dee, Hey, you looking for Rob. He just left."

"I stood there about to faint. I couldn't believe that nigga was playin' me like that."

"Oh, she's Rob's friend?" the lady asked.

"Yeah." Courtney answered, with a pleading look in his eyes for me not to reveal the truth.

"Well you could introduce us she kept pushing, and Courtney looked like he wanted to die."

"Oh, Ummm, Michelle this is Dee, Dee this is Michelle. I extended my hand out to her, and that's when I saw the ring, and I swear I wanted to throw up. I knew immediately she was his wife because the ring was his taste. It looked exactly like a ring he'd shown me one day when we were in Tiffany's. I remember browsing around in there and him asking me what kind of ring I would pick. After I showed him, he showed me the ring he'd pick for his lady. And the one he chose was big and gaudy. Just like the one that was on her hand.

Finally I was able to say "it was nice meeting you," and she responded with "Maybe we'll see each other at some of the games. I'm sure your ticket will be in the same section as mine."

"Maybe so," I answered back.

D.C. started to cry again. "I'm in love with him."

"We know," I answered softly as I rubbed through her hair.

I thought about Michael and our situation. Maybe he is married too.

17
My Secret

D.C.

Courtney really came into my life back in November when I went to a party with Lori, one of my co-workers. Now, I know I told Jada I met him when I was eating lunch with a client, but I lied. I lied about something so trivial because I just couldn't tell Jada I met him through Lori, the woman I said got on my nerves. Jada knows me too well. She would've immediately figured out that I had a motive for hanging with her, and to be honest, she would be right on this one.

Well, back to my story. Lori had been telling me about his guy she was seeing and how gorgeous he was, but I never thought he played professional football until she begged me to accompany her that evening. Going to an event like that was right up my alley, however I dreaded going with her because she was one of those white girls who got drunk everywhere she went, and probably had trains pulled on her a thousand times. I didn't feel like being bothered, but I choked that attitude up and tagged along just in case I ran into the NFL, or NBA player I was looking for.

Lori reminded me the entire week prior to the party that there was going to be plenty of food and drinks and she could guarantee me a great time. I wanted desperately to tell her I had been to more NFL parties than her little heart could handle, and I knew exactly what to expect. My only concern was whether there was going to be only white players there, getting drunk and acting like idiots, or whether there would be some brothers around too?

Since I wasn't for sure, I didn't want to sound too ghetto by asking her ahead of time. I developed a plan of how I was going to escape if it happened to be something I didn't want to be bothered with.

When we got to the neighborhood I was surprised. Not only were we not on the side of town where most of the athletes lived, but the houses weren't major. The homes in the area started at around three hundred fifty thousand., which were shacks compared to some of the real baller's homes I'd seen. I was expecting a gated subdivision that started at a half a million and went to a million plus, but this neighborhood was one of those business men, and doctors' areas, where the wives didn't work, and thought they were something. Little did they not know, they were broke as hell compared to an athletes' wife. An athlete's wife could pretty much buy whatever she wanted when she wanted.

Cars were lined up on the street. We walked toward the house, and I noticed most of the cars had rims, tint, and some were even dropped low. That's when I got a little excited because those were signs that brothers were in the area. I knew my men, and only Negroes plushed their cars out like these. White boys hardly ever bought rims like Sprewells, Twenty Two's, and Twenty Three's. If they did, they would probably put them on a corny car like a Camry. Not saying I didn't like Toyota's but I'd rather something in the Benz, Lexus or BMW family.

"Goodness, this must be some kind of event," I told Lori, still playing the nut roll.

"I told you it was going to be packed," she responded excitedly. "Jason said there is going to be a live band here and everything."

Lori looked too happy for me to crack her face and tell her I didn't give a hoot about a damn band, let alone the food and drinks. I was only interested in the men.

****

The house was nice. It was your typical Texas style mansion, complete with red brick and beautiful flowers. It kind of reminded me of the home my mother had off of highway two ninety with her second husband, the surgeon. That poor man worked his tail off trying to please Momma, and she still left him. I guess after he got sued, and lost his practice, she said screw him! Now, he has been replaced with a guy that owns about ten Wendy's restaurants, and has a real estate company. I don't know how and where she met her men, but she kept one, and of course they were always rich.

When we got to the house there were signs directing us toward the backyard, and as we walked we could hear the band playing. When we got around back, I saw all walks of life partying, drinking, swimming, and having a good 'ole' time. There were mostly black people there which surprised me, because as white acting as Lori is I never imagined her wanting to hang out with a bunch of us. She is one of those blonde hair, blue eyed rich kids from the suburbs that didn't really have to work, but did only to prove the point to her father that she could stand on her own two feet.

Lori's looks were ok to me, but I am sure in white world she is drop dead gorgeous, because she was blonde with blue eyes.

"Hey, let's go over here." I see Jason," she said.

We walked past the pool and toward a bar area where a lot of folks were gathered around getting drinks. As we got closer I didn't see a white boy in the area, so I started wondering where he could have gone, or how she thought she had spotted him when there was nothing but brothers taking up the space in the direction she was headed in.

"Guess who?" she said as she happily put her arms around a big black man. My mouth was on the ground. There was no way in hell Ms. Southern Belle was sneaking around with this big chocolate brotha'.

He turned around, and gave her a hug and a kiss. "Hey L baby," he replied. "I was wondering where you were."

They talked and I stood, still amazed at what was taking place before me. Lori had given me no indication she had Jungle Fever, but the more I thought about it, I realized the subject never came up. I automatically assumed she would be with a white guy from the same kind of perfect world she came from, but she proved me wrong because this Jason dude was definitely far from Caucasian. This man was full blown African American. There were no traces of another race in him at all! *I bet her parents had a fit when she brought him home for dinner!*

I checked him out from head to toe, and he wasn't' anything I'd take interest in. For one he was too big, and had too many damn braids in his hair. I hated braids. The diamond earrings in his ear were flashy, and he wasn't dressed nicely either. He had on some baggy jean shorts, a white t-shirt, and some Reebok flip flops. He looked exactly like one of the football players that I took pride in dogging out when I saw them on television being interviewed. He wasn't an ugly brother, but there was no way in hell I could see him with a pretty woman. A pretty black woman, that is. I guess that's how he got with Lori.

"Oh, Jason, I want you to meet my friend D.C." Lori happily introduced.

"What's up D.C.?" he said real cool with his hand extended.

127

I could barely speak for looking at the diamond-faced watch he was wearing. The damn thing almost blinded me it was glistening so much.

"Hi, nice to meet you," I smiled.

"Ya'll better get on over there and get you some of that food. They have shrimp and everything."

I was smiling as he talked, but in my mind I was talking shit. He knew his country ass had no business messing with a white girl. He probably came from a ten-child family straight out of Alabama somewhere, with a mother who would whoop his tail if he came home with anybody lighter than she was.

"You know Jason, I'm going to go over there and get me a bite of something. Lori, I'll catch up with you later."

I waited patiently in line for my shishkebab and then I strolled inside the house to give myself a tour.

The music was blasting and people were mingling about the house like it was theirs. Men dressed in their casual clothes and women dressed in those pieces of material that were supposed to be dresses, showing all curves and flesh. Most of the ladies looked like they were about to pose for Playboy. I couldn't believe how tacky some of them looked. There was no way I would have shown up looking tasteless, especially on an outing like this that was filled with athletes. The sad thing is the more I observed them the more I started feeling overdressed in my Dolce & Gabbana hip hugger blue jeans with the gold studs down the leg and my blue silk wrap shirt with the three quarter length sleeves.

I strolled toward the bar to get a margarita, and that's when I spotted Courtney, the man of my life, and he was gorgeous! He was a fair skin, very tall man, and I liked that.

Since I focused in on what I wanted, I had to figure out a way to make him notice me. All he needed was one good look, and that would be it. I was confident he would be interested, so I got up, straightened my clothes and strutted down toward his end of the bar.

I squeezed in between him and another lady and that is when I got a good look at him. I could smell the Armani cologne he was wearing. He was a light caramel complexion with a nice grade of hair, faded just right. His eyes were a very light color and the muscles in his arms and legs were bulging out of control. He definitely had the body of an athlete; but that wasn't the feature I liked most. It was his ring finger that was bare. That's what got me excited. He was *fair game*, and I was about to put the moves on.

"So how are you?" I asked when he finally received his drink from the bar tender. The girl next to him turned bright red because I stopped her plan. She should've moved a little faster.

"Fine," he answered in a sexy tone. "And you?"

He was definitely a flashy dresser in his jeans and red and yellow, plaid jacket with a white tank top underneath. His matching plaid hat was a bit much, but obviously he was from the East or West Coast. That was their style. We definitely don't roll like that in Texas.

"I'm doing pretty good." I smiled. "I must say this party is a bit too much for me though. Too many people."

"I know, it is crowded, he agreed.

"Would you mind stepping outside for a bit? I mean if you're not here with anyone," I said like I really cared.

"No," he responded, totally shocked at my proposition. "We can go on out."

I grabbed my drink, took a deep breath and put my strut back on. I knew he was going to check out my hind view as we made our way to our destination. He couldn't help but notice how my jeans were hugging my behind, and if I were to bend over, he would get a quick glance at the top of my thong.

I dropped my coin purse on the floor as we headed outside, and of course I had to bend over to retrieve it. "I'm so clumsy" I chuckled, hoping he got a good look.

We decided to go to the front of the house where there weren't as many people. There was a marble bench out there with a birdbath and a fountain, so we grabbed that spot.

"May I ask your name?" he said, looking me straight in my eyes.

"Deidre Carol, but everybody calls me D.C."

"Oh really, D.C." he smiled, licking his lips as he slightly scanned my body, "I'm Courtney Vincent."

"It's nice to meet you," I said.

"Who gave you the name D.C.?"

"My grandmother started calling me that, and it just stuck with everyone in my family I guess."

"I see. Well D.C, are you from here?"

"Yes, but not this area. I'm from Missouri City, which is south of here. I take it you're not from here?' I asked, knowing damn well he most likely wasn't if he played ball.

"No, I'm from California. I'm just here for work."

There was a moment of silence, and during that moment I debated over whether or not to call him out about his career or to wait. Obviously, he didn't want me to know right off that he played ball because he didn't mention it. That was nothing but a test, and unfortunately it was a test I'd already passed a number of times before. I'd dated enough athletes in the past to know if you showed the slightest bit of interest in their careers, you were setting off a read flag to them that you were a potential groupie. I immediately changed the subject to make him think I wasn't the least bit concerned with any of that. Too bad he just didn't know who he was messing with. If he wanted to play a game, I could definitely go there.

18
New Years Eve

Jada

$\mathcal{A}$ new club opened on Westheimer and Mara and D.C. were dying to go. They were on their hate men kick again and were eager to be on the scene to meet new men to torture and dog. My heart was still broken from the drama with Michael, so I wasn't quite ready to be out trying to scheme brothers out of dinner and dates. We were too old for that, anyway.

There wasn't a day that went by after Michael left that I didn't think about our relationship. Never had I fallen in love with somebody that quickly. I plundered over and over in my mind reasons why he hadn't called me but nothing made sense. I felt like if he cared about me or felt anything, he would've at least tried to contact me. Since he hadn't, as bad as it hurt, I was going to have to get over him. It was obvious he'd replaced me with one of his other women, or just wasn't, feeling me anymore because we had not spoken in days.

Like Momma said, I didn't need to be with an NFL player anyway.

****

The line to get inside the club was from the door to the parking lot, and I was turned off immediately. First of all I didn't want to be there, and secondly, I hadn't waited to get inside a club or a party since I was in college. It wasn't that serious that we be there anyway.

"Why don't we grab something to eat and head back home you guys?" I suggested as we headed toward the front of the line.

"Girl, we're getting up in here." D.C. answered. "We're not waiting in line either. So come on."

We followed D.C. to the front of the line, and people were looking at us like we were crazy as we walked past them. I was trying to figure out what she was up to.

"What are we doing?" I whispered impatiently to Mara as I witnessed women looking like they wanted to jump out of the line and beat us down.

"Girl who knows."

"He-ey Luke," D.C said to a man that was dressed very nicely at the door. "I haven't heard from you in a while. Why you can't call me back," she smiled.

"Get outta here Dee." He laughed. "You know you don't want to talk to me. I don't make enough money for you remember?"

"Ah, that's not true Luke. I can't believe you think that."

D.C. leaned over his shoulder and whispered something in his ear, and he started grinning from ear to ear. I shook my head because it never failed, she always got exactly what she wanted.

We were about to go in when I heard loud music coming from the parking lot. I turned around and there was a black Escalade cruising through. It looked like Courtney's. When I got a clear view of who it was show boating, my stomach quivered because it was Courtney with Michael on the passengers side. He appeared to be admiring a few of the ladies in the line.

"Damn. Who is that?" I heard a woman behind me ask her friend.

I hid behind Mara, so he couldn't see me. I was hoping and praying he wasn't coming inside.

I couldn't believe it was him, and I didn't know whether to call out his name so he could know I was watching him, or leave it be. Actually, I didn't have the right to clown him because I didn't know where we stood anyway. He hadn't shown any interest in letting me know his whereabouts, so I guess that meant we had nothing.

I went in the club with them, but I really didn't want to be there after seeing him. I made sure I didn't tell them I had just seen Michael because I didn't want their input on what I should do, so I kept it to my self.

"Ya'll I think I should go on to the house. I'm just not in the mood for all this tonight," I said once we got inside.

"Girl, please, you're not going to no damn house and sit and mope over that man. We're going to have us a nice little evening and get our groove on," Mara said as she started bouncing her head to the beat of J.A. Rule's song "Living it up."

We found a table directly off the dance floor; one where we could see every person that got on and off of it. Good, we got us a good seat. D.C. said, as she bounced her head "I plan on dancing the night away."

D.C. and Mara were both getting on my nerves with their new attitudes. No matter how hard they tried to play it, both of them were hurting and there wasn't a club in the world that was going to make that pain go away. D.C. had been on her 'forget the world' kick since she found out Courtney was married, claiming she was going to get him back in due time. I never asked her how she had planned on doing that, and honestly, I didn't want to know because there was no telling with her. Mara on the other hand, I didn't quite understand where she was coming from with her attitude toward men, other than the fact that she couldn't get Colin to make a commitment to her. He was the only man I'd ever heard her gripe about. *(She kept saying she thought he was bisexual, because he didn't like to have sex as much as she did, but I figured she was pressuring him into something he wasn't ready for.)*

An hour had passed and I still hadn't had a single dance. Every brother that came along, I brushed away. At one point the D.J was playing jam after jam and I almost went out there, but the crowd on the floor made me change my mind. I didn't feel like finding a spot and bumping into others around me, saying "excuse me" over and over.

"It's live in here tonight isn't it?" D.C. said when she came off the dance floor for the fifth time.

"There are some fine brothers in here too." Mara agreed.

"I'm still ready to get out of here. It's the same old same old thing to me just like all the other clubs." I said.

"Oooh, you are so funky tonight, D.C. said "Snap it together."

I ignored D.C.'s irritating statement and turned to watch everybody dance.

"Will you dance with me?" a voice whispered in my ear from behind. I was a hundred percent sure I knew the voice, but I was too scared to turn around.

"Well look what the wind blew in?" D.C. said before I could say anything.

I hated I told her anything!

I turned my body slightly around, and there he stood looking good as ever.

"How are you, Ms. Jada?" He whispered in my ear, totally ignoring D.C.

Goose bumps were spreading down my spine. I was ashamed of it, but I had a weakness for the man. A weakness I was afraid would make me say and do something totally out of character.

"I'm fine, and you?"

Our eyes were glued on each other, and I wanted desperately to kiss and, hug him and tell him how much I'd missed him, but I couldn't.

"Oh shit" D.C. said. "Let me get away from this table. I'm not trying to see none of this tonight."

D.C. walked away, leaving Michael standing next to me. He sat in her chair and we started having a general conversation about the club and how crowded it was. Then we went on to the wild folks on the dance floor. It was a start, but definitely not what I wanted to discuss.

Then a slow song came on, and everyone coupled up. "Will you dance with me?" he asked grabbing my hand.

"No. I'm not in the dancing mood right now."

"Please, Babe," he asked softly.

Michael's eyes always did something to me, and I got weak, and couldn't resist him. I could feel in my heart he had something to say to me, something that would make things a little better for us.

"Yes, I'll dance with you." I whispered.

Michael led us out onto the crowded dance floor, and surprisingly found us a little spot in the back. Once out there he wrapped his arms around my waist, and it felt like they were supposed to be there.

We danced in silence, and he began to caress my back. That's when I got irritated. "Ok. Michael, what the hell is up with you? You haven't called me or even tried to talk to me in days, and now you see me in a club and start hugging all on me like everything is fine. What do you think this is?"

"I have so much to tell you Jada. So much," he whispered in my ear. "Will you let me explain?"

I pulled away from him and looked him in the eyes. Our bodies stopped swaying to the music.

"If you hadn't seen me here tonight, you weren't ever going to call me were you?" I asked.

He stood for a moment, and dropped his head.

"Yes I would have called you, Babe, but I didn't know what to say. The last time I saw you it was horrible. Everything was messed up. I hadn't forgotten about you, I swear. Hell I can't forget about you. I love you."

Hearing those words eased my heart just a little, but I needed more. I needed a full explanation as to why he did me the way he did.

"Can we go somewhere and talk? I mean, if you feel like it? He asked humbly.

I inhaled, struggling to keep the tears back. "Yes, we can."

We walked hand in hand off the dance floor and back to the table where Mara was sitting with a guy who had a curl. She was talking loud and laughing with him like she'd known him for years. *He looked a mess!*

"Mara, I'm going with Michael. I'll see you guys later."

"Where are you two going?"

"None of your business," Michael answered jokingly.

"Alright. Don't start nothing and it won't be nothing."

"Baby, did you drive?" Michael asked.

"No I didn't, so I guess we can't go anywhere then."

"Yeah, we can. Let's catch a cab." He said with a smile on his face.

"Are you serious?"

"Yeah, I mean we're on Westheimer, the heart of Houston. There's got to be cab drivers everywhere on this street that will take us somewhere."

"You don't mind getting in a cab in front of a club?" I asked him, still caught off guard by his suggestion.

"Look, I come from the projects, and catching a cab was a luxury to me back in the day. I'm not ashamed of anything."

I was impressed with how down to earth he was.

"Well, we can do whatever." I softly whispered.

Michael grabbed my hand and walked toward the door like we had a car outside valet parked. I thought it was flattering he was willing to do something so extreme as catch a cab so he could have some quiet time with me, but in the back of my mind I was still wondering what was up with him.

When we got outside there wasn't a cab driver in sight. "So what do we do now?" I asked.

"The Westin Galleria Hotel is just down the street, and they have a lounge area where we can go for some solitude. Do you mind walking down there?" he suggested.

I was still amazed the brother wanted to walk down Westheimer at ten thirty at night on New Year's Eve.

"That's fine with me."

Off we went, hand in hand, down Westheimer on a beautiful, cool night. In all my years living in Houston, I had never done that. As we walked, I admired the city's scenery, which consisted of bright lights, and tall business buildings, and just like any other big city, there were cars speeding to their destinations.

"Jada, I'm really sorry for everything," he said, breaking my nervous thoughts.

I said nothing because I was wondering if I was doing the right thing.

We were at the hotel within fifteen minutes.

"That wasn't bad now was it?" he said once we got there.

Michael walked straight to the check in counter and pulled out his wallet. "Yes, I would like a room please,"

As the receptionist began tapping on her computer to see their availability, I got pissed and tugged on his arm.

"Excuse me. What are you doing?" I asked with an attitude.

"Oh, I thought we would get a room so we could talk. I know how it looks—but I'm not trying to be funny Babe. I just want to be alone with you. Is that alright?"

His eyes always melted me on the inside.

"I suppose, but how am I getting home?" I responded still trying to be defensive.

"Jay baby, do you think I wouldn't get you home safely?" he asked, picking up my chin.

I blinked my eyes and surrendered. "Never mind."

****

When we got to our room on the tenth floor, I didn't know what to do. I wondered what Michael was really thinking. Did he think I was going to have sex with him after he'd gone a week without communicating with me?

"This is pretty nice?" he said as he placed the room key on the dresser.

"Yeah, it is. Is this a suite?"

"No, just a regular room I think?"

I sat on the bed and started fidgeting with the Coach tag on my purse. My leather jacket was still on, and my posture was straight and tense. I looked like I was waiting to receive life threatening news.

Michael came and sat alongside me. He put his arm around my shoulder like we were pals. "Relax Jada. I'm not trying to do anything, I promise."

He smiled.

"Seriously," he began as he turned my body toward his.

"Jay, I haven't ever met a woman like you that I really enjoy being with. Since I've been in the league, I can't ever tell if a female is really interested in me, or my name. That is why I got a divorce the first time because she was all about the money and I found out too late. I mean in the beginning when I was twenty two, just coming into the league, it was cool to have all the women on my tip, but now it is played out. I'm getting too old for that shit, and these women are so damn scandalous. I'm not trying to get trapped like everybody else in the league; having babies in every city. I know you may not believe me, but I'm ready to chill. I know we haven't known each other long, but I know when the feeling is right, and everything is right when I'm with you."

I had been waiting for Michael to say all the things he was saying and his words were taking some of the pain away, but I still had too many concerns I had to air out before we went any further.

A welcomed silence fell over us.

"Jada, are you messing with someone else?"

"No." I responded surprised. "Why are you asking me that?"

"Well because you never called me to say what's up or anything. I didn't hear from you the entire time I was in Chicago."

"Michael I did try to call you two times. Every time your voice mail picked up. I thought you were avoiding me, or you just didn't want to be bothered. I'm sorry, I'm not accustomed to jocking anybody. To me, you were sending a clear message that you didn't want to have anything to do with me."

"That's furthest from the truth Baby. Jay, there's something about that incident I was too embarrassed to share with you.

He closed his eyes briefly.

"Shit, where do I start?"

Silence

"First of all, I've never had a seizure before. I mean not to my knowledge anyway. Remember when you asked me if I had a problem, you know after you'd seen me taking that medicine?"

I nodded my head yes. I was scared to death of what kind of information he was going to reveal.

"I'm so ashamed to say this, but I do. I'm hooked on painkillers—I think. Well, I know I am, and have been for a year or so now."

I knew it!

My eyes were directly on him. I wanted him to know I was attentive and there for him, so I didn't say a word.

He got up and paced the floor. I could feel his nervousness, so I stood up with him.

"It's ok Michael," I said as I rubbed his back.

"I don't want you thinking I'm some crack head or something. After that night with you, in the park, I got scared. That's when I realized I had a serious problem."

"Well what happened to make you start taking the pain killers?"

"I had a back injury about two years ago, and the doctors gave me all kinds of stuff to get through the pain of the rehab, but nothing worked. I guess my body is so banged up, that each pain killer they prescribed wouldn't be strong enough after a while, so I'd keep going back for more. First, it was the Tylenol with Codeine, then it went to just the anti inflammatory pills, and those things didn't do anything. I started messing with some pills called Vicodin. It's the Vicodin that I can't kick. I never thought I was hooked until a few months ago when my doctor wouldn't give me anymore, and I started calling around to friends I knew who had a hook up with prescription medicines until I found one. I called all over the world trying to get somebody, and finally I did. Now I can get them whenever I want."

I sat with a dazed expression on my face because I couldn't believe what I was hearing. My level of respect for him tripled because he confided in me. The conversation we were having answered all of my questions about him.

"The night I had the seizure I mixed two pills together because I was out of the Vicodin. I took them in the bathroom at your mom's place, and I guess I'm allergic, or I'd taken too much, which is what sent my body into shock. It's a miracle I didn't kill my self. I'm not for sure Jada, but I asked a doctor friend of mine back home about it, and he told me it was possible that my body was rejecting what I took. I guess my dumb ass had taken a bad combination."

Michael sat back down on the bed and put his head down.

"I don't know what to do, Jada. I don't want to be a drug addict.

"You're not a drug addict, Michael. You just have a problem with these pills, and I know a lot of people are probably in the same situation. What we have to do is get on top of it now before it gets out of hand. Do you feel like you can't make it through a day without taking something?"

"Sometimes, I do. What's scary is most of the time if I can't have a pill, I have to have a drink. I'm not even a big drinker. I never have been. I used to talk about brotha's I saw popping three and four Tylenol's or taking pain killers with alcohol. I'm telling you there are dudes out on that field that are drugged up, and the worst thing about it is, all of the coaches and doctor's know it. In all my years, I've only had one doctor ask me about how many pills I was taking and turn me down. He's the one I just told you about. All the others do whatever you ask or what the coaches suggest just to get you through the season. It's messed up Babe, and I'm pissed I let myself get in this situation."

I continued to rub his back as he talked, but I didn't know what to say to him.

"Baby we're going to figure out something. Everybody makes mistakes, and we can get past this, but you have to be strong and want to give up the habit. I know it won't be easy, but you can do it if you put your mind to it."

"I don't know, Jay. It's January and I report to a mini-camp in March. It's going to take longer than a month to kick this I know, and I sure as hell can't have any more surgeries on anything before this season. They have already given me a signing bonus. If they detect the slightest thing wrong with me they'll get rid of my ass in a heart beat.

Michael and I spent the remainder of the night talking about everything from his family to his career. We finally came to the conclusion that he was going to have to visit some kind of rehab facility before the season started, but we didn't know where.

His concern was making sure the public didn't get a hold of the information, for fear of ruining his image.

"Happy New Year, baby," he said when the clock struck twelve, as he planted an unforgettable soft kiss on my lips.

"Happy New Year to you."

Michael Riley

I'm coming to you Lord in an attempt to state my New Year's resolution. I have to kick the pills. I can't possibly enter into another year still taking those things. I have to kick this habit before I self destruct.

So, What's up God? You gonna stand by a brother or what? Just let me know what I'm supposed to do. What do you want from me?

Look, I'll do whatever, because all I know is right now there is no way I can continue to run out on that field in this much pain. I can't survive out there without the help of some kind of drug. Please make it easy on me! I know I haven't done all the things I'm supposed to be doing, but I swear God, I'll change if you just help me this one time.

I'm feeling pain all over my body. My neck is stiff, and I keep a headache from that. I have four broken fingers. My arm has paralysis in it, and my lower back is killing me. Not to mention the knee injuries. I'm about to be more bent over than O.J. and you know that brotha' walks like an old man.

Anyway, is it time for me to quit? If so, please send me a sign. Let me know, cause' I can't keep popping pills and drinking. I swear I'm an alcoholic. I never thought I'd admit to that, but I am. Just to think I used to talk about players that were on cocaine, pain killers, or drinking every damn night. Well, look at me now. I wake up to a sip and go to bed with one. The bad thing about it is I don't really know when it got out of hand. For the longest I thought it was after my baby brother Flip got shot up two years ago, but I think it was before that. I think THAT made matters worse, but it didn't start with his death. This situation started way before him.

There's no way a man living the life I have lived should be a substance abuser. I make too much money and I've been too blessed to be doing this! I'm so mad at myself!

It just crept up on me. One minute I was Michael Riley, the big Pro-bowler, and the next minute I'm Michael Riley the drug addict.

I'm on my knees begging for relief, while I got beautiful Jada sleeping peacefully in the bed right here next to me. If she could see me down here humbling myself to you, she would trip.

God, I'm really feeling her, and I'm hoping I haven't spooked her with all my drama. You know I haven't had too many women that I've opened up to, and you really know I haven't EVER brought a woman as fine as she is to a hotel, and didn't get busy. That's a trip ain't it.

I'm proud to say that Jada and I brought the New Year in right. We talked and got to know each other, and that's how it's supposed to be.

Believe it or not, I don't want our relationship to be based on sex like all my others. I want this to be special. I want her to be my lifelong friend. It's scary, but I'm hoping she'll someday be my wife.

I'm glad you sent her my way, because she's been listening to my crazy situation, and that's what I needed. I just hope she really understands what your boy is going through, and will be patient with me, because it's about to get rough.

I think what I'm trying to say is I'm tired God. I'm tired of the fast pace living, the groupies in my face, the mind games the coaches play, and the most serious thing, I'm tired of being in all this pain. Something has got to give, and I guess it's the NFL.

I know they told me ten years ago it wouldn't last forever and to enjoy the ride. I understood what they were telling me back then, but to be honest, me and hundreds of other brothers are really hoping and praying it will last forever. Running that ball is our life, and we don't know what to do without it.

Jada's moving now God, so I guess I'll go. I wouldn't want her to hear me. I won't take up too much more of your time because I know with it being New Year's Eve and all, you got a whole lot of people to watch over.

Before I go, I do want to say I'm thankful for the ten years you gave me, all the loot I've made, and actually I'm glad I was able to help everybody and their momma out. *(Even though most of them nigga's didn't appreciate it.)*

I guess my time is about up on that field. My body doesn't want anymore hits, and for real, neither do I.

Deliver me God.

Amen

19
Shocking News

Jada

*M*ichael and I decided to catch a cab to my house since I lived closer to the Galleria. As the driver drove us down the street, we laughed and talked about being in the same clothes and our stroll down Westheimer. He joked on me about not being spontaneous and looking nervous once we got to the hotel. "I'm not giving you none!" he said, waving his finger in the air with his hand on his hips, trying to imitate me.

"Whatever, Michael I'm getting in the shower before I take you home," I said unlocking my front door.

"I can get in with you?"

"No. I won't bathe if you're in there."

"I'll let you bathe. I promise," he pleaded as he began unfastening my pants.

I couldn't believe I was giving in to him like I was. Did the man have me whipped? He always said the right things at the right time, leaving me a little more vulnerable each time.

We were kissing and half dressed when Michael's phone rang. He ignored it the first two times, which made me immediately suspicious. Was it the Angela chick again?

"Michael, your phone." I whispered in his ear.

"That can wait babe. This right here is more important."

"Answer it Michael. It could be an emergency." I explained, when in actuality I wanted to see his reaction to whoever it was.

Frustrated, he pulled away from me, and took it out of his jacket pocket.

"What's up?" Michael said when he answered.

I decided to not be childish, so I went ahead to get in the shower. I gave him one last kiss and ran my half nude body to the bathroom.

While the hot water splattered against my skin, I reflected on our night together. How he shared everything with me, and held me the remainder of the night. It was the best New Year's Eve I've ever had. I hoped he was telling the truth about everything because it felt pretty good to be in the arms of a man I could trust. I hadn't had a trusting relationship in years and didn't know the steps to take to keeping it the way it was. I wanted what Michael and I had to last. I wanted him for more than just a man I was seeing on a regular basis. I was envisioning him as my husband. He had all the characteristics I was looking for. The only problem we faced was getting him off the Vicodin, and with the support I was going to provide him with, he was bound to get through that.

I was rinsing my face cleanser off when Michael knocked on the bathroom door.

"Jay babe, can I come in?"

I smiled, because although I hadn't made love to him before I got in the shower, I was more than refreshed and willing to then.

"Come on in," I answered, as I dried my face and dropped the bath towel from around my chest so he could get back into the mood.

He opened the door. "Whoa" he said with a half smile on his face.

I walked up on him and began pressing my body against his. His shirt was already unbuttoned from us starting earlier.

"Babe, we can't he said, stepping away from me. "There's been an accident."

"What? Who?" I said, pulling away and picking my towel back up.

"Your friends had an accident last night after the club. That was Courtney calling."

I couldn't believe what I was hearing. "How bad is it?" I asked nervously.

"I don't know babe, but we need to get over to Ben Taub Hospital. Do you know where that is?"

I stood motionless "Oh My God!"

Ben Taub was one of the best trauma units in the world, but it was also the hospital daddy had passed away in. I had promised myself I would never set foot inside that place as long as I lived in Houston, no matter who checked in there.

****

When Michael and I got there all my fears returned and I started to panic. What if the end result was like it was with my father? Death. I knew if that were the case, I wouldn't be able to handle it. Mara and D.C. were like sisters to me, and life without them, or even one of them, would shatter me forever.

Mara and D.C.'s mom were in the waiting room when we got there. They were sitting next to each other holding hands.

"How are they?" I asked as soon as I ran over to them.

They both gave me intense hugs with reassuring half smiles that let you know things didn't look good.

"D.C.'s mom grabbed my hands and sat me in between both of them. Well, I just spoke with the doctor and he said D.C. has a broken arm, and a few cracked ribs, but she will be fine. Her blood pressure keeps rising, so they are watching her carefully."

"What about Mara," I asked, turning to face her mom.

They said she has a slight concussion from her head hitting the dash, and her face is cut up from the glass. I hear she was pinned in the car, and they had to cut her out, because they were hit on her side. But, Jada, they are also saying she's pregnant. Did you know?"

"Pregnant?" I repeated "N—No, I didn't"

"Well, I was wondering because you know Mara is so private. She never tells me anything until the last minute. I guess I wasn't going to know until after the baby was born. Lord, I just hope my child is going to be ok."

The room got silent for a few minutes, and then Michael came over to us and asked if we wanted him to get us anything from the cafeteria. I had forgotten all about him being with me because he was so quiet.

"Oh, I'm sorry Michael, I haven't introduced you to D.C. and Mara's parents. Michael this is Mara's mother and this is D.C.'s mother.

"It's a pleasure to meet you," they both said.

Michael smiled and said he hoped the best for both of their girls, and then he went on to get a cup of coffee.

"Jada, we're not for sure what happened. We were hoping you knew." D.C.'s mother said.

"No, actually I don't. I was with them last night, but I left early."

"The police are saying D.C. was chasing another car and she lost control of it and side swiped a truck which caused them to spin around and hit a light poll. I don't believe one word of that. Why in the world would my Dee be chasing a car down a street as busy as Westheimer, especially on New Year's Eve? That's bull, and I swear on my mothers grave if they are lying about my Deidre, I'm going to sue the hell out of the entire Houston Police Department."

While D.C.'s mom complained, I thought back to who made the initial phone call to us. Courtney. I knew instantly he had something to do with it because how else would he have known to call us. The only thing I could come up with was they must have been together or she saw him and they got into an argument. But I still thought it was out of character for D.C. to chase him down.

"I guess we're never going to know until we hear what really happened from one of them," I said.

"Well, I'll tell you what, I'm going to figure it out and when I do, somebody is going to pay." D.C.'s mom announced.

D.C.'s mother hadn't changed a bit. She was always talking about suing somebody, or making somebody pay. When we were kids, D.C. could tell her mother anything, be it the truth or a lie, and her mother would listen. Most of the time Dee would be lying her way out of something, and she would still get away with it. Mara and I on the other hand, our mother's didn't believe anything we said.

When my mother finally arrived, I asked her to go in with me to see them. I was too scared to go by myself, because I couldn't imagine seeing either of them hurting. After momma said hello to everyone and gave her hugs, we went to D.C.'s room first.

I held momma's hand firmly, and followed her lead into the room, where D.C. lay wide awake. She appeared to be in deep thought about something when we entered.

"Hey sweetheart," Momma said "How are you?"

"Hey—Ms. Ballard" D.C. answered with a raspy voice.

Momma bent over and gave her a hug

"Hi Dee," I said softly "How are you?"

"Hey Jay. I guess I really did it this time huh." she smiled "You better be glad you didn't ride with us?"

"How is she Jay? Did I mess her up?" she cried.

"No, no. I'm going to her room now. She's going to be fine, both of you are." I responded.

I gave D.C. a hug and left to go where Mara was. Momma reminded me the entire walk down the hall to be strong and pray. I was listening to her, but I still didn't think I was strong enough to handle it.

When we got to her room I said a prayer before opening the door like momma suggested.

She'd been cut by the glass, and her face was swollen. I closed my eyes and took a deep breath before getting any closer to her bed. Thank God she didn't look as bad as I'd imagined.

"Mara, I'm here," I whispered in her ear as I stroked the top of her head. "It's me Jay. Your shadow."

She didn't move.

"She doesn't look bad, Jay" Momma said "She will heal pretty well baby. God takes care of his children."

I kept trying to talk to her, hoping she'd open her eyes, but she wouldn't.

"Mara, remember that time when we were in first grade, and I spent the night with you and you cut your hair?" I smiled "I'm still mad at you for telling your mother I did it. Momma gave me a whooping for that, even though I tried to explain to her it wasn't me."

Mara squeezed my hand.

"Momma she can hear me."

Mara opened her eyes, and squeezed my hand again.

I knew you were faking," I smiled as tears rolled down my face.

HALF TIME

20

Training Camp

Jada
(July 2002)

I was falling in love and there was no doubt about it. Every moment of my day I had Michael on my mind. He was all the man I ever wanted. We developed a very close friendship which lacked in my other relationships.

I enjoyed sharing my thoughts, dreams, and plans with him because he was an excellent listener. He gave me more attention than I could handle. I could ramble on and on about a topic I knew most men would find boring, but he didn't. He not only gave me his undivided attention, he also asked questions to let me know his mind was totally with me. It seemed like after we had our discussion on New Years' Eve, everything was smooth sailing. Matter-of-fact, things were so smooth, and I was so happy I began to fear the time when it was going to end.

****

The season was upon us, and you could tell. Everybody in Houston was going crazy as the first game drew near. I didn't think I would get that excited, but I did. I found myself reading articles about the Bulls even when I wasn't with Michael. Of course he provided a daily report on what took place in the locker room, but strangely that wasn't enough for me. I still had developed somewhat of a fixation on them. Me and millions of other Houstonians couldn't wait for that first game to arrive.

****

It was hotter than hell outside and I was standing out in the sweltering heat watching the Bulls practice. Michael was in training camp for six weeks, and I guess you could say on lock down. He tried to warn me ahead of time of how difficult it was going to be for us to see each other during this time, but I didn't believe him. However, after the second week, I understood clearly. I was dying. I was so desperate to see him. I took off work one day and headed downtown to the Reliant Stadium to watch him practice.

When I arrived, I was shocked to see so many fans in their Bulls gear. I guess if you are a die hard football fan, with nothing better to do, you wouldn't miss an opportunity to watch a new expansion team practice. Of course, there were a lot of women observing the practice as well, and I couldn't tell if they were wives, girlfriends, or groupies. It was funny to watch a few of them prance around in the hot heat wearing their Sunday's best.

Training camp according to Michael was a very crucial time. During the six weeks a lot of men would be sent back home. Nobody was protected during this time. Coaches were on the players like white on rice, fining them large amounts of money for being late to practice, or late for check in. I blocked the thought of Michael leaving out of my mind.

Regardless to whether a player signed a nice contract or not, they could rip it up and bring in somebody else. This was all new to me. I still found it hard to believe that a man could do all that work for a team, and still get the axe.

I spotted Michael when I got to the field, and immediately felt sorry for him. He had on pads and a helmet, standing dead in the sun.

Coaches were blowing whistles, and fussing at the same time. The whole situation appeared stressful.

I headed inside the stadium to find something to drink. There was a group of women standing near the fountain and bathroom area. They were all dressed in hottie shorts with tops that showed a lot of cleavage and skin. As I approached them I thought, "I am not in the mood for any fake smiles, and generic conversation."

"Hi," I said.

"Hello," only one of them responded dryly.

I knew they were staring me down as I drank, but I ignored them.

"Excuse me, but who are you here to see?" one of them asked, catching me totally off guard. She was the same woman I'd seen Michael with at the café. I immediately became defensive. I didn't know whether to say none of your damn business, or to answer, her. I remembered what D.C said about claiming your man, so with an attitude I said "Michael Riley." Why?"

"Oh, Michael," she said with a seductive smile. I know him very well."

I couldn't believe the witch was saying that!

"We were just trying to figure out who was with whom. You know how it is girl?" she continued. I was thinking, *"No the hell I don't know because I'm not a groupie."*

"He's not married is he?" heifer number two asked.

By then I was furious!

I had never had a woman be that damn bold. I started to lie, and say we were engaged, but since I didn't know the details between him and the witch who had asked the first question, I left it alone.

"No, he's not, but we are dating."

"Humph" she said, with a grin, "Thanks."

How immature I thought as I headed in a different direction, pissed at what had gone down. Was the chick from the café one of Michael's women, or what?

Is this what I could expect if I were with him?

21

Confession

Since Michael didn't have curfew until eleven, after practice we headed to Uno's Pizzeria. On our way there, it was a struggle, but I managed to keep quiet about the stadium incident while we were driving.

"So what's on your mind, Sweetheart?" Michael asked as he kissed me across the dinner table.

"Nothing. Why?"

"I don't know. You have this look on your face, like you're deep in thought about something."

He hit it on the nose, and I didn't know what to say, because he was right. I did have something on my mind, but I didn't know how to share it with him. I kept wondering, "Do I tell him I met one of his women at the stadium, and she tried her best to intimidate me, or do I let it ride?" "Would he think I'm a wimp if I come to him with a situation like that?"

"Look here, Baby, whatever is on your mind, I want you to share it with me. I'm trying to be straight with you Jada, and you're going to have to do the same with me."

We sat quietly as the waiter placed our large gourmet pizza on the table.

"Umm," Michael said. "Babe you don't know how long I've wanted this pizza. This shit is the bomb back at the crib!"

Michael talked on while I thought about the situation. Something was telling me deep down that he was lying about her just like he did about the pain killers. That woman had a look in her eyes that told me she either had Michael or wanted him. It was a vicious, scandalous look, that made me feel very uncomfortable.

"I'm glad you suggested this place. Do you come here a lot?"

I smiled, but didn't answer.

"Did you hear me, Jada?" he said, touching my arm to get my attention.

"Yes, I heard you."

He looked at me for a moment.

"Alright, what's the deal?" he asked as he put his fork down.

"I already told you."

"No, Jada, there's something wrong, and I want you to tell me."

He held my hands. "Be honest with me. What's the problem?"

I looked deep into his eyes, and inhaled before I asked— "Michael are you involved with someone else?"

He looked at me with sincerity and said "No baby. Where is this coming from?"

I explained the incident at the stadium, and I even described the woman. Michael denied knowing her.

"Jada baby, I want you to trust me, and I'll do whatever it takes to get you to believe in me."

"What about all the women? How can I be sure you're strong enough to handle them?"

"Jada, there are women in my face on a regular basis, but they don't mean anything to me. Hell, ninety percent of them are groupies and have been passed around throughout the NFL and the NBA. I don't want a woman every man has had. I don't care how beautiful she is."

"You know what, Michael? The bottom line is I don't want to waste my time. I've been in plenty of relationships that were a waste of time, and I'm not trying to do it again."

Michael gently stroked the side of my face.

"I understand sweetheart, and please believe that I'm not trying to waste my time either," he said.

"I don't want a relationship filled with the other woman drama" I said "I know people go through things in a relationship, but I don't want to go through that madness. I'm sorry."

"Jada are you trying to get rid of me? Michael asked in a low serious voice.

"No—I'm not Babe. I answered nervously fidgeting with my bracelet.

"Well, give me a fair chance. I'm not like your other men, nor am I like the impression you have of athletes. See, you have me stereotyped just like the rest of the world. All athletes are not womanizers, and party goers who want to have a good time. To be honest with you, a lot of us have morals and values just like you do. But when a few of us mess up, we all get lumped into that one big pot of stereotypical judgment without ever having the opportunity to defend ourselves.

I felt bad as Michael continued.

"Jada, I'm just a man who happened to be blessed with a talent. Trust me, I never thought having a blessing bestowed upon me would be this difficult to deal with."

Michael's serious tone and straight face made me feel worse, so I began to apologize.

"Michael, listen, I...."

Putting his finger to my lips, he said "Don't worry about it. Just promise me in the future, when you hear something about me, you'll come and ask me about it before jumping to any conclusions. Can you do that?"

"Yes," I softly responded, kissing his lips.

"There we go. That's my girl."

22
Stalker

Michael Riley

*J*ada dropped me off at the hotel around ten forty five, feeling a little better about what had taken place at the stadium. She's such a beautiful woman, and I can't mess things up with her. That's why I lied.

I knew it was Angela and her crew of groupie friends that Jada met at the stadium, and I am so sick of those bitches! See, Angela has been following me from city to city since I got in the league. She just can't accept the fact that I filed for a divorce and moved on. Who does she think I am?

When I found out she tried to holler at another player on my college team named Gant, I was done. I had fractured my foot right before draft, and couldn't play, so she thought I had ruined my chances of getting signed. It was her loss because I still got drafted and went higher than Gant did. In a way, I needed to thank Angela for fucking up the way she did, because if she hadn't I would be looking quite stupid right now like a lot of brothers who don't know who they're married to.

I spotted Angela as soon as I entered the hotel. I tried to walk past her, but of course she wasn't having that.

"Angela, you can't keep doing this!" I said as calmly as I could.

She pulled the back of my shirt and I knew if I didn't stop to listen, she was going to cause a scene; and I didn't need another one.

"Michael, will you just talk to me for a minute please?"

"I would but I have curfew in about five minutes. You know the deal. Can we talk tomorrow?" I calmly replied.

Her eyes watered, and I knew it was going to be trouble.

"Michael, I was your wife. Have you forgotten that?"

I took another deep breath, and reached for the elevator button.

"No, Angela, I haven't forgotten that, but we are not married anymore and I don't owe you shit, so please stop this!"

She grabbed my arm and yelled, "You owe me brother! Do you want the Houston Chronicle to do an article on athletes and pain killers, because you know we both know a lot about that topic, now don't we?"

With fire in my eyes, I ignored her.

"I hope you're listening to me, Michael, because I'm sure it would draw a lot of your fans attention, especially since you've been on the shit since college."

I stared at her, feeling hatred like I've never felt before. She had been blackmailing me for years, and I'd already given her over a half million to shut up and go away, but she kept returning.

"Michael, who was the woman at practice today?"

"Why, Angela? That is none of your damn business, and you and those groupie friends of yours need to stay away from the stadium."

"I'm going to ask you one more time." She said with one finger up. "Who was the bitch at the stadium?"

"Please leave, Angela, before I call the police. Please!"

"Oh so now you want to talk that shit again! Haven't you figured out by now that that doesn't scare me! I love you Michael. I made a mistake. Will you please give me a second chance?"

Reaching for the button again; I stared at Angela in disbelief. I couldn't believe she thought I'd take her back after what she'd done. After at least ten years she still pops up in every city I live in, from Chicago to L.A. to Houston, trying to get me back through manipulation.

"Ok, you won't talk to me, so guess what? I'll ask the bitch myself. I know everything about her little ass, and if you keep fucking with me, I'll go to every paper in town and let them know Michael Riley's big secret!"

The elevator doors opened and I quietly stepped inside.

"Did you hear me, Michael? I know where the little bitch lives! I'm going to tell her who I am?"

The elevator doors closed, and I hit the walls. I didn't know what to do especially after I'd just looked Jada in those beautiful eyes of hers and lied. For some reason, I felt the need to protect her, and maybe I just didn't want her to think I was another no good brotha with a bunch of issues.

The elevator doors opened, and my coach was right in my face.

"Good evening Michael. Long night." He said. I shook my head yes, while thinking, I didn't need any shit from him about being past curfew.

"Yeah, it's been a long one," I smiled.

Ding—the elevator doors opened to my floor.

"Have a good night, Coach." I said and stepped off.

"You too."

I headed to my room, thinking about all the years I'd put up with the curfews, fines, and all the other bullshit that came along with the league. If my family back in Chicago didn't rely on me so much for financial support, and if I knew what life after football would be like, I would walk.

23
Check up

Mara Sampson
September, 2002

"Well Mara it looks like you and the baby are doing just fine," Dr. Young said as he felt my round stomach. "Have you been experiencing any pain, or having contractions?"

"I haven't been in pain so far, but I am having a lot of those Brachston Hicks contractions. Is that what the real contractions are going to feel like?"

"Not quite, but close. When you have a real contraction, you will know. I've heard they feel nothing like the Hicks ones," he smiled. "Well, we're all done here. Let's see, your delivery date is September fifteenth, which is next week, so you better make sure you have a bag packed. You're running out of time."

"That's done. I just have a few more things to do around the house. But tell me, doctor what happens if she doesn't come on the due date? Will you still take her on that day?" I knew I was asking a million questions, but I had to because I didn't know anything about babies, especially having one.

"If she doesn't come on her due date, we will give her an extra week. If she doesn't come by then we will schedule a date to induce labor. How does that sound?"

"Pretty good, but I'm still scared about all of this."

"That's normal. Most women are a wreck with their first child, but by the second, third and fourth ones, they turn into pros."

"Trust me, Doctor Young, there won't be a second, third, or fourth here. I'm afraid this may be my only one."

"That's what all the ladies say in the beginning, but they end up coming back to visit me not even two years later. You will change your mind. Trust me."

When the doctor left the room I thought about how much time I had left. It didn't seem like nine months had gone by as fast as they had. I still had a few things to do before the baby was born, like get the carpet cleaned in the house, get all my bills paid, and call around to find a good pediatrician. It wasn't a lot, but I was running out of time. The most important thing on my to do list was to tell Courtney he was the father. I'd prayed and prayed about it, and my heart kept telling me he needed to know. Whether he decided to acknowledge me or not, that was information I couldn't keep from him.

****

I was surprised Courtney agreed to meet me on my first try. I just knew with the season being two days away, it would be an on going thing of me asking and him being too busy. After all, we hadn't talked since January. We hadn't seen each other since the incident at the club when D.C. went crazy. I still don't even know what triggered her. All I know is we were walking out of the club heading toward D.C.'s car laughing and talking when she spotted Courtney. He was in his Escalade with another guy, cruising through the parking lot, stopping ever so often to check out women. All of a sudden D.C. started yelling obscene things at him. "Courtney Vincent is a lying son of a bitch!" she screamed at the top of her lungs.

"Come on D.C. don't go out like that," I said trying to calm her down.

Courtney and the guy he was with turned around to see who it was, and when he saw it was D.C. he threw his hand up at her in disgust, and kept on doing what he was doing.

"Why in the hell did she do that?" I thought. Before I could finish my thought, she was running toward his car, and was swinging at him through the driver's side window.

"Get this crazy bitch out of here!" He screamed at me.

"I got your bitch motha fucka!" She shouted back as I tried to pull the back of her dress for her to come with me.

"Your ass won't be talking shit when I tell your wife now will you?"

"Stop it Dee!" I hollered "Stop it now! Let's go home."

Courtney drove off and I had her calm. Everyone watched us leave.

"I swear I'm going to make him pay, Mara. I'm telling his wife every damn thing and fuck his marriage up, you watch me! Plus I know some more shit on his ass. His career is in my hands! That nigga owes me, and I'm gonna get mine!"

"Just calm down, Dee. Let it go! You can't keep tripping with this man like this. It's over!"

D.C. got quiet and I thought she had cleared her mind and was calming down, until she spotted Courtney's truck at the traffic light in front of us, and she sped up.

"Don't start this shit again!" I screamed at her "Don't start driving crazy because you see him in front of us Dee!"

D.C. ignored me and pressed her foot to the floor, weaving in and out of cars on Westheimer.

"Slow down, Dee!" I kept yelling.

I guess by the time we caught up to Courtney, he had already spotted us coming in his rear view mirror, so he picked up speed. We were all racing full speed down the street at two o'clock in the morning, when out of nowhere a doughnut truck pulled slowly out in front of us. The rest is history. I don't recall anything else from that point on, but I knew God had spared me again. That was a night I'll never forget, especially since that's how Momma and the rest of the world found out I was pregnant.

****

Courtney was about ten minutes late meeting me at the California Pizza Kitchen off Post Oak Boulevard. I was already seated and munching on a medium vegetarian pizza when I saw him park his car. I was ashamed to say, but I felt queasy as I watched him walk toward me. I wasn't sure if it was the baby, or me having feelings for him, but something was going on inside of me. Courtney and I had only clicked because he liked to talk trash and he could screw. At least that's what I thought in the beginning of our fling, but somewhere down the line I guess I started developing feelings for him. He was really a good brother. That's why when D.C. announced that he was married, I got sicker than she did. Not only was I fucking around with my best friends man; he was married. That is something I have never done and wasn't about to do, so I broke it off. He was disappointed in my decision, even after I told him I knew he was married. He wanted to continue our little sex sessions, but I couldn't. He even tried to convince me he was getting attached to me.

I had already done too much lying and was now about to become a single parent; all because I had those sexual encounters with Courtney Vincent.

"What's up Mara? He said, when he got to the table. His eyes bucked wide as he noticed my full face and stomach. "Damn, when did that happen?"

We hugged each other and took our seats.

"You look nice." I said ignoring his question.

"And so do you. A lot different than the last time I saw you, but nice," he smiled

"Well how's life been treating you, Mr. Vincent?"

"Better now that I'm sitting across from you."

Why was I blushing? I wasn't for sure, but I was positive he could tell.

"So, are you nervous about the game?"

"Naw, not too nervous. I've been doing this for eight years now, and I really don't get excited anymore. It's a business baby. Just a cut throat business."

Pause

"Forget about me." he said "What's up with you?"

"Courtney, look I won't keep you, and I know you are wondering why I needed to meet with you since we haven't talked in months. First, I'll just say it has nothing to do with D.C."

He breathed a sigh of relief.

"Good because she is still leaving crazy messages on my pager, and threatening to tell my wife. She keeps saying she has something on me that will ruin my life, but I don't know what the hell she's talking about. I wish she'd go away. Actually, I wish I had never touched her fatal attraction ass. You know she's a big time groupie don't you? I found out there's a couple of brotha's on the squad that has been tagging that too."

"Look, I don't want to talk about D.C. right now. What she does is her business."

I knew all along D.C. was a groupie. Brothers just kept falling for her look.

"I need to tell you first of all thank you for calling the ambulance for me the night of the wreck. I remember hearing your voice when they tried to get me out of that car. I remembered him saying **"Hold on Baby. Don't go out on me like this."** I will always be indebted to you because you could have left and called from anywhere else, but you didn't. You stayed" My eyes watered as I rubbed my hands nervously together trying to get to the point of us being here.

"Can I get you anything else? The waitress asked.

"No thank you," I answered.

"I'd like a Pepsi," Courtney ordered.

He reached across the table and caressed my hands. "You know I was at the hospital that night with you too" I looked surprised.

"Yeah, I followed the ambulance there, and I stayed until your mother got there, but I don't think she saw me. Mara, I still do care about you, more than you'll ever know, and if the situation were different I would be trying to have a relationship with you because you're so different from the usual selfish, non-conversation having women I usually attract. I'm so sorry for lying to you the way I did. And as far as my marriage, I can't even go into detail about that. It has been on the rocks since the first month of the entire six years. That's another story that I don't care to get into right now"

I was nervous as he talked, and I couldn't believe it, but as I sat face to face with him I made up my mind that if he rejected us I would deal with it. If he didn't, that would be cool to. The bottom line was I had feelings for him and I wanted my child to know her father.

"Oooh" I said, taking a deep breath and grabbing my stomach.as I felt it tighten and loosen again.

"Are you ok.? he asked.

"Yeah. Just another contraction."

"A real contraction?" he asked surprised.

"No. I'm having those Brachston ones.

"Whatever those are." He answered.

"Are you serious with the father, or have you already gotten married on me?" I looked down at my huge belly as I prepared myself for what I had to do.

Then Courtney's phone rang, giving me more time to think.

I began to sweat as I pondered how I was going to deliver the news to him. There was no easy way to tell him that he was the father of my unborn child.

"Ok, back to what we were saying," he said as he hung up his cell.

"No, I'm far from being married." I said softly.

"Oh, you are." He smiled as if he were relieved to hear that news.

I inhaled one last time and then I blurted it out "Courtney you're the father of this baby."

His face went blank instantly and a look of bewilderment came on it.

"What did you say?"

"You're the father of my baby." I repeated softly

He sat speechless, and I felt like I should have kept my secret.

"Are you sure?" he asked

"I'm very sure, and it's a girl."

"Damn," he whispered under his breath as he looked out the restaurant window. "I have really fucked up this time."

Silence

"You know what, Courtney. I'm not telling you this story to get money from you or to try and ruin your marriage, but I thought you should know. You don't have to do anything for her, or even see her, but it was only fair that you know."

"Can we take a blood test once she's born? I mean I have to be sure."

My initial reaction was to curse his ass out, but I didn't—I couldn't. He had the right to want to know, and I was more than one hundred percent sure it was his, in spite of the world assuming it was Colin's.

"Sure. Whatever you want," I replied. "I'm not due until next week, so we can have it done immediately."

I reached inside my purse and took out the piece of paper where I'd written the hospital name and number. "Here is the hospital name and number, and like I said I'm not expected to deliver until around September fifteenth sometime."

While I talked, Courtney sat with a confused look on his face.

"I—I don't know what to say, Mara. I need some time to think."

"That's cool. Here just keep this and if you decide to call that number to find out when she's born then that's fine. If you decide not to, I hope you have a great season and I wish you the best. Just call me if you want to talk."

Courtney sat and stared at me. "I can't believe you're not yelling and screaming at me. Why are you so calm?"

I shrugged my shoulders like a little kid, "I really don't know. I guess I've come to the conclusion that I'm going to have to do this on my own. It may be hard in the beginning, but I'm a fighter so we'll be alright."

"I promise you'll hear from me next week if not sooner." He softly stated.

He stood up, gave me a kiss on the cheek and said goodbye. As he walked away the tears I struggled to hold back finally slid slowly down my face. I knew I'd never see him again, and I knew my daughter, my Courtney, who I was naming after her dad, would never meet her father.

24

Game Day

Jada

*B*utterflies fluttered through my stomach as I drove down highway 610 headed for the Reliant Stadium. The stadium was adjacent to the Astrodome (our old stadium) on Kirby Drive. It featured the NFL's first retractable roof and grass playing surface. Of course I didn't know crap about retractable roofs or grass surfaces but I'd taken a strong interest in anything relating to the Bulls since I'd been dating Michael. The Houston Bulls were playing their first game of the season against the San Francisco Forty-niners and I was hyped!

I had never been to a professional football game before and you could tell by how nervous I was. Unlike high school or college, this was the real thing, the NFL, and I was excited to be attending it as Michael Riley's woman.

On the way there I imagined what the other ladies would look and act like. The times I'd seen athletes wives on television, I got the impression they were not very personable. I looked at my outfit and wondered if it were dressy enough. When I asked D.C. her opinion, she said I had to be the sharpest one there and I needed something from the Versace store. Of course Versace costs a fortune and the accessories she mentioned were well out of my price range. I didn't see the need in buying a Prada purse and Prada shoes for a football game. The purse alone was a thousand or more, which made me eliminate the shoes real quick.

Mara, suggested jeans and a cute top because she couldn't fathom the idea of dressing up for a football game either. She said she didn't care if Will Smith himself had invited her, she would never dress to attend such an event.

I didn't go with either of their suggestions. I decided to wear a linen sundress with spaghetti straps, to show off my cut arms, and my khaki colored BCBG sandals that strapped around my ankle. My toes were freshly manicured in the French way and so were my hands. Everything was together, including my hair which I decided to wear down since Michael hadn't seen it that way in a while. I admit with it being a high of ninety three degrees outside, my hair was hot as hell on my neck, but after sitting in Toya's Salon for three hours to have it flat ironed, I was determined to leave it down.

Around eleven o'clock I pulled into the stadium parking lot. There were people tailgating everywhere. I couldn't see anything but Bulls jerseys and t-shirts throughout the parking lot. Folks had tents set up with barbeque pits smoking and televisions playing. My mouth hung in disbelief. I could not believe the level of tailgating that was taking place. I mean, I'd seen tailgating in college, but this was quite different. There were men relaxing with beers in recliners and on couches, watching screen televisions like they were at home.

Here it is an hour before kick off and I could barely get through all the fans. Houston had gone a long time without a team and the fans are excited. It is amazing to see so many smiling red and blue faces with the teams paraphernalia plastered all over them. The more I watched them, the more pumped I became.

Michael gave me a parking tag to hang from my rearview mirror. The pass allowed me to park in a special section. The stadium workers guided me to their special parking area where a man was guarding the section. He smiled and opened the fence to let me in. I parked my car next to a red convertible Mercedes and left the parking lot to find my way. I guess the attendant could tell I was confused, so he asked to see my ticket. He offered to take me to a tunnel where an elevator would land me directly in front of my section. That way I wouldn't have to deal with the hassle of walking through the crowd. I had never heard of such, but of course I hadn't been hanging out at a lot of stadiums either.

When we got to my floor, a sign stared me in the face reading sections twenty-three through twenty-eight. I smiled. I was already enjoying the NFL treatment.

I took my time walking down the concrete steps, studying each and every one carefully. My stomach bubbled as I glanced down at my ticket stub, then back to each row as I passed them by. I could feel eyes on me as I walked and I could hear whispering the closer I got to the field. Finally I heard someone say, "I wonder who she's here to see?" and that's when I knew I'd made it to my section.

Excuse me, excuse me," I said with a smile as I crossed over a few women trying to get to seat twenty eight C. Not one of the ladies returned the smile, but trust me, I was honored with looks of impatience.

"Hello," I said to the lady sitting next to me when I finally reached my seat.

"Hello," she replied dryly.

I tried to avoid looking in her direction because I could feel she was not in the mood for chit chat. It was difficult, considering how close our seats were to each other. She focused her attention on the field, letting me know she cared little about becoming acquainted with me.

I hated to admit it, but she was an attractive lady. She looked like one of those island women—like the ones I'd seen when I visited the Bahamas. Everything about her was natural and beautiful, and her demeanor let me know she knew that.

I was thumbing through the game program looking for Michael's picture when I heard "excuse me" all over again. I looked up and there was another black woman headed in my direction. The seat to the right of me was empty so I knew she was coming for it.

"Excuse me, I'm so sorry," she said with a southern drawl.

"Oh that's ok." I replied, loud enough so the funky woman to my left could hear what kind words sounded like.

"Girl, I had a time finding this damn place, she started right in. "See, I'm from Tennessee and I don't know anything about Houston. Are you from here?"

"Yes, I am, and I still get lost. Houston is an easy place to get turned around in if you're not familiar with it."

"Girl you ain't never lied. I been driving for almost an hour trying to get to this stadium. Hell, I'm tired now," she chuckled.

This woman was a very pretty woman as well, with a deep brown complexion. Her features were very dark, and her hair was cut in a short funky style. The sister was together from head to toe, and I was glad she and her personality had come to save the day for me.

"I've talked your head off and haven't even introduced myself. My name is Vickie, Vickie Keith, she said with her hand extended. My husband, Darren Keith is the running back.

"Oh, ok." I said, like I knew who Darren Keith was. "I'm Jada Ballard, and I'm not married to anyone," I smiled.

"Well, it's a pleasure to meet you, Jada." She laughed "Now let me warn you, I get really excited during the games and can act crazy sometimes. Just pinch me if I get too wild ok?"

"I'm sure you won't scare me. Feel free to do all the yelling and screaming you have to."

The game music started and the crowd got crazy. Everyone jumped up and started dancing and clapping as red, white and blue confetti was thrown throughout. I couldn't believe the crowd was so rowdy. Even Ms. Sidity, next to me clapped her hands and patted her feet to the beat.

"Girl, this team is going to be off the hook! I can just feel it. Look how pumped up these folks are" Vickie said as she clapped and screamed along with them.

"I've never seen anything like this," I answered as I tried to move to the beat like they were.

Then the guys ran onto the field and chills shot through my body. They looked so handsome in their fitted uniforms, with their shirts and socks tucked in to perfection.

"Oh my, God, they look so good," I mumbled

"Don't they girl. I love the dark blue helmet."

The music stopped, and we took our seats, but my rush was still there. I felt like a little kid waiting for a surprise. I was that pumped up!

"Look, I think number twenty nine is trying to get your attention."

I looked down at the field and there stood my baby looking extra fine. He winked and put his thumb up and I waved and smiled back blushing from one end of the stadium to the next.

"Isn't that cute?" Vickie said, "I remember when Darren used to do those sweet little gestures to me. I could always count on him to look for me in the stands after he'd made a big play. But now girl, that brother hardly ever pays my section any mind. I guess that's what happens when you've been playing for eleven years."

"You guys have been in this for eleven years?" I repeated, totally surprised.

"Girl yes, and I tell you what, we have been through it all. We've been cut, traded and signed a million times. Baby, nothing shocks me anymore. You'll see what I'm talking about. Actually our time is almost up, and to be honest, I'm glad.

We've saved us a little money and Darren made his pension, so I don't care anymore. You know you have to have three years to make that? Has your friend made his?"

"Yeah" this is his tenth year." I didn't know why I proudly answered as if I knew what I was talking about. I wanted to tell her I had not been dating Michael a complete year yet, and I did not know where our relationship was headed, so I did not really know if I would learn the tricks of the NFL or not. We were still in the beginning dating stages.

"Girl, the NFL is serious," she continued "When they love you, they love you, but when they don't, you're out! That's why these brothers need to start saving, stop flossing, and leave these, excuse my French, Groupie Bitches alone!"

It was horrible, but I instantly thought of D.C.

"Go! Go! Go!" Vickie yelled along with the crowd.

"Jada, you better pay attention, that was number twenty nine that just made that touchdown!" Vickie announced very excited.

I looked down on the field and the play was over. The announcer was saying Michael's name and they were replaying the play on the screens. Michael had a beautiful interception and smoothly scored. I was staring at him down on the field, hoping he'd look up at me, and he did. Our eyes met and he put his thumb back up.

****

The final score was fourteen to twenty one, the Forty-niners had defeated us, but in spite of the loss the crowd still cheered. They cheered until the last player jogged of the field.

Vickie and I followed some of the other women from our section down to the tunnel where we were going to meet the guys. We stood to the side and waited for our men to come out the locker room along with about fifty other women. Everybody was staring, trying to figure out who was with whom and who had on what. The stares made me feel a little uncomfortable.

"This tunnel is different from the one we had last year in Jacksonville," Vickie said as she looked around with her nose in the air. "Girl down there, they have snacks for you while you wait for the guys, 'cause Baby sometimes it takes them forever to come out of that damn locker room, especially if they have to get something taped up like Darren usually does."

I couldn't respond to her because I didn't have a clue what she was talking about. The only tunnel I'd been in was the one I was standing in right then, and it looked fine to me.

"Here comes Darren."

I looked up, and walking toward us was a tall slender chocolate man with a bald head. He didn't look like a football player at all. More like a basketball player. He could've easily passed as Michael Jordan's twin. He was very handsome in his black suit, with a light blue shirt underneath. The diamond in his ear glistened against his flawless skin tone.

"Hey baby," he said to Vickie, bending down to give his five foot wife a kiss.

"Hey Man. You played good," she smiled.

"I did alright."

"Oh Babe, this is Jada. We just met. Jada this is Darren."

We shook hands.

"It's a pleasure to meet you Jada," he said.

"Same here."

"Check you later girl," Vickie said.

I watched them walk off hand in hand and I pictured me and Michael. I wanted to be there for him after each game like she was. I wanted to compliment him on his every move and mistake like I knew Vickie was going to do with Darren.

"PSSST, PSSST" I heard. I looked toward the locker room and there was my man. Why he came out in sunglasses and we were indoors, I don't know. They did look suave with his suit, adding more flavor to the outfit. I didn't know where he gets his clothes from or who tailor made them, but whoever it is needs a reward because the dude is sharp!

"How's my lady?" He said as he kissed me lightly on the lips.

"Fine and you?"

"Oh I'm cool," he grinned, showing off his dimple.

Michael grabbed my hand and our fingers intertwined, and even though I wasn't Mrs. Riley, I felt good just being on his arm.

25

Crab Cakes

Jada

$\mathcal{M}$cCormick and Schmicks was more crowded than usual. Michael had never been before, and since he asked me to choose our restaurant I chose McCormick's because they had excellent crab cakes too. Plus, the ambience there was outstanding. You can always get a nice quiet seat to sit and talk by candlelight. If you are alone, it is the perfect place to think.

"I have passed by this place a million times, but never stopped to eat here. What kind of food do they have?" Michael asked.

"Mostly seafood. I chose it because I love their crab cakes. You like crab cakes don't you?"

"Babe, I don't consider dishes like crab cakes real food. Brothers don't walk around trying to find the best crab cakes in town. That's a woman thing. I'm looking for some real food, and not any of those cute and danty dishes."

"They have a nice selection. Trust me," I said slipping my arms around his waist.

Michael and I had been getting along wonderfully since we cleared the air about his problem. He swore to deal with the Tylenol with Codeine in moderation until the season ended so he could wean himself from the Vicodin.

I thought that was fair enough, although I didn't want him taking anything. The reality of the matter is that the pain in his lower back and neck is going to be there until he has surgery, which he has absolutely refused to do for fear of it ending his career. I hate to inform Michael that every client I helped with that same herniated disk problem, required surgery because the pain was too unbearable.

We sat on a bench and watched people come and go from the bar. A lot of them had on Houston Bulls clothes, which led me to believe they were coming from the game like we were.

"Would you like a drink?" Michael asked.

"No, but I will take some water if you don't mind."

Michael didn't move. He sat and smiled at me. "Did I tell you how nice you look in that dress?"

"No you didn't."

He touched my arms.

"Well, I apologize for that. Baby you are looking fine as hell in that dress, and I love those shoes."

I glanced down at my feet, and I was quite pleased with my selection.

"Thank you Michael."

"And you are welcome."

Michael gave me a nice wet kiss on the lips. "You know I'm falling for you don't you?" he said, still staring me in my eyes.

"That's part of my plan."

"Oh really," he laughed, giving me one more kiss "I'm going to the bar. Do you want something?"

Michael got up and went to the bar to get our drinks. I sat in a daze. Everything was going perfectly. I couldn't believe I had finally met a fine, intelligent man who knew how to treat a lady. He was sensual, complimentary and attentive. He was also very domestic, and I loved that. I was most impressed with his household skills. My mother always said a man that could take care of himself, surely could take care of you.

"Michael Riley, that was a good game you had today sir," a man said at the bar.

While I daydreamed about Michael and watched him sign a few autographs, my cell rang. When I saw D.C.'s number blinking, I laughed because I knew exactly what she wanted.

"Hello."

"Damn it, Girl. I told you to call me at halftime, and here it is six o'clock and I'm calling you."

"Calm down, Dee," I chuckled. "I started talking to this lady who was sitting next to me at the game, and I forgot. Plus there were so many people getting up at half time, I changed my mind.

"Heifer, didn't nobody say you had to get up. You could have called me right from your seat. That's why you have a cell phone, remember?"

"Whatever. Anyway, the game was good. They lost, but they did a good job. I was . . . "

D.C. cut me off. "Did you see Courtney's wife? Did you see him after the game?"

"You know, I didn't see him. He must have come out the locker room after Michael. I saw him down on the field, but not after the game."

"Damn Jay, you're no help."

D.C. started mumbling about how I was supposed to be on the look out for her, and then she started asking me how many single men I'd seen coming out the locker room. *As if I could see which players were wearing wedding rings.*

Out the corner of my eye, I noticed a Caucasian woman come behind Michael and whisper in his ear. "No this witch isn't," I mumbled to myself.

"Jada,!" D.C. yelled through the phone. "Are you listening to me?"

"Oh—I'm sorry Dee. You know what? I'm going to have to call you back."

I hung up in her face, turned my phone off and threw it in my purse.

What should I do? I asked myself. Should I go up to them and nicely remove my man away so that witch will know he is already taken, or do I sit and wait for him to come back? Would I embarrass myself if I were to go over there? I hated when my mothers' old school thoughts popped in my head when I was in a crisis with a man. I need to let those rules go because in the new millennium it doesn't work. Women are stealing husbands everyday, and they sure as hell are stealing boyfriends.

With that in mind I got up, straightened my dress and walked over to where they were standing. As I got closer, I wanted to smack her right in her mouth. She was still giggling and trying to get conversation out of Michael, even though he was half listening to her.

"Hey, Baby. What's taking so long?" I said, wrapping my arms around his waist. *Men are so damn dumb, or should I say they play dumb when it came to recognizing when a woman is trying to holla'. It's very interesting that a man sure as hell could spot when a brotha' is trying to hit on us, but they never recognize when a woman is doing the same.*

A fly could have flown in her mouth, as wide as it hung open. We gave each other those stares that let each other know what we were thinking. (BITCH)

"Here they are, Babe," Michael said with a smile, as he turned around and handed me my glass of water.

"It was nice meeting you Mr. Riley," she said with her hand extended out for him to shake it.

"Same here," Michael responded, nodding his head, but not acknowledging her hand.

We walked away, and left her standing there. "Thanks, Babe for rescuing me. I was wondering when you were going to show up."

"You're a big boy. You can handle yourself can't you?" I winked.

****

Our table was ready by the time we got our drinks. The waiter escorted us onto the patio.

"This is nice, Jay. Is this your spot?"

"No, not really. I only come on special occasions with special people."

"Hmm, well I guess that means I'm special," Michael smiled.

Michael pulled out my chair just as a gentleman would, and again I felt love flutters in my stomach.

"Hey look, there's Courtney and his wife," he said. "Let's go over there real quick, I want to holla' at him about the game."

I looked at him like he was crazy. He knew Courtney wasn't at the top of my list. "Michael, you know I don't want to meet his wife," I whispered.

"Come on now, Babe. I swear it will only be for a second."

I turned around slowly, hoping Michael was wrong about who he'd seen, but I wasn't. There sitting calm and cool was Courtney "the playa" Vincent, and sitting directly across from him was that evil woman I sat next to at the game. The snooty, stuck up one. I strained my eyes once again to see if my vision was deceiving me, but it wasn't. It was her. I had sat next to Courtney's wife the entire game and didn't even know it.

I looked at the table one more time and closed my eyes. What in the world were we going to talk about? I hesitantly picked up my glass of water because I knew it was going to be a long, long evening.

26
Classless

Jada

"So what you think man?" Michael asked Courtney at the table. "You think we're going to be any good?"

"Yeah Man. I think we did a hell of a job out there today to have such a young team.

I mean don't forget our quarterback is straight out of college, and most of the other players have only been in the league for two or three years. Shit, we did alright in my eyes."

Courtney's wife, Michelle talked on her cell phone the first ten minutes we were at the table. That was a relief because I didn't feel like straining to carry on a conversation with her anyway. Despite her attitude, she was a pretty woman. She had a gorgeous tan that made her a flawless honey brown. Her long wavy hair was slicked back into a ponytail, and she was a tall, thin woman. She probably could have been a model. She too was wearing a sun dress, but hers was longer than mine. She sort of had a classy look, but the platinum in her ears, around her neck, on her arm, and around her ankle, was too much!

"Jada, what did you think about the game? Courtney asked.

Michael smiled, because he knew damn well I didn't know anything about football. I was sure he couldn't wait for my response.

"Well Courtney, I don't know much about football, but I do know enough to say you guys did an excellent job out there, and you have a hell of a fan club. Those people were so hyped out there, they got me excited. My adrenaline flowed the entire game."

"Good answer, Babe," Michael smiled.

"I'll talk to you later Kima," Michelle said, as she prepared to end her pointless conversation. Courtney gave her a look of frustration.

"I didn't get your name, she said with her hand extended after she hung up.

The princess cut rock on her finger was exquisite.

"Jada. Jada Ballard," I answered with a fake smile on my face, to match hers. "We sat next to each other at the game."

"That's right," she replied. "We sure did."

I shook her well manicured hand, and noticed the charm bracelet dangling from her arm. It wasn't your usual charm bracelet with simple sized charms. This thing looked like it was heavy as lead. It was white gold, or platinum. I'm sure it was platinum, and it had about eight charms on it about the size of nickels. I saw the number thirty-two, Courtney's number dangling from her arm in diamonds.

"So did you enjoy the game?" she asked, like I was a kid from out of town that had never been anywhere before.

"Yes, I did."

The table got silent.

"So where are you guys buying your house?" Michael asked, trying to break the silence.

Michelle butted in "Oh Michael, you have to come and see it. *I noticed she didn't say "we" had to come see it.* "It's in Sugarland on the golf course, you know by First Colony Mall where most of the other athletes live, and it is beautiful. They say Charles Barkley lives out there as well."

Michael gave her the attention she demanded but Courtney tried his best to review the menu so he wouldn't have to get involved.

"Anyway, the house is a little over ten thousand square feet, sitting on two acres of property. I haven't decided if I want it to be stucco or not, but most likely. We're going to have a pool with a Jacuzzi and a wet bar out back for when we entertain, and the media room, oh my God, the media room is off the hook! I designed it myself."

She was annoying me with all of her I's. It was very clear to me that she didn't come from anything because her conversation was one about material things.

Everything she said was I, I, I, which was sickening. It was sad to say, but I could see why Courtney was cheating on her. She never once mentioned his name as she dominated the conversation about their house. She was talking so fast and so much, I hated Michael had even asked the question.

Finally Courtney cut in and asked what we were ordering.

"I always get the crab cakes and a dinner salad," I said.

"Oh, you come here often?" Michelle asked.

No she didn't. I knew that witch wasn't trying to imply I couldn't afford to eat at a nice restaurant. I swear project ass women get on my nerves. Here she was riding her husband's damn coattail, and she was questioning me.

"Yes I do," I answered sharply. "They have excellent crab cakes."

"Hmm, maybe I'll try the crab cakes too," Courtney said. "I'll take your word for it, Jada."

"Courtney, Sweetie, I thought you hated crab cakes."

"I never told you that."

Michael gave me a look that let me know he was starting to feel uncomfortable. *He should've listened to me and stayed at our table.*

"I think I'm going to try the salmon," Michael said.

"That sounds good, Babe. I've heard that's good as well." I replied.

The waiter came and took our orders, and I couldn't wait for our evening with them to end. Michelle and I had nothing in common. Matter of fact, she was the kind of woman I never gave a second thought.

"So what do you do for a living?" she asked, as she took a sip of her red wine.

"I'm a physical therapist." I proudly responded.

"And a damn good one," Michael added.

"Thanks Sweetheart."

"Oh my goodness, I just don't know how people get up and go to work everyday. I mean I can't work for anyone. I would have to have my own therapy place, or whatever you guys have.

See what I mean. Her dumb ass didn't have the common sense to know that therapist usually work in hospitals or rehabilitation clinics of some sort. I despise women who turn their noses up at people, when they have the brains of a bird. Where would she be without her husband? Probably working at Burger King some where. Remember the song from back in the day "Captain save a ho? There was a lot of that going on around the NFL from what I could tell.

Courtney looked up at her.

"So what was your major? I asked, trying to blow off her third knock to me and resume with kindness.

"What major?" Courtney intervened "She didn't go to college."

The look of embarrassment spread across her face. The husband she took so much pride in bragging on. The man she had obviously used so she could live the lifestyle of the rich and famous, had cracked her face and I didn't feel the least bit sorry for her.

Courtney Vincent

I'm just sitting here wondering, why in the hell I didn't make Michelle's ass sign a prenuptial agreement. The woman is crazy!

I can't believe she's sitting here saying all this crazy shit in front of my friends. I know Jada is probably calling her all kinds of names, and I can't blame her! I'm trying   to play it cool, but I'm pissed. How could she sit here and say she could never work when she worked at that cheap ass clothing store at Foxhill Mall back in the day. She had to work, to help take care of all them damn kids her momma had. Hell, we both are straight from Nickerson Gardens, the projects in Watts. Everybody that lives in Los Angeles knows that Nickerson ain't no punk!

I don't know why Michelle always clowns like this when we get around other couples. I think she is just intimidated by women that have an education. Maybe that's why she feels she has to put on her snooty role. She's had more than enough time to go to college, and probably get a Ph.D., but no, she wanted to keep f---- around with cosmetology school. Thank God she finally finished that. But what good is that when she hasn't done anybody's hair but her momma's and sister's when they bring their free loading asses to visit.

She's just not the same girl from back in the day. We met at Banning High School, and were the couple of the year for all four years there. I loved that girl to death, and everybody knew it. We were with each other morning noon and night, until I went to college. I got a full ride to UCLA, and she went on to seek her career doing hair. I never understood why she wouldn't go to college with me, but I guess when you come from a ghetto ass family like she did, where nobody went to college, it's not a priority.

187

We had problems when I left because she didn't want me talking to anybody. I guess the whole education thing freaked her out a little bit. She would come on campus acting like a damn fool in front of all them white people, and it would piss me off! Michelle clowned me so much, and so frequent, the ladies on campus started joking on me about her.

I tried to break up with her a number of times, but I couldn't. For some reason I felt obligated to her. I was her only way out the projects and the rest of her family. That was alright with me then, but now I don't care anymore because she doesn't appreciate anything I've done for her, and neither do they.

I came to that conclusion when I found out she aborted our child because she didn't want to be strapped down with a bunch of kids like her mother was. *(And who do you think gave her that advice. Her mother)*

Forget what I wanted, it was only about what she wanted. That's when I knew we had outgrown each other, and her ass was a straight demon. Too bad now, there's no love there. I mean, I love her as a person, but I'm nowhere near in love with her anymore. She has spent too much of my money, and she's very disrespectful. The money has changed her, along with everybody else in my so called corner. In this profession, you have a lot of people loving you for the wrong reasons. You have to be very careful about who you let in your circle. God forbid if you let a person in that you don't really know. Man, you can immediately become *fair game* and get used. In this business, everybody uses you. Women, men, family, preachers, whatever. Everybody just wants a piece of your pie and those MF's will do whatever it takes to get it.

I mean I'm not going to be too many more MF's, and bitches! When Michelle decides to go off, she starts calling me all kinds of names, hitting on me, and throwing shit! I lived through that when I was a kid, and I'm sure as hell not going to endure that as a grown man.

The bottom line is I can't take it any more, and after this season with the Bulls I'm going to ask her for a divorce. I tried to stay true to her because I wanted to be with a woman from my home, a woman I could trust. But the real deal is, you can't trust anybody nowadays, especially when money is involved. Hell money changes everyone.

I'm tired of feeling unappreciated, and getting disrespected. I've bent over backwards for her and too many other folks. I'm about to put my foot down and cut a lot of folks loose. The game is now going to be about me, Courtney Vincent. Not my family and their needs, and my boys and theirs. Who said once I made it, everybody else had to make it?

I'm just waking up and realizing that I'm not obligated to take on everybody's troubles. Their bullshit isn't mine. From now on, I'm only watching after Courtney, and I don't give a damn whose toes I step on.

I tried to save the world, and because of that, my damn investments and bank accounts are very low. Hell, if the truth be told, I'm almost broke. That's why I dibble in a little bit of everything, so I can stay on top, cause' I'm not going back to those projects. EVER!

Lord knows I don't have anyone to fall back on if I do go down.

It's my world now, and everybody else can go to hell!

27

Drama

Jada

$\mathcal{A}$s we were leaving McCormick and Schmicks, walking hand in hand two women in a black SUV slowed down in front of us.

Michael stopped and by the expression on his face, I could tell he knew them, and something was wrong.

I didn't' recognize the driver, but the lady on the passengers side was the same woman I'd asked him about before.

"Well look a here, if it isn't Michael Riley," the familiar woman said. "How are you this wonderful evening?"

Michael looked at me, closed his eyes and inhaled before responding with a dry, "Pretty good."

The driver laughed to herself as she looked at both of us and rolled her eyes.

"Excuse me, but I didn't get your name the last time we met. My name is Angela." She said with her hand extended out to me. Michael grabbed my hand and pulled me toward the car. As we walked away she yelled, "It was nice meeting you Jada."

I stopped.

"Michael, who is that woman, and how does she know my name?"

"Jada, I'll explain it to you later. Can we just get in the car?"

I was pissed beyond belief because he was for sure busted now. There was no explanation that was going to get him out of this one.

I got in the car and slammed my door. Once Michael was in, Angela appeared on his side.

"Michael, get out and talk to me or your girlfriend here is going to find out some shit about you that will break her heart."

"Fuck!" Michael yelled as he hit the steering wheel with his fist.

"Michael who the hell is she?" I asked louder this time.

Angela beat on his window for him to let it down.

"She won't leave me the fuck alone, Jada!" He said with apologetic eyes that I wasn't trying to feel. "The bitch is crazy as hell!"

"Just drive off, Michael. Let's just go!"

Instead of Michael driving off, he got out the car.

"Tell her Michael. Tell her that I'm your wife!"

My stomach dropped instantly, like the feeling you get when riding a roller coaster.

I got out the car and ran around to where they were.

"Michael, get back in the car," I yelled as I tugged on his shirt.

"Angela, if you don't get your crazy ass out of here, I'm going to call the cops!" Michael yelled.

"Call the cops! What can they do but listen to my side of the story, and after I tell them how you are on drugs and enjoy beating on women, your career in this city will be ruined!"

As she yelled, I continued to try and get Michael out of her face for fear that he might snap and hit her. She was punching him in the chest and screaming at the top of her lungs. I was a nervous wreck. The look Michael had in his eyes frightened me. I had never seen him look that angry.

"Leave him alone!" I screamed in her face.

"Oh, so now you want to get in this. Look you don't want to mess with me little girl.

I'll hurt your little ass, so gone and get back in that car!"

Angela and I were in each others' face, going toe to toe.

"You need to gone home, and get yourself together!" I said

"Bitch, you don't know me. Who the hell are you to tell me what I need to do?" she screamed back.

Just as I was feeling the urge to beat the hell out of her, a Houston police officer pulled up.

Angela backed away, and Michael turned his head the other direction, I guess hoping the cop wouldn't recognize him.

"Is there a problem?" he asked when he got out the car.

"Yeah, there's a problem" I spoke up first. "This woman right here is disturbing us!"

The officer turned to Angela, who automatically turned into an angel.

"I'm on my way out of here officer. There is no problem anymore." She said in her sweetest tone.

"Is everything alright with you Mr. Riley," the officer asked politely. I wondered how he knew Michael's name.

"Yes, we're fine," Michael replied.

"Alright, alright, let's clear out of here before I have to write a report."

Michael and I got in our car and so did Angela, and as we drove off, I noticed that a crowd had formed outside the restaurant. I was so ashamed when I realized they had probably watched the entire ghetto scene.

****

Michael and I rode in silence. When we got to his place, I was still in shock and couldn't say anything. I guess he was at a loss for words too because he was quiet as well.

He parked his car and turned it off. We both sat, still struggling for the right words, to get us through the tense situation. The evening started out perfect, but ended in hell.

"Jada, I'm sorry. I'm really sorry," he said with his head down.

I didn't look at Michael nor did I respond to his apology because I was hurt. Words can not explain the disappointment I was feeling.

Since I was in no mood to curse him out, or even to slap him, I decided to sit quietly.

"Jada. I'm sorry." He repeated, this time, turning my face to look at his.

"Ok." I replied as I got out the car.

I walked to his front door, not knowing what to do, or what to feel.

It's funny when I'm with my friends, I'm very confident saying what I would do if I caught my man slipping. But now, that I was in this situation, I am stuck. Stuck with no answers.

28
Flashback

D.C.

*T*he room was small, plain and white with not enough pictures on the walls to deter my mind for even a second. The medicine like aroma made me nauseous; more nauseous than I already was, so I struggled to breathe only through my mouth while I waited for the procedure to begin.

I wondered if I was doing the right thing because, this was my second abortion. This time I wasn't in college and couldn't use the excuse of not being financially stable. God knows I made more than enough money to take care of myself plus two or three kids.

****

Courtney promised he would meet me at the clinic after his work out at the stadium. I gave him very explicit directions on how to get here, and my appointment time, but he wasn't here. I looked at my watch and it was twelve on the nose, which meant the doctor would be starting at any minute now. I was beginning to get nervous as the time drew near. There was still time for me to pull out. All I had to do was get up and put my clothes back on. It was that simple. But I couldn't because I wasn't for sure if it was my mind that was messing with me, or the last words from Courtney's mouth which clearly stated he wasn't ready for children. I wasn't quite ready for a child either, but I didn't want to ruin my body for child bearing later, because I kind of loved the thought of having a little Courtney running around.

"Good Afternoon, Ms. Thompson" the doctor said as he entered the room. "How are you doing?"

"Fine," I whispered softly, trying not to show my indecisiveness.

"Have you given this a lot of thought and are you sure with your decision?"

I hesitated, as I gave my watch one last glance, checking the time. It read twelve thirty. Courtney was thirty minutes late, and I was pissed! I was about to endure something that would scar me for the rest of my life, and he didn't have the decency to be on time or call. What could he be doing that was more important than what was about to take place with me?"

The more I thought about it, and envisioned his face, the more I realized I didn't want to be stuck with a child because I knew that he would be nowhere to be found.

A baby would be the ticket to my future financially because with Courtney making over a million a year, I would get paid. On the low, me and a child would be worth at least four thousand a month, and with that kind of money who would give a rip if he saw the baby or not. But then I thought about my father, my baseball playing dad that only came around during the holidays. He played for the Houston Astros, got my mother pregnant and later decided, with his career keeping him on the road, he didn't have time to take care of a family. Momma said he wanted her to have me, but he just didn't want to get married. I beg to differ. The brother hardly ever saw me. He just sent his monthly check to shut her mouth, but did nothing to make sure we had a secure relationship. Still doesn't! Jack ass!

"Yes, Doctor, I'm sure."

I put my legs into the assumed position and closed my eyes. I prayed to God to help me through the mental pain I was about to endure.

He began. The feel of the cold, steel utensil inside of me vacuuming my child's body parts was making me crazy. I wanted it to end. I wanted to change my mind while tears flowed uncontrollably down my face. I didn't know if it was a boy or a girl. I didn't know if he or she had my eyes or his. I would never know.

"Try to relax," the doctor said. "We're almost done."

No sooner than he said that, he was finished. I was glued to the bed. My body was numb, and my mind had blackened out. It was like I was dreaming with my eyes open, but all I could see was a dark room. I could hear the doctor and his assistant talking to me as they prepared me for departure, but I couldn't respond. I was out of it.

****

I don't quite remember how Lori got me home, but she did. She was very helpful and patient. She tried hard to assist me once we got to my place.

"Lori, thanks for everything, girl." I told her repeatedly.

"You're welcome, Deidre. You just make sure you get plenty of rest ok."

Lori let herself out and I grew angry at myself again for not having Jada or Mara with me. But I knew if they had known I was pregnant, they would have talked me out of having an abortion. Jada was with me the last time, when I swore I'd never do it again.

My couch was as far as my legs would take my chilled body so I cuddled into the cracks of it with my favorite throw, and I tried to grasp solitude. The phone rang almost an hour after I'd gotten comfortable but I couldn't lift my arm to reach for it on the coffee table. It rang and rang until I mustered enough strength to grab it. When I heard Courtney's voice, the pain along with the tears returned.

****

Courtney and I flew to Cancun a week after my abortion so I could sort through my feelings. He owned a condominium there, so he offered to take me on a get away since he felt horrible for what he'd done.

He swore the coach had called a meeting at the stadium, but I didn't believe him. Anyway, the fact that he'd taken time out to help me, soothed my mind just a little.

We had a wonderful weekend, and he was very attentive. We chilled on the beach, did a little shopping, and got our sleep on. It was the perfect setting for us to make love, but because of my situation, I couldn't have intercourse for a few weeks. It didn't matter though, because I had a good time getting to know my man. I had my camcorder, and my camera, and I took all kinds of pictures of us. I even got shots of him and some other brothers that were down there, playing volleyball on the beach. Later, I found out Courtney knew the guys, and they were all interested in investing in the same company.

I almost got angry when I realized he was planning to come to Cancun anyway for business. He had me thinking this trip was just for me. By the time we were on our way back, I had almost forgotten about my abortion. My mind was strictly on him. Never had a man made me feel special the way he had. It became ok that I had a second abortion because I knew someday I was going to have children. I knew he was going to be the man that I would spend the rest of my life with. I was sprung, but when I found out about his wife, I was devastated!

My dreams crumbled. How could he do that to me? How could he be that good to me and be lying the entire time?

I made up my mind I was going to make him remember our affair, so I decided to stalk him once his wife moved to Houston. I called his pager and his cell at all times of the night until he got them both changed. I left notes on his car and added a few scratches to his cherished Escalade. I sent mail to his house every week, reminding him of all the times we'd made love, all the gifts he'd purchased, and my horrible abortion.

Courtney shouldn't have played with me. I was determined to make his ass regret what he'd done, especially after I started bleeding two weeks after the abortion and had to rush myself to the emergency room. That's when I found out I had a puncture in my cervix, and would never be able to have children.

29

The Arrival

Mara

*J*ada informed me of how crazy D.C. had been acting over Courtney—paging him all times of the night, writing crazy letters, and following him around. I thought after we had the accident she'd gotten a little better, but I guess I was wrong. It just wasn't like her to go out like that. I knew something else must have taken place that she wasn't telling us because her actions weren't normal. She was usually the kind to never let a brother see her sweat, especially since she always kept one or two on the back burner. Through the years we'd never witnessed her go crazy over a man the way she was doing with Courtney. Well, maybe except for the ball player in college. Now I admit, in the beginning when she first started bragging on him, I thought it was only because he had money, but now I was starting to believe she really was in love with the man.

The more I heard about how insane she was acting, the more guilty I felt for doing what I'd done. Now that I think about it—me movin' in on her man is something that a "chicken head" would do. I mean, I have talked about women that screwed their friends man, and here, I had eaten my own words and done the same thing. It was time I faced up to Dee and tell her the truth. Even if she didn't ever speak to me again, I wanted her to hear who the father of my child was from me, and not anyone else.

I picked up the phone and dialed her cell. It was five thirty and I knew she was usually on her way to the gym at that time, which was near my house. I was determined to get the truth out before my baby was born.

"This is Deidre," she answered.

"Hey, Dee. Where are you?"

"Hey girl, are you about to have that baby?" She asked excitedly.

"No," I smiled "We are still sitting here. I guess she's going to wait until her actual delivery date, which is tomorrow."

"She's just like her momma. Always doing her own thing, whether it messes up the world or not."

I sat quietly for a second as I thought about what she'd said.

"So would you like to come over and take me to Chili's restaurant so I can get one of their Cajun chicken sandwiches and fries?"

"Girl, you're still eating spicy foods."

"I surely am," I said with confidence.

"Did you call me for that corny request?"

"Yes, I did. I'm really craving it and you know I'm too scared to drive in all that traffic. People drive crazy in the evenings, and I don't want to take any chances."

"Ok, I'll come get you. I should be there in about fifteen minutes."

We hung up and I sat down and rubbed my stomach. I could feel my baby kicking and rolling around inside of me and it felt wonderful. "Courtney, Baby, I'm going to love you so much. More than I can ever describe. It won't matter if your dad comes around or not. Maybe one day he will. I just know when he gets one good look at you, he'll be hooked just like me. I only hope your Aunt Dee will forgive me and be a part of your life as well."

I went to the restroom one last time before she came, because the further along I got with this pregnancy, the more frequent I had to go to the bathroom. I got my purse and was turning out the light when I felt water trickle down my leg. I went back to the restroom because I assumed I had had an accident. Then more water came. I knew my water had broken. I panicked. I felt it flowing down my leg like a running faucet.

The doorbell rang.

"D.C. is that you?"

"Yeah, it's me."

I opened the door, and before I could tell her what was going on, she spotted how wet my clothes were.

"Oh shit!" she screamed. "Are you getting ready to have her?"

"Yeah, I think my water just broke."

"What do you mean, you think? Don't you know?"

"Hell, I don't know. I haven't done this before!"

I went to the back and got my bag that had been packed for nearly two weeks, and grabbed a pair of sneakers and we went out the door.

D.C. drove like a bat out of hell trying to get me to Memorial City Hospital where I was due to deliver. There was traffic everywhere, and she cursed and honked until folks got out of our way.

"Aren't you going to call the father?"

I didn't know what to say. "I'm going to call him later. Right now, I'm trying to get to the hospital."

"Whatever you say," she responded.

I wasn't in any pain, and shockingly, I was calm, so calm that I dug through my junky purse for my cell and called Jada and my mother to come and meet us at the hospital.

I knew D.C was thinking why call them before the father, but I didn't care.

"How are you?" D.C kept asking. "Are you in any pain yet?"

"I'm fine, I'm fine. You just focus on the road."

It was kind of funny seeing her freak out the way she was, because she was acting like she was the one having the baby.

When we got to the emergency room entrance, they took me to the back and D.C. couldn't go with me. That's when the tears came. I wasn't for sure why I was crying but I couldn't stop.

****

I pushed as hard as I could, but it seemed like she wouldn't come down. I could hear Momma and Jada getting excited when they saw the top of her head. "Wow, she's got a head full of hair just like you Mara," Jada announced. I could hear her, but I was too tired to respond.

I wondered if the pain I was experiencing was a part of my pay back for all that I had done, or did every woman delivering a baby feel what I was feeling. It hurts!.

My mind reflected back on all the times I hooked up with Courtney, even after I found out he was married. I knew damn well I didn't need any more sins on my wayward soul, but I still continued to mess with him. Sharp pains began hitting my lower back area. Damn!

"Oh, Momma, please tell them to get this girl out of me!" I screamed.

"Just keep pushing Mara. Just keep pushing!" Momma encouraged.

Tears were cascading down my sweaty face, and I wasn't for sure if they were tears of joy or pain. Then, I thought of the weekend getaways Courtney and I had together. The trip to Cancun and the one to South Padre Island were the best weekends I'd ever had.

In Padre Island, he wined and dined me from the time we got there until the time we set foot back on that plane Sunday evening. Everything was beautiful, especially the love making. Actually that is when I think I conceived.

If he hadn't invited me to go with him to take care of business down there, I probably wouldn't be pushing in the delivery room, screaming and hollering like a damn fool right now!

****

Courtney was born at 8:05 p.m. and she was the prettiest little girl I've ever laid my eyes on. She weighed nine pounds, three ounces and came out kicking and screaming.

Momma, Jada and D.C. were in the room with me. Momma cried the entire time, while D.C. rubbed my face and stroked my arms. Jada was down at the foot of the bed along with my doctor, talking me through the whole thing.

When I heard the baby crying, more tears came. Words could never describe the joy that filled my heart. "What's her name?" Momma asked again, even though she was well aware that I was thinking about naming her Courtney and not Shae which is what she had picked out.

I was about to say Courtney, but I noticed a smile on D.C.'s face, and I couldn't do it.

"I think I'm going to name her after me. Mara—Mara Sampson." I announced proudly.

"Oh that's cute," Jada said with tears in her eyes.

"She's gorgeous like her mother, so why shouldn't she be named after her," D.C. replied.

They brought little Mara to me after they'd cleaned her up. As I held her I was amazed how God could create something so wonderful. She was absolutely precious, with a head full of black hair that lay smoothly on her head. Her skin color was light like most babies when they are born, but the tips of her ears and knuckles were brown, which let me know she was going to get darker. She had my nose and her dad's funny colored eyes. Every time she opened them I thought of him.

30
Disaster Day

Jada

These flowers are because I can finally say I love you to someone
And really mean it.
Jada, I love you!

Michael

*I*sat at my desk teary eyed admiring the twelve red, roses sitting in front of me. The moment had finally come. Michael had said the words I'd been dying to hear. We had been through much drama in our few months together, but now it was smoothing out. He explained to me that Angela was the only other person that knew he had been hooked on pain killers, and he had been paying her to keep her mouth shut for years. Not to mention the fact that she wants him back.

My mouth hit the floor when he told me he'd given her at least a half million dollars since his career began. I couldn't believe Michael could be that naïve to allow someone to blackmail him like that.

Each time he paid her a lump sum of money, she'd disappear for a few months and then she would reappear, starting the process all over again.

Naturally, I questioned Michael repeatedly about his addiction because each story he shared with me was different. The truth finally came out through that nut case Angela. Michael had been using Vicodin since he was injured in college, but the addiction wasn't as bad as it is now. Angela apparently had covered up for him back in college. His coach had instructed him to cut back on the pain killers, but he wouldn't because he was hooked. As a result, Michael would get his pills from "the pill man" on campus, since he couldn't get them from his coach anymore.

The "pill man" got busted one day, and Michael's name was one of the names he called out as a frequent client. This incident could have ruined his college career, and almost did until Angela took the blame and said Michael was buying the pills for her. *(I couldn't believe that woman stuck herself out there like that. I couldn't have done it)*

Michael went on to explain to me that his chances of getting drafted were looking slim because some of the NFL coaches were still skeptical about whether he was really addicted. Then he fractured his ankle, which made matters worse. That's when Angela obviously gave up on him, and began to seek another athlete. I guess she figured she had invested enough time in Michael, and she needed to seek another meal ticket.

Michael and I agreed to inform the police about Angela and make plans to get her out of his life. She hadn't appeared since the parking lot incident, but Michael was positive she would show up eventually. Her laying low meant trouble to come.

****

Well, well, well, looks like somebody has an admirer," Dr. Rotsworth said, interrupting my daydream.

"Oh hey, Doc. I didn't hear you come in."

"I know you didn't because you were floating in space."

We both laughed.

"I guess I was."

"Michael is a nice man, and you two look good together. I hope everything works out for you."

"So do I. I'm trying to take it slow and not get too excited, but it's hard. He's like everything I've been looking for."

"Well that's nice to hear because I was worried that no man would be able to reach your expectations as high as they are. I'm glad Michael came along, because Denzel is already taken."

"Funny, Doc."

Colin walked past my office, not saying a word.

"You know, he's been acting really strange since Mara had that baby. Do you think he thought it was his?"

"Hell, we all thought it was his, even me, but Mara says it isn't, and I suppose she would know."

"Did she tell you who the father is?"

I shook my head no, even though I knew deep down in my heart that little Mara had to be Courtney's baby.

"Hey beautiful," Michael said as he peeped his head through my office door.

"Well speak of the devil," Dr. Rotsworth said as he walked toward him to shake his hand.

"Hey, Doc. What's going on?"

"Nothing, Mr.Riley. You're looking good out there so far. I've been checking you out."

"Thanks, Man. We still need a lot of work though."

"It's only been one game, and I think you guys look great for a new team. Matter of fact can I get an autographed picture for the clinic?"

"Yeah man, I'll get that for you next week."

As they talked, I admired Michael. He looked good in anything, including the navy blue Nike shorts and Houston

Bulls t-shirt he was wearing. His baseball cap fit his head perfectly, making him look like a college student. I checked him out from head to toe and was very pleased. I had finally found a man I was crazy about. God had answered my prayers.

"Well, let me leave you two alone. Take care, Man," the Doc said.

After the Doc left, Michael looked at me and smiled. "Who sent you those flowers?"

"Hopefully you," I said giving him a gentle kiss on the lips.

"Can I see you tonight?"

"If you want to."

"Hey," he said, pulling back just a little "I came to show you something. Can you come outside?"

"What have you done now?"

"Just hush and come see. Close your eyes."

We walked slowly to the front of the clinic, and I could hear him opening the front door.

"Ok, you can open them now."

There sitting in front of me was a white, 1989, 300zx. My favorite sports car.

"What did you do?" I smiled, as I noticed the car, still not for sure what he was up to. "Is this yours?"

"No, it's yours."

"What!" I screamed. You heard me, Girl. It's yours. Didn't you say this was your favorite old car. Well, I happened to luck up on a deal and I got it for you. I mean clearly it's not like your Lexus jeep or your 3000 GT, but it's your favorite vehicle right?"

I looked at him in amazement. "Are you serious?"

"Yes. This is your car, Ms. Jada Ballard, so go and look at it, please."

My feet wouldn't take me, so Michael gave me a nudge.

"Michael, you didn't have to do this. I mean I can't believe you. What am I going to do with three cars?"

"I don't know. That's your problem."

I looked at him and a tear dropped from my eye. "Thank you, Michael. I mean I don't know what to say. I'm not even sure if I should take such a gift from you."

"First of all," he said, wiping my tears, "You have to take it because it would be rude for you not to. I went through too much to get it. Secondly, I'm not going anywhere, so you can wipe that thought out of your mind."

I pulled him close to me and kissed him again. Our bodies were in sync as we held each other, and I could feel him being turned on.

"See what you do to me?" he smiled as he ran my hand across the front of his shorts.

"Let's take it for a ride." I suggested.

NFL players were always off on Tuesdays and that was when Michael would go shopping to buy all kinds of gadgets that he would excitedly share with me at the end of the day. I never expected him to come with a car, especially for me, but he had. I was quite impressed.

Thank goodness Tuesday mornings were slow because I wanted desperately to take my new car for a spin before Michael had to go. I ran inside to tell Dr. Rotsworth I was leaving for a few minutes and I happily jumped inside my new ride.

"You look good in this, Jada, he said as I burned rubber out the parking lot.

The leather interior looked great, and the car had that new smell to it.

"Michael this thing looks brand new. Where did you get it?"

"I can't tell you all of that. Just ride and enjoy yourself."

I love driving a stick shift. It always makes me feel like I'm going faster than everyone else.

I took pride in shifting those gears and pressing the gas, making the car roll back and forth at the stop lights.

"I cannot believe you did this, Babe." I said as I glanced over at him. "You're something special."

"Happy Valentines Day, Baby," he said, reaching over and giving me another kiss on the cheek. I smiled.

"Michael, Valentines day is four months away."

"Oh well. You're my Valentine, twenty-four seven. Can I buy you a present when I want to. You got any complaints?"

"No, I can't say that I do."

When I got back to the clinic, I didn't want to get out. I fantasized about leaving with Michael and driving off into the sunset, like they do in the movies.

"Well, Babe, this is it," I said as I looked at him with sexy eyes. "Now get out my car!"

"Whatever woman. I'll get out when I feel like it."

I released my foot from the clutch too soon, and the car jerked.

"Oops, I guess I'm a little rusty."

"You think?" Michael replied sarcastically with a smile.

"What's on the floor" I asked, glancing down.

He was busy messing with the radio trying to see if it picked up all the stations clearly.

I looked in the back seat, where his gym bag had turned over and I repeated, "What's on the floor?"

He finally heard me and looked down. He closed his eyes, then looked at me.

"It's not what you think Jada."

"Let me see it Michael."

"Jay, don't ruin our day. I mean everything is under control with all that. Just don't start tripping."

"What are you talking about, Michael?" I raised my voice "If it's nothing to trip about, then why don't you just show me the damn bottle?"

Michael slowly bent over and picked up the medicine bottle.

I snatched it out of his hand, while my heart pumped extra fast. I was hoping it wasn't anything related to a painkiller. Sure enough, it was a full bottle of Vicodin.

I was hurt, and I know Michael could see it on my face.

I threw it at him, and got out of the car, tears flowing down my face. **He lied to me again!**

Usually Michael would try to offer an explanation, but this time he didn't. He didn't even try to chase me, because he knew there was nothing he could say. Our perfect Tuesday had ended in a disaster!

31
Surprise Visit

Mara

*M*y little angel Mara was killing my breast as she struggled intensively to breast feed. Motherhood was the most beautiful thing life had to offer, but breast feeding on top of labor and delivery was hell! No matter how relaxed I tried to be, I was still in pain. My breasts were swollen twice their usual thirty eight D's and the slightest brush against them brought tears to my eyes. Mara gnawing on them had my nerves on edge.

The nurse continued to tell me little Mara could sense my tension, which was why she was so aggravated and my milk wouldn't come down. I was trying to focus on things that would put a smile on my face like the nurse suggested, but even that was difficult. I wanted to do the natural thing and feed my child from my body, so I switched my mind from the pain to happier things like the day of her birth. The day I conceived her. It was a shame that every time I thought about Courtney, a smile appeared on my face. He was special to me, and his child was even more special.

I propped my pillows again, with her still in my arms and tried to relax so I could give it one last try before buzzing the nurse to bring me the Enfamil. "Come on, Mara, Let's try one more time. Momma is sorry she can't get you comfortable and feed you the way you want. Just be patient with me, Sweetie." I closed my eyes and asked God to help me, and I gave it one last try. Her little lips attached to my breast, and I sang "Jesus loves me" softly. A calm immediately came over me, and the milk finally came out. Tears came to my eyes as I watched her little mouth and body move. It was still hard to believe she was mine. She was my responsibility.

Mara fell asleep in my arms and I didn't want to wake her by placing her in the cold hospital baby bed because I wanted her to sleep peacefully with me. I gently placed her down, and I was standing over her watching her little chest go up and down when I heard my hospital door open. I knew it was one of the nurses coming in to poke around on one of us like they'd been doing since she was born. "So who do you have to check now?" I asked without turning around

"I'm here to check on you." Courtney said.

I turned around slowly, and there he was, the person I'd been thinking about the entire day.

"How are you, Mara?" he asked as he stepped toward me and gave me a light peck on my cheek.

I couldn't believe he'd come.

"Can I take a peek?"

Courtney stood next to me and stared down at little Mara. "Man, a baby girl." He said with a faint smile on his face. "What's her name?"

"Her name is Mara. Mara Courtney Sampson."

He looked at me. "You gave her my name?"

"Yes. Do you like that?"

The look on his face as he stood over her was that of a proud father, and it gave me hope that he'd be in her life someday.

"Yes, I'm flattered." He said still staring at her in amazement.

I could feel he wanted her, that he would love and accept her.

"Can I hold her? I mean I don't know if I'll do it right, but I'd like to try, if you don't mind?"

"Sure you can hold her. She just ate and fell asleep, but that's ok."

Courtney reached his muscular arms over the bed and as gently as he could, he picked Mara up.

"I'll schedule a blood test for today while you're here if you want me to." I said. "I mean I know we agreed to do that before."

Courtney ignored my suggestion. He was still in a daze staring down at Mara.

"Damn," he smiled. "Look, she has my eyes."

He swayed with her back and forth. "You're a beautiful little girl. Do you know that? You have your daddy's eyes."

A tear fell down my face as I watched him with her. It was a moment I'd never forget.

To break my emotional moment, I began rambling on about delivery and how Mara was hard to breast feed.

"Does she have my last name?"

"Well no, because I hadn't spoken with you, and I knew you wanted a blood test first."

Courtney looked at his daughter again and smiled. "I don't need a blood test. She has my eyes, and my exact birthmark on her arm. Did you see it?"

I walked closer to him. Sure enough, there was the same mark on little Mara's arm that was on his.

"Mara, I know she's mine because she looks just like me." Courtney said as he stared at her with starry eyes.

"Courtney, she is yours, but like I said we can do the blood work now if you want? I want you to know for sure."

"I don't want to offend you by requesting the test," he said apologetically, "But athletes get stuck all the time. I know you wouldn't do that to me. I guess I'd feel a little better if I had test results."

"It's no problem. I understand."

I pushed the button for the nurse to come in so I could tell her, and while I waited I admired Courtney and Mara together. They were going to be good for each other, and I couldn't help but wonder if my father had ever held me the way Courtney was holding our child.

32
Missing Him

Jada

Momma and I sat at the dinner table eating, talking, and partially watching the football game as we sometimes did on Sunday afternoons. She was discussing Bin Laden and the whole depression of September eleventh, while I sat quietly with my mind rested on the Bulls and their game against the Dallas Cowboys. I hadn't spoken with Michael since the day he showed up at the clinic with the car, although he did call at least three or four times.

After the drama with Angela and all the promises he'd made to change, I finally realized the relationship was hopeless. He was willing to stay addicted to drugs as long as he could hold on to his career.

I reflected on my relationship with Shakeem.

I couldn't walk down that path with Michael like I did with him. Shakeem was on cocaine, and toward the end of our relationship I was positive he was using crack.

When I thought back to the night he broke into my place while I was asleep and was standing over my bed, I became

215

terrified. It's weird how God wakes you up just in time, because I felt him over me, and when I opened my eyes, He was standing there smiling.

"Shakeem are you alright?" I nervously asked after I jumped, letting him know I was scared of him.

"Don't be afraid, Baby. I'm just here to hold you."

I turned on the lamp next to my bed. I couldn't believe how deranged he looked. His eyes were glossy, his usually neat hair was not cut or combed and his clothes were filthy.

"You think I ain't shit? Don't you?" he asked.

"No," I answered, trying to ease my way out of the bed.

"Yes you do, Jada. You're a bitch just like all these other Houston 'Ho's'! Think ya'll better than somebody!"

I was really scared then, so I tried to make a run for it. He grabbed the back of my gown and threw me on the bed. His kisses on my neck and his touch on my breasts was making me sick! Tears rolled down my face when I felt my panties being ripped.

"Please no, Shakeem! Please don't do this to me" I screamed.

"You used to love for me to make love to you. What's wrong now? Are you fuckin' somebody else?"

Shakeem started fidgeting with his pants trying to get them down, while keeping my arms pinned behind my back. I squirmed and kicked until I was able to turn and bite him on the arm. I sunk my teeth deep into his skin, making him loosen his grip, and I ran to my bathroom and locked the door.

"Bitch, why'd you bite me?" He yelled.

I pressed my back deep into the door, hoping to keep him out. After about five minutes of him cursing and kicking, I heard the front door slam.

I almost got up, but I was frightened by the thought that he may still be out there, so I sank back down to the floor in a fetal position and cried myself into the next morning.

****

"Jada, you didn't eat your food, and I fixed all of your favorites. Are you feeling alright?" Momma asked, snapping me out of my thoughts.

I looked down at my plate of collard greens, black eyed peas, baked chicken breast, and a slice of warm Jiffy cornbread. I felt my stomach turn. My appetite had gone.

I hadn't told momma anything that had happened between Michael and me because I knew she wouldn't understand. The world of football, and painkillers would definitely be too much for her innocent brain to process. I didn't want her getting Michael's addiction to Vicodin confused with a person who is addicted to a drug off the streets. Since I know how her brain operates, I realized that if I tried to explain it to her, all she would hear would be that word 'addiction,' and nothing else. Plus, I know if I don't fully understand the situation myself, I wouldn't be able to explain it to her. All I know is I can't fall in love with another drug addict.

Even though Michael and I weren't on good terms, I still wanted the best for him, which is why I stopped contemplating whether or not to turn on the television to see what was going on in the game. It was too hard to sit, knowing he was playing without taking a peek at the score.

Michael had left a message for me about going to Dallas for his game. He even went as far as to offer to buy my plane ticket, but I never responded. I desperately wanted to go, and be supportive of him, but I was hurting too badly. To go would give him the impression that everything was ok.

A commercial was on when I found the game on the Fox channel. Cedric the Entertainer was doing one of his Budwieser commercials. It is the one where he goes to get his date a beer and accidentally shakes it up while he's in the kitchen dancing. "Momma have you seen this before?" I yelled to her so she would come and take a peek.

When Momma came around the corner, Cedric had just done the funniest part by accidentally spraying his date with the beer.

"These commercials are getting sillier and sillier as the years go by." Momma laughed.

The game came back on to the first quarter and the score was thirteen to fourteen, Dallas' favor.

"This is one heck of a game" the announcer stated "Here we have two Texas teams who both have a good defense. I wouldn't be surprised if the game went into overtime."

I got in a comfortable position on Momma's leather sofa so I could see the television good. I tried to find Michael on the sideline, but I spotted Courtney first. He was sitting on the bench sipping out of a cup. He didn't look like he'd been in the game, or cared to go in. Then I recognized a couple of other guys I'd met through Michael.

"I tell you what, John" the announcer said "For these Bulls to be a young team, they are doing a hell of a job out on that field. I mean their quarterback Hank Jones is doing work, making plays that count. He seems very confident."

I'd met the quarterback before, and he was a cute, young white boy, but I was getting tired of hearing about him All the tabloids in Houston talked about how wonderful he is and how much of an asset he is to the team. Personally, I wanted them to start mentioning some of the veteran players like Michael. The veteran guys are the ones that are solid. They are the ones that will have to teach the young guys what to do.

Just as I was having more bitter thoughts, the cameraman flashed Michael's number, while he was jogging on to the field to get ready for the play. I watched intensely trying to see if he was covering who he was supposed to. Number twenty-seven was quick, but Michael broke away, and when the football came his direction my heart pounded out of control. An interception! I screamed at the top of my lungs. "Run, Michael! Run!"

Momma came back into the room and joined in the excitement.

Michael was almost in the end zone when Dallas' number thirty eight came from behind and tackled him.

My adrenaline stopped flowing. Number thirty eight crashed helmets some kind of way with Michael and about four other guys jumped on top of the pile.

"Get off of him!" I yelled.

I knew it was part of the game for the guys to be rough and do the things they were doing, but damn, I didn't think they purposely tried to injure other players that were trapped in positions they couldn't get out of.

I remembered Michael saying he'd been scratched and bitten at the bottom of the pile, and I got scared because he was at the very, very bottom.

Slowly the guys got up, but when they reached the bottom, there were two players still lying there. Number thirty-eight, and Michael.

"Oh my, God! Look Momma, that's Michael down there?"

The announcer gave background information on Michael and the other guy that was down with him. The other guy got up. The crowd cheered as the camera zoomed in on the player limp off the field with help from his coaches.

Michael wasn't moving.

"Come on, Baby, get up, I said with my hands folded in a praying position.

"That's Michael Riley down right now," the announcer started in again, and then they replayed the hit and I was able to see from which direction the other player hit Michael. It appeared to be a head on collision, and I noticed how limp his body became as he fell

to the ground.

"This team really needs Michael Riley. I mean he's a ten year veteran and has been to the Pro-Bowl two or three times.

This man has always been a solid player. The Bulls will be hurt without his smarts on the field."

They flashed one of those small snapshots of Michael, and I got teary eyed.

A Heineken commercial interrupted.

"Momma what do you think?" I nervously asked.

"I don't know baby. They didn't really show much," she said as she sat next to me on the sofa.

I closed my eyes and said a prayer, "Please. God, let him get up. Let him be alright."

It seemed like they showed ten commercials before getting back to the game. When the game came back on, the ambulance was driving onto the field. Michael's head was taped down.

"Oh my, God!" I cried out.

Momma grabbed my hand, not saying a word.

"We always hate to see guys go down like this," the announcer continued, making the situation worse for me. "But I just got word that he is moving his feet, so there isn't any paralysis, which is good."

"Thank you Jesus," Momma whispered.

"Momma, I should be there with him. I should've gone when he asked me too."

Momma rubbed my back. "He'll be fine, Jada. He'll be just fine."

33
Just Listen

Jada

It was nine thirty and I sat outside of Michael's townhouse complex, waiting for him to return from the game. I'd been calling his house and cell every hour leaving long drawn out messages about how worried I was. Finally, the anticipation got to me and I hopped in my car and headed over to his place.

The guard at his complex wasn't the usual nonchalant guard that I was used to seeing.

This guy was an older man that looked like he took his job as a security officer seriously. His uniform was nicely creased to perfection, with his stick and little handgun hanging on his waist. His Barney Fife hairdo was parted neatly on the side of his head, making him look crazier. I didn't attempt to ask if he'd let me in, because I knew he was the kind that goes strictly by the book, so I simply parked over to the side, and looked at him with a smile.

****

Around ten fifteen, a white Denali with chrome rims pulled to the gate. I didn't know the guy that drove the vehicle, but I knew he played ball by the Oklahoma tags and the Bulls hat he was wearing. A lot of the players lived in the same complex off of Highway 288.

Shortly after he arrived, a black corvette pulled in and the guard let him through with the same smile he'd given to the Denali man.

Finally, Michael arrived in his Jag, and I honked my horn. The guard pointed in my direction and Michael backed up alongside of me.

I was nervous, because of our last encounter, and I didn't know if he would accept me being here to offer support, or if he would tell me   to go to hell for not understanding his problem.

"Hey," he said in a deep, low voice, "What you doing out here so late?"

"I saw your game, and I was worried about you."

"Why didn't you return any of my phone calls?" Michael asked.

"I didn't know what to do, Michael. I mean I was hurt that you lied to me."

"Jada, look, I didn't lie to you. I have to do what I have to do, right now and that is to continue taking the pills. I know that may sound crazy to you, but football is my life. I'm not ready to throw it all away just yet. I've been in this game since I was eight years old, and with the dream of becoming an NFL player. I finally made it, and I put in a lot of hard work. I'm not giving it up. Not yet. That's why I wouldn't let Angela's crazy ass ruin what I've worked for years to build."

"Can I come in?" I asked softly, interrupting his speech.

He paused and put his head on the steering wheel.

"Not if you're gonna hassle me, Jay. I can't handle that right now."

I sat looking at him, and at that moment, I realized I had to do whatever necessary to prove I would stand by his side.

"Michael I'm not here to hassle you, I promise."

Silence

"Come on," he said.

I felt a sense of relief as I followed him through the gate.

****

Michael and I sat up until two in the morning discussing what had happened to him in the game. He told me he had a mild concussion, and it was nothing to be concerned about because players get them all the time.

Of course I couldn't understand how a man could and would continue to play a sport where he was constantly in pain or in danger. The game was too life threatening for me. I guess making the kind of money they make, and living the life they lived, makes a concussion here and there worth it.

****

"Good morning," I said as I entered the den where he was reading the newspaper. "You're up pretty early."

"Yeah, I couldn't sleep. Too much on my mind."

"Do you want to talk?" I asked as I grabbed his hand and sat down next to him. "I know you don't think I can handle what you're going through, but I can. I just don't agree with your solution to the problem. I am going to stand by your side if you let me."

"Well you didn't stand by me when you found the pills in the car the other day. You ignored me like I was a bum off the streets. What was up with that?"

"I told you I was scared. I don't want you to take those things because I know you're addicted to them. I can't say that I want to sit here and watch you hurt your body more by using them. Even though you may not see it now, trust me, if you continue to take that stuff, your body will be affected later. I know I don't understand the NFL and what goes on, but I do know that I love you and I don't want to see you go down the drain taking painkillers.

"You love me Jada?" Michael repeated.

"Yes, I do."

"Well, support me then, be here for me."

Damn that was the same thing Shakeem said when I confronted him about being on cocaine.

"I need your encouragement, not your lectures and you skipping out on me. I need your help."

I grabbed his hands. "I'm willing to be all of that for you, but don't ask me to go against what I believe in and I don't believe in drugs. Those painkillers can lead to you being addicted to something else. I just want you to promise me again that you'll at least try to go and seek counseling or help after the season is over."

Michael didn't answer me. He got up and walked into the kitchen and I thought I had pissed him off again, until he returned with some papers. He handed them to me.

The pamphlet on top was about drug addiction, and the second was for a rehabilitation clinic in Austin. I looked up at him.

"I told you I was going to try. I'm scheduled to go at the end of January, after season ends."

I didn't know what to say, so I got up and gave him a hug to let him know I supported his decision. He held me closely, "Thank you Baby," he whispered.

****

The hot water and the touch of Michael's hands washing my back was soothing.

"You're so beautiful" he said, as he turned me around to face him. "Your skin is so soft."

We stood wrapped in each others arms, and I felt like a queen that had just been rescued by her king.

"Will you make love to me Jada, right here, right now?" he whispered in my ear as he kissed me on my neck. We stared into each other's eyes, my hand caressing his body.

"I'll do whatever you want me to do. Whatever."

"But do you want me?" he asked with a look of doubt on his face.

"Yes, I do."

My heart was pumping blood at an unbelievable high rate.

Michael lifted my body and I wrapped my legs around his waist. He positioned me on top of him, and we made passionate love as the water bounced off of our bodies.

****

The smell and sound of bacon sizzling in the skillet woke me up. It was like waking up in my bed back at home with Momma, except for the jazz music playing downstairs. I laid there with a smile on my face as I reflected back on the activities from earlier that morning.

Was this how life would be if Michael and I made it? If so, it would be heaven. I don't know of any married women that had their husbands bathe them, make love to them and then make them breakfast.

I got up and went downstairs where he was, but when I got there, I didn't see him.

"Michael!" I called "Where are you?"

I didn't get an answer, so I opened the door off from the kitchen that led to his garage to see if he might be outside, but he wasn't.

"Michael, stop playing. Where are you?"

Still no response.

"He must be upstairs in his office," I said to myself.

I went into the kitchen and turned off the skillet of turkey bacon, and made sure the eggs were off too. I smiled when I saw two trays out with napkins and juice. Just as I suspected he was going to surprise me with breakfast in bed.

I was headed back up stairs when I heard a loud thump behind me. I stopped for a second, assuming I was hearing things but—I heard it again.

I slowly backed down the steps and moved back toward the kitchen.

"Michael" I called one last time, much softer than before, because by now I was getting a little nervous.

Then the thump came again. This time I knew it was coming from inside the bathroom that was off from the kitchen.

I stopped.

"Michael," I repeated.

I stood close to the door and called his name again, while putting my ears close to it.

I heard moaning.

Scared to death of what I might find on the other side of it, I slowly opened the door. There he was lying on the floor in a doubled up position.

"Oh my God, Michael! Baby what happened?"

He didn't answer me. He just lay there moaning. I tried to turn him over, but he was too heavy.

Finally, I thought to run in the kitchen and get the phone to call 911, like I should've done when we had the incident at the park.

"Michael, Baby, can you hear me? What's hurting you?"

He still said nothing.

Michael, I called for help. You're going to be ok baby."

"It's just an upset stomach," he mumbled.

"No it's not. We're going to the hospital."

I got him up without any more fight. I was able to clean his shirt just a little, and wipe his mouth just in time as the ambulance arrived.

We walked slowly together to the door, me struggling to hold up all two hundred fifteen pounds of him. Finally, I made it and was relieved to see the paramedics. I told them what had happened to the best of my ability.

It was amazing how calm I was. But when they closed the ambulance doors I broke down.

I felt the anxiety of entering into another hospital. I hate them! I mean everything about them. They make me nervous as hell every time I set foot in one. Now I have to face this and find out what's going on with Michael.

I was sent on a wild goose chase for nearly an hour. I finally found the floor.

St. Luke's hospital is entirely too big for me and just knowing it is full of sick and dying people, makes me even more shaky.

When I got to Michael's room, I took a deep breath before I entered. I knew the situation had something to do with those damn pills. I wasn't sure, but I have a gut feeling he overdosed, or had taken the wrong thing again.

****

I opened the door, and I saw him facing the wall. He didn't turn around when he heard the door open.

"Michael, Baby, it's me," I said slowly walking to his bedside.

He turned to face me, and I swear he had the saddest look I'd ever seen. His eyes were red, like maybe he'd been crying.

"Hey, Jay," he said softly.

I bent over to hug him and he squeezed me tightly.

"Look, Jada. I'm so sorry you had to go through this with me again. I'm so ashamed you had to see me on two different occasions in a state like that. I know I probably scared you to death and I wouldn't blame you if you wanted to end your relationship with me altogether. This is too much for me, so I can imagine what you must be feeling."

I sat next to him, and held his hand. "Michael, you can't get rid of me that easy. I've already fallen under your spell Baby, so whatever you go through, we're going through it together." *I couldn't believe I was saying that.*

He smiled, and squeezed my hand.

"But I do need you to be honest with me. I know we are just starting this relationship, but we've been going pretty strong since day one, so I feel it's only fair that you be on the up and up with me. What is really going on with you?" *For some reason, I kept thinking Michael was on something other than painkillers. I prayed I was wrong.*

Michael looked up at the ceiling and grabbed his head with both of his hands.

"Aw Jay, you just wouldn't understand."

"Try me."

He sat up in the bed, and turned to look at me.

"I don't know how you're gong to feel about me after I tell you this.

I was thinking "Oh no, what next?

He stopped for a minute, and I caressed his hand to reassure him I was still by his side.

"I've been in so much damn pain, that I've been popping all kinds of shit, and washing most of it down with alcohol. It not only soothes my mind, but it takes the pain away. Jada, I'm so fucked up right now, I don't know what to do. I've been on this shit for years! It's a wonder I haven't overdosed or killed myself by now. I guess God keeps sparing me for some reason.

Michael's voice shook and I knew he was about to cry, so I held him. That's when he let it out. "Jay, I'm scared."

"It's ok. Baby. You're right, God is sparing you, and he's going to continue until you figure this thing out."

228

"I just wanted to play ball, Babe. "That's all" he said, looking me in the eyes.

"I know, and it's not over yet." I said softly.

"Yeah, it is, Babe. I think I'm going to retire."

I couldn't believe what I was hearing, and I knew for him to say that, things must be bad.

"What did the doctor say?"

Michael shook his head. "He said I have a bleeding ulcer, and basically it's coming from my body being messed up—Hey, it's my fault. I fucked myself."

"Michael you did what you thought best to make it. Don't be so hard on yourself."

"Jada, I knew what I was doing. I knew I could get hooked. I've seen too many guys in this same situation."

"Well, now you have to do what's necessary to get out of this situation. I know you can do it…we can do it."

Michael closed his eyes and shook his head. "I got so many damn people depending on me. I got to play ball."

I wasn't sure who the people were he was talking about, but I had an idea he was talking about his family and friends.

"Jada, can I have some time alone, Babe. I just need to get my mind right."

I didn't want to leave him, but I knew he needed to think, so I gave him a kiss on the forehead and left.

34

Devastated

D.C.

*L*ori and I had to be in Kansas City for a three day conference. Each day we tried to eat at a different restaurant. We ate barbeque the first two days because we fell in love with the famous Gates and Sons. Since Kansas City is known for barbeque, we decided that should be our first dining spot.

Me, Lori and two other pharmaceutical reps that we met at the conference had Gates for dinner. When we got there, the waitress yelled very loudly from behind the counter "Hi, may I help you?" She almost gave us cardiac arrest. A lady in front of us smiled and said, "That's their trademark." *I guess she could tell we were from out of town.*

Out of all my travels I had never been to a place where they did something that drastic to grasp their customers' attention.

Since we ate too much barbeque, the Cheesecake Factory was perfect for us on our last day.

The Plaza was a hot spot in Kansas City. There were a few hotels there with lots of shopping places. It kind of looks like an outdoor strip center for Yuppies, complete with FAO Schwartz, Ann Taylor, Barnes & Noble, The Gap and pretty much all of the stores I could find at home in the Galleria. There were also restaurants, but most I was already familiar with.

"I'm starving," Lori said, looking over the menu after we had taken our seats.

"So am I. We've been shopping since eleven thirty. It's almost two o'clock. Besides, all we had this morning were bagels. We walked that off two hours ago."

"I think I'm going to get a Philly cheese steak sandwich. What about you?"

"I don't know. I want something spicy. Maybe I'll try one of their Cajun pasta platters."

As Lori was ordering, I couldn't help but feel jealous about the three carat engagement ring she'd just gotten from Jason. Here I couldn't even get a man to commit and be faithful to me, let alone propose. **Now** here's this white girl who not only snatched up a black man, he was a rich one at that.

"So have you picked a date yet?" I asked, faking like I really cared.

She smiled as she glanced at the rock glistening on her finger.

"I'm thinking it will be sometime during this off season. I kinda' want to go to Hawaii or something like that, but Jason wants a big traditional wedding. You know he's an old fashioned country boy."

I could feel my temperature rising as she innocently talked. Now, I was getting pissed off at Jason's big country ass for falling in love with her.

"I can't believe he wants a big wedding," I answered "Most men don't want to be bothered with all the planning, nor do they want to spend all that money. Girl you must have him whipped," I smiled.

"Yeah, I think I do," she laughed.

That's when I knew the damn world was coming to an end, because she proudly agreed with me.

"Deidre, I'm really sorry about Courtney." She changed the subject. "I didn't know he was married. Honestly."

"Girl don't worry about that. I'm moving on. That man will have his day and I mean it's going to be a *helluva* time when it gets here."

"Have you left him alone. I mean are you still taunting him like you were?"

I couldn't believe she was asking me that shit. I closed my eyes and took a deep breath,

because I didn't want to go off on her. Like I said, we were cool, but not that damn cool.

"Look here, Lori. I didn't taunt him. I just gave that man what he deserved. He played with my feelings and I don't just let folks do shit like that to me and get away with it. I don't know who told you that bull, but obviously they don't know what the hell they're talking about."

Lori sat looking nervous, probably wishing she hadn't said anything.

"Look," I said in a calmer tone "Nobody knows what happened between me and Courtney, and I choose not to talk about it. I mean I'm trying to forget about it and move on with my life. Does that make sense?"

"Yes, it makes sense, and I did not intend to upset you the way I did. I know it's hard finding out the guy you are interested in is not only married, but . . . has a child with your girlfriend."

I looked at her confused.

"What? What are you talking about?"

Lori's blue eyes got big.

"What the hell are you talking about Lori? What baby with my girlfriend?"

"I—I thought you knew." She said in a shaky tone.

"No, I don't know, and I still don't know what you're talking about. So since you've said this much, could you please finish informing me?"

Lori pushed her sandwich away from her, and started

fidgeting her ring.

"Well, Jason told me Courtney was worried that the baby your girlfriend had was his. He said they had a one night stand a long time ago, and she told him a couple of weeks ago that he was the father."

My mouth was on the ground. She had to have been talking about Mara because she was my only friend who had just had a baby girl. She was the only friend who wouldn't reveal who the father was.

"Oh my God!" I whispered as tears came to my eyes. Lori reached across the table and grabbed my hands.

"Deidre, I'm so sorry you had to find out like this. I really thought you knew."

As Lori talked, the tears poured. I was hurt and angry. How could the two of them do me like that? I never came on to any of Mara's men, so why would she do me like that? We'd been best friends since kindergarten and had never had any problems.

Lori handed me a napkin. "Deidre, why don't you talk to her? Because I'm sure she's feeling really bad for what she's done, especially since she hasn't told you yet."

I couldn't respond to Lori's statement, all I could do was shake my head and think about the delivery room when little Mara was born. I was the one who drove them to the hospital and I was there in the room the entire time. How could she play me like that? How could Courtney do me like that? There were a thousand questions roaming through my mind.

"Lori, I'm sorry, but I'm going to head back to the hotel room. I have to lie down for a while."

I dismissed myself from the table and slowly headed toward the door. I was completely out of it. It was kind of chilly outside, and the cool breeze hit me in the face. I had my jacket, but I couldn't think quick enough to get it on. I saw one of those decorative cow statues, and I leaned against it to keep from falling over.

35
Confrontation

D.C.

I called three times, but Jada would not answer her cell phone. I left her messages clearly stating it was urgent that she get in contact with me because I had something very important to discuss with her. I couldn't sleep the entire night for replaying the situation over and over in my head. I tried to figure out when and where Courtney and Mara had screwed. I wondered if they were in love. I thought of Jada. She had never betrayed me in the past. Did she know too?

I drove down the highway coming from Hobby airport, tears flowing down my face. I thought about the horrible day I had that abortion. It was a nightmare I'd never forget, and it left me unable to have children ever. I was enraged that I had aborted a child for Courtney because he didn't want any children, and here Mara had just had a baby girl with him. That should have been me having little Mara. Courtney was supposed to be the father of my child.

My cell phone rang, and it was Jada.

"Hello" I answered, sounding groggy from all the crying.

"Hey, girl. When did you get back?" she asked cheerfully.

"Oh, I just got back. I'm on my way from the airport right now. Where are you?"

"I'm headed over to Momma's real quick. I need to get some stuff out of the attic. How was Kansas City? Did you meet Dorothy or see Toto running the streets?"

I cut her off

"Jay, why didn't you tell me that Courtney was the father of little Mara?"

Silence

"Jada!" I said louder.

"I—I didn't know Courtney was the father. Mara never told me who the father was, and for the longest I thought it was Colin, but he started acting strange after she had her, and then I assumed it was someone she'd had a fling with that she cared not to tell us about. Who told you that Courtney was the father?"

"Lori did. She didn't know she was delivering new information to me, seeming that Mara is supposed to be one of my best friends."

"Dee, I'm so sorry. I would have told you if I had known for sure. You know how private Mara is about stuff like that. I mean if you think about it, we never know half the people she messes around with, now do we?"

"Jada that's not the point. I need to know why she stabbed me in the damn back like that. Shit, we've been together too damn long to start fucking over one another now!"

"I know, Dee. Why don't you meet me somewhere so we can talk about this. I can't imagine how you feel."

"No, you can't imagine! Hell if I can't trust my own fucking best friends, then damn who can I trust?"

"Dee, please meet me real quick so we can talk about this. I'm right at 59 and Kirby. I can meet you somewhere."

"No, I don't want to meet you. I'm going straight over to Mara's, I want her to tell me in my face why she fucked my man!"

I hung up on Jada because I didn't want to hear any more of her rationale. She didn't know how I felt, and I didn't want her making any excuses for Mara. The bottom line was she screwed the man I'd fallen in love with, and I needed to know why.

****

Mara answered the door with little Mara in her arms. It was only their fifth day home from the hospital, and she looked tired.

"Hey, Dee," she said strangely once she noticed I didn't have a happy look on my face.

"Are you alone?"

"Yeah. Momma just left to go shower. What's wrong?"

The tears came back before I could get through her door good.

"Oh my goodness, Dee. What's the matter?"

I went and sat on her couch and put my head in my hands, because for once I was at a loss for words. Usually I never had a problem voicing my opinion or telling a ho what I felt about her, but this was different. This was Mara, my best friend, my ace, my sister. I couldn't call her a bitch or a ho, because I loved her, and I damn sure loved that baby.

She went and put Mara in her room, and came back and sat down next to me.

"Dee, please tell me what's wrong?"

I turned and looked at her, tears flowing down my face.

"Why didn't you tell me about you and Courtney?"

She didn't say anything.

"Why did you do me like that, Mara?"

Mara got up and walked over to her fireplace and put her head down. She stood there for a moment in silence. The house was still.

"I'm sorry, Dee." she said when she turned around. We had dinner that night Duwayne stood us up, and too many drinks. It started out as a shit talking session, and then the next thing I knew he was over here. Dee, I'm so sorry. That was the biggest mistake I've ever made in my life. Now look, I have a child that probably won't ever know her father all because I had a one night stand."

I didn't believe the two of them had only hooked up one time.

Mara talked and I listened. I couldn't offer her any sympathy because I didn't believe in the "I got drunk" crap. Matter of fact, I hated when women pulled that line. It was so weak.

"Dee, I think it was a self esteem booster for me. I know that sounds stupid, but I have always been the one out of our group to be the third wheel, or the one who was dating the wanna be drug dealer type, and I'm sick of that! I'm tired of meeting these broke ass, needy brothas. You and Jay always get the ones with the money and education, not me. I get the losers. I haven't had a brother take me on a shopping spree let alone buy me an expensive gift yet, and you've had diamonds and all kinds of shit thrown at you."

"Mara, I didn't even think you cared about that kind of stuff. I mean you're always acting like nothing matters to you but your career. You've never insinuated to us that you wanted to be in a long lasting relationship. Hell, I always thought you just used men to get what you wanted and that was it."

"Sometimes things are a front Dee. Sometimes I'm just covering up the hurt."

"Do you love Courtney?" Dee interrupted

"No, but I do want him to be in my daughters' life. I don't know if he will, but I have asked him."

"Oh, so he has seen her?"

"Yeah, he saw her the other day, and he said he would make sure she is taken care of. I mean I don't know if he's a man of his word or not, but he knows he has a daughter and if he chooses to be in her life fine, and honestly it's fine if he doesn't."

Mara's doorbell rang, and Jada came in with a concerned look on her face.

"Dee, are you o.k.?" she asked when she came in.

"Not really Jada. Why don't you talk to Mara, so she can tell you what's going on. That's if she already hasn't.

Truth of the matter is I didn't care about Mara's damn self esteem. The bottom line is she should've never messed with anyone I'd been with, let alone had his child.

"Come on now Mara, let's talk this out," Jada said in her usual calm voice.

"No, Fuck talking now! Nobody gave a damn about me when this shit first kicked off, so fuck it now!"

Mara walked up to me, with a sad look on her face. Tears streaming down.

"How could you? You were like a sister to me."

I could hear little Mara crying, but all three of us were frozen, stiff as boards.

"Forget it," I said as I threw my hands up and headed for the front door.

"Wait, Dee" Jada pleaded softly.

I stopped and looked at her.

"I've never been stabbed like this before. Not ever!"

I opened the door and slammed it behind me. When I got to my car, I sat there for a moment. I couldn't believe little Mara was Courtney's child. The thought of them together made rage come through my body. "Fuck them! Fuck all of them!"

36
Pop In Visit

Mara

I gently placed Mara in her car seat and took her in the bathroom with me. It's a shame I am too nervous to leave my baby in her bassinet while I take a bath but I'm scared something will happen to her. She's only three weeks old, and after reading those articles about Sudden Infant Death Syndrome, I never let her out of my sight.

My bath water was steaming hot, just the way I like it, and the bubbles were filled to the rim. I haven't had a bath in months because my doctor advised me against it while I was pregnant. Showers were all I'd been getting and they are always rushed so I can finish doing house work or feeding Mara.

I laid in the relaxing water looking at my little angel God had blessed me with and I closed my eyes and thanked him.

It's still hard to believe I am a mother, because I thought I'd never have children at the rate I was going. Between my mouth and my impatience, there is no way in hell I would be any mans first pick to marry, let alone bear his children.

I was never too big on marriage after watching how my alcoholic father treated my mother. He was always drunk and ready and willing to fight when he came home from work. I used to hate when he picked and picked at Momma until she'd say something that would provoke him to punch her.

The last time I saw him, I was in the fifth grade, and he and Momma were doing their usual. It hurt like hell for me to sit in my room and listen to her scream and cry, so I got up enough nerve to go in and jump on his back, and that's when things changed. I started kicking, hitting and biting him to get him off of her, and he let go, but he flung me across the room, causing me to hit my head against the corner of Momma's dresser. Momma started screaming at the top of her lungs, and ran to my rescue. I was out of it, but before totally blacking out, I remember him yelling "That's her big ass fault for fucking with me! Ain't nobody gone want her just like don't nobody want you!"

Tears came to my eyes as I reflect back on how crushed I was then. My own father had talked about me, slung me across the room, and punched on my mother. At that moment I made up my mind no man was going to determine my happiness, and he surely wasn't going to badger my self esteem the way Daddy had done Momma's. I didn't care if I were big as Free Willy, I was going to be the biggest, sexiest woman to walk the planet, that's why I let Colin's gay ass go. After I continued propositioning him to take trips with me and asked him to date me exclusively, and he continued to act like a bitch, I knew. At first he was doing everything to satisfy me, but that didn't last long at all. When he came from Washington D.C., where he went for Christmas to see his so called cousin and came back talking all that shit about we shouldn't have sex before getting married, I was through! Plus I found some exotic male magazines in his bathroom linen closet. I don't think too many straight brothers take pride in looking at other men.

****

Just as I was drying off, my doorbell rang. I hurried to finish, and put on my robe. According to my watch it was only four. I knew Momma wasn't off work yet, because she always came to help me before going home.

Mara was still sleeping peacefully in her chair, and had been the entire hour I was in the tub. I took her into my bedroom and ran to answer the door. When I looked through the peephole I was surprised to see Courtney standing there.

As much as I didn't want it, a smile came across my face, and before I knew it, I was straightening my robe and trying to fix my hair. *I still looked a mess, but at least I smelled good.*

I opened the door slowly, smile still in place.

"Hey this is a surprise." I greeted pleasantly.

"What's up? He smiled "Are ya'll busy?"

"No, no, come on in. I just got out the bathtub, and Mara is in there sleeping"

"She's always sleep when I come around."

"Well, babies sleep a lot, but her little butt isn't sleep at night around eleven. She definitely has her days and nights mixed up."

"Courtney smiled. "Well, you look good. Motherhood is doing you right."

I hadn't blushed in front of a man since I was a teenager, but after that remark, I was blushing from ear to ear.

"Thank you, but you don't have to lie," I laughed. "I know I look a mess."

"Honestly, you don't. You look really nice."

Silence

"Do you mind if I take a peek at her?" He asked nervously.

"No, Come on back."

I switched my behind as hard as I could as he followed me toward by bedroom. I wasn't for sure why I was feeling the way I was, but something inside me wanted him to pick me up, propose, and make love to me.

Mara's little eyes were wide open when we got back there. "Well, look a here, she's up." I announced

Courtney's face lit up. "Hey, girl," he said happily "How are you?"

I stepped back and let him have his moment with her, and it was beautiful. He held her in his arms like she was his prized possession. The way he swayed and stared at her made me want to cry. "You're growing up girl. You're starting to look like your Auntie Raquel. He turned to me proudly and said, "Raquel is my youngest sister."

I nodded my head, and gave him another smile.

Mara started doing a little squirming and Courtney got nervous.

"She's hungry," I smiled.

I took her and went to the rocking chair Momma had bought me. I cautiously positioned her on my breast so she could eat.

Courtney stood with his eyes glued to us like he'd never seen breast feeding before.

"Is this scaring you?' I smiled.

"No, I guess I still can't believe she's mine."

"It is hard to believe isn't it. I find myself looking at her and wondering the same thing because she's so beautiful. I never thought I could love someone the way I love her," I said as I placed a kiss on her little cheek.

Courtney sat down at the edge of my bed. He appeared to be troubled about something.

"Is there something on your mind?" I asked.

He paused and took a deep breath.

"Yeah, there is just a little something I need to tell you."

My stomach started rumbling, and my mind was thinking AIDS, or something that was going to ruin my life.

"So, what's up?" I tried to ask calmly.

"I was released today."

I didn't know what to say because I didn't fully understand what he was talking about.

"Released. What does that mean?"

"I was cut from the Bulls. They let me go."

I couldn't believe what I was hearing. How could they cut one of their big time players?

"Well, damn. That's messed up. They can just get rid of somebody in the middle of a contract like that?"

"Yeah, they can pretty much do whatever the hell they want to do."

We sat for a moment, and I began trying to rock Mara back to sleep

"My agent is working on it, and he says I should be picked up by the end of this week. There's supposed to be a few teams interested in me."

"I'm sorry to hear that, Courtney. I know you're pissed off."

"Well, yeah but that's how the game goes, and I'm used to it now. I got some other stuff working, so if I don't get picked back up, I'll have something to fall back on."

"Well, that's good."

I got up and placed Mara in her bassinet, and sat back in my seat. I felt awkward because I didn't know what else to say to him other than sorry.

"I won't keep you, Mara. I just wanted to give you this check to help you out for a minute, and I want you to know I'm not going to skip out on her. My dad did that shit to me, and I promised myself I would never do it to my child."

He laid the check on my dresser, and started walking toward the door. "Do you have my cell phone number?" he quickly turned and asked.

"Yes"

"Here let me give you my sister, Raquel's number, in Atlanta in case of an emergency. She always knows how to reach me. Not that I won't be calling to let you know where I am."

I handed him a piece of paper and a pen. While he was writing, I thought about his wife, and got a little ticked. *As if I had the right.*

"I know your wife wouldn't want me calling your house."

He looked up at the ceiling. "You mean my soon to be ex wife. I filed for a divorce last week."

My heart fluttered. "Was it because of Mara?"

"No, it was because I don't think she ever loved me anyway. She was all about the money, and I felt that before I married her. I don't even know why I did it."

Courtney had a disappointed look on his face, and my heart was telling me to give him a hug, but my feet wouldn't go toward him for some reason.

"Well, I don't want to talk about that. Just know I'm not going to run out on you guys.

You take care, Mara, and please take care of my little girl. She's all I have."

"I will."

He turned around and gave me a hug, and a soft kiss on the lips.

"You're a good woman" he said as he stroked my cheek. "Take care of yourself."

"You too."

When I closed the door I felt like I'd lost a best friend. Tears came to my eyes, and I fought to hold them in. I headed toward my room to put my clothes on, and that's when I remembered the check he'd laid on the dresser. I picked it up. It was made payable to me in the amount of twenty thousand dollars. I couldn't believe it. I had to take a seat to make sure I was focusing right.

In the memo section, he wrote: "For my girl, Mara Courtney."

37
Game Time

Jada

*M*omma looked nice in her Houston Bulls shirt, Capri jeans, and Bulls sun visor. She was determined to wear her paraphernalia to the game. When Michael called her personally and invited her, she went out that day and searched for the perfect game day outfit. I couldn't believe she was as excited as she was, because I'd never seen her really watch a football game, and I surely had never seen her get excited about anyone I was dating. When I asked her about her enthusiasm over Michael, she said she thought he was a nice, God fearing young man. I didn't bother questioning her on how she could tell Michael was God fearing because I didn't want to get her started about men that went to church and men that didn't. Even though the conversation wasn't originally about me it would end up back on me some kind of way.

Michael wasn't playing in the game because of his bleeding ulcer. He stayed in the hospital two days, and once released he told his coach just a little about his pain killer addiction.

Of course he never mentioned the overdose, but he did inform him of his situation.

Michael had to have a doctor's release to show to the coaches, which I thought was ridiculous for a grown man to have to do, but like he said, football is a business, and he is a part of their business going right.

Retiring was still on Michael's mind, which I encouraged. However, I didn't think it was going to be as easy of a transition as he was trying to proclaim. In my opinion a man that has been as blessed as he has, and has gotten ten long years in the NFL, should be willing to move on to the next phase of his life, especially if he is as banged up as Michael is.

He still had his appointment set to go to rehab at the end of January, and I told him I was going to make sure he got there and stayed the duration. We even researched some AA groups that he could attend, but the problem was visiting the local meetings. Michael was worried about the press getting a hold of his personal information, so therefore, I found some meetings in Austin since that is where the other rehabilitation clinic was.

"This is so much fun" Momma said as she bounced in her seat to the game music. I looked at her in amazement. When the Bulls ran out onto the field, Momma jumped up and started yelling along with the other thousands of fans. "They look really handsome in those uniforms. I like these a lot better than that Oiler uniform, don't you?" *Her attitude was tripping me out.*

I smiled and nodded 'yes'. "Look Momma, there's Michael."

Michael looked up at us at the same time we were looking at him. He smiled and put his thumb up like he always did

"I tell you, Jada. I really like him. I wish your father could have been here to meet him."

I looked at her, and she had a very serious look on her face.

"Your daddy would have loved to be at this game, and he sure would be proud to have a son-in-law that plays in the NFL."

"Momma, who said Michael is going to be your son-in-law, we haven't even dated a year yet."

"Jada, you can't put time on love, Baby, and I can see love in your eyes. I saw something in his way back when I first met him. That man knows what he wants out of life, and if I'm not mistaken you are one of those things."

I didn't want to sound too cocky and say we were going to be together and then he turn around and crack my face, yet I didn't want to say anything negative, and curse myself either.

"Jada, look at that woman's ring down there." Momma whispered in my ear "It is huge."

I glanced down to where she was pointing and the lady she was describing was the wife of the running back Les London. Felicia London was her name, and she and her husband were truly paid. He was one of the highest paid players on the team. I had already seen the ring before, so it was not a big deal to me.

"Momma, her husband makes millions a year, and from what Michael tells me, he's old as molasses and has been playing for an eternity."

"That is some kind of diamond. I haven't ever seen anything that big. It's beautiful, but I don't think I would have placed a diamond that big in white gold. It just doesn't do anything for it."

I looked at momma like she'd lost her mind. "Momma, I'm sure that is not white gold. It's probably platinum. Matter of fact, knowing Felicia, as snooty as she is, I'm sure it is Platinum."

"Platinum, what is that? It looks like white gold to me."

"Platinum is the most solid and strongest metal you can buy." I explained as if I owned any. "It's like the most popular thing now. White gold and gold are out, and platinum is in. Ghetto and rich people both want to have it."

"Well, about how much do you think it costs?" Momma asked innocently.

"That ring she has on, I would probably say it cost around fifty thousand, maybe more."

"You have got to be kidding me Jada. Fifty thousand dollars for a ring, that's ridiculous. That's more than some people make a year."

"Well Momma that's nothing to most of these guys. Some of them make thirty thousand in two games."

Momma sat, staring at the lady's hand in amazement. What kind of money do these guys actually make Jada?" I thought around fifty to a hundred thousand a year."

I listened to Momma and I realized we both have a lot to learn. She knew absolutely nothing about any profession other than her world of educators. We were an upper middle class family that lived comfortably in our Texas style home. We lived nicely, and I never had to want for anything, but Momma and Daddy worked and studied hard to make their household total of a hundred and eighty thousand per year. I knew if God had Michael in His plan for me, it was going to be very interesting when momma found out that Michael made more than she and Daddy made their entire lives the first year of his career. This was a whole new world for us, and though I'm still learning, I have a lot to teach her.

38
Pushy

Jada

I hadn't heard from D.C. since the day we'd seen each other at Mara's. It had only been four days, but we usually talk everyday, unless she is out of town on business.

I couldn't get the disappointed look she had on her face out of my mind. I had never seen D.C. look like that. Even after she'd had her heart broken, she still managed to put a smile on her face.

I hate I didn't tell her about Courtney and Mara, but if I had that would have made things bad for Mara and me. Mara should have told her months ago like I suggested and maybe things wouldn't have turned out the way they did. Maybe Mara should have told me the truth when I asked. She could have sat D.C down and explained the situation from beginning to end right after it happened. Since she didn't it was all out of control, and we probably would never get our relationship back.

It was eight o'clock on Wednesday evening and I decided it was time I tried to talk to her. I pulled into her driveway directly behind her, and the look on her face told me she wasn't happy to see me. It wasn't her usual wide, bright smile that always let me know I was her girl.

"Hey Dee," I said softly, as I took off my sunglasses so I could see her facial expression clearer.

"Hi, Jay. What brings you this way?" she responded like I'd never been over there before."

"I haven't heard from you in a while, and I was wondering if you could go and have a banana split with me at Baskin and Robins. I know that's your favorite."

"Girl, I don't think so. I just came from working out, and I really don't need one. Maybe some other time."

D.C. coldly turned away and was headed up her sidewalk like she didn't have time for me. What had happened to us? Was this the end of me, Mara and D.C.?

I stood there not knowing what to say or do, as I thought about all the years we'd been together. I couldn't let it go. If I turned away now, then it would only get worse, so I turned right back around and strutted up her sidewalk and rang her doorbell.

She didn't answer the first three rings, so I pressed and pressed on it like a crazy lady, until she returned.

"Yes, Jay," she answered somewhat annoyed. I pushed my way past her and walked in. "We need to talk, and we need to talk right now."

"Look, Jada. I'm not in the mood for this discussion. You and Mara have made it crystal clear that I'm not worthy of being your true friend. You both tip toed around me, keeping a major secret from me like I was some outsider or something, so we don't really have anything else to discuss."

"D.C. please know that I didn't have a clue Courtney was Mara's father. Now I will admit I did figure out that Mara had slept with him but she swore she'd tell you, plus she said it was nothing but one of those things that happened after they had too much to drink."

"Yeah, whatever with that "too much to drink" bullshit! Do you walk around fucking your friend's men when you have too much to drink? Hell no!"

"D.C. I believe Mara. I mean she doesn't have any reason to lie to us. I clearly don't think she liked him before. I really think she let her alcohol and whatever she's been going through lead her into a bad decision.

"Well she and her bad decisions can to go to hell because things won't ever be the same between us. I have never even thought about boning any guys that liked either one of you, even years after you weren't talking to them, if they tried to holla', I'd quickly remind them that we were tighter than that, and the shit wasn't going to happen. But she didn't do that for me. She only thought of herself."

I sat down on D.C.'s couch and noticed her place. It wasn't as neat as it usually is. Papers and books were spread about her living room floor. Her kitchen had dishes on the counter and in the sink. It was really out of character for her to be so untidy. That's how I could tell that the entire situation had her really upset.

"Look, Dee. None of us are perfect, and Mara's not proclaiming to be. She apologized for what she did, and I know she is truly bothered by it but there's nothing she can do now but step up to the plate and take care of her responsibility. Hell, I don't even think Courtney is good enough to even be little Mara's father. We both know he's not going to do a damn thing for her, let alone be a part of her life. That in itself is going to drive Mara crazy, and we need to be there for her. She's a single parent now, and will always be one."

"Jada, please stop taking up for her!" D.C. screamed at the top of her lungs. "This is not some shit that will go away. The bottom line is she fucked my man, and got pregnant! That's it in a nutshell! Now you want me to forget about that, and go over there and help her with the baby. Well, I'm sorry I can't do it. I mean I'll always love her and care about her child, but it's going to take me a hell of a long time to get over this one, and to be truthful, I may not ever."

"Will you at least try, D.C. I mean will you try if she tries?"

"I don't know, Jay, I need time. I got too much shit on my mind right now. I don't need the pressure."

D.C.'s eyes watered.

"I mean it's hard getting your heart broken all the damn time, and it's even harder trying to play like nothing bothers you. I'm tired of playing that role. I want to be loved, and I want my man to love me back. I am not that bad of a person, and I think I deserve that."

"D.C. nobody ever said you were a bad person, but I will say that I never thought you were ready for a relationship. You've always given us the impression that you just needed a man for money. We didn't think that love was ever in your vocabulary."

"That's not true, Jada" she defended. "I've always told you guys when I was in love.

"Yeah, you have, but your next word after that was always how much money he made. I mean I've always thought you didn't really believe in all that love stuff."

"Well, I guess that's something about me that you never knew. I am human you know.

Shit I'm not trying to be like my mother, bouncing from rich man to rich man, not feeling anything for any of them. I want to be somebody's real wife. I want to say "I love you' after we make love and mean it.

You don't know what it was like growing up with a woman that married men only for what they could do for us. Hell, I can't even say all that was for us, because the older I got, the more I realized she did all that for herself. That's just the kind of woman she is. I guess my Dad could see through her bullshit and was smart enough not to marry her."

I listened to D.C., and was totally shocked. I never thought she felt that way about her mother, I knew she had developed some of her ways, but I didn't think it was something she despised. I always thought that was exactly how she wanted to be.

"Dee, I'm sorry. I didn't know."

"I know," she said as she started straightening up.

I walked around looking at pictures on her mantel of the three of us, and pictures of her mother and other family members. It was interesting how the older we got, the more our issues surfaced. We had been around one another since kindergarten, and it wasn't until we got in our thirty's that we started figuring out each other's personalities.

Here I was afraid to be with a man because I didn't think he could be as good to me as my father was. Mara was so scarred from her upbringing that she pretended like she didn't need a man or a family to bring her happiness, and now D.C. who I thought was a little more content with her life revealed that she really wanted to be in love, because she didn't want to be like her mother. After all the years we'd been together, everything was just beginning to make sense to me.

I was about to take my seat when I noticed a package addressed to Mrs. Michelle Vincent, and another to the Houston Police Department behind her leather sofa.

I bent down just a little to see if I was reading it correctly, and I was. I looked into the kitchen, but she hadn't noticed what I'd discovered. What could she be mailing to them? I wondered. I thought she was moving on with her life.

"So, Dee. Will you meet me at Pappadeaux's on Friday.?" She looked at me like I was crazy. "Please" I begged.

D.C. ignored me and continued washing the dishes.

She never answered.

39

Reunited

Jada

The crowd at Pappadeaux's was not the usual Friday night crowd. Things had changed. It appeared to be a much younger group, and I wasn't too particular about how they looked or acted. The age group appeared to range from around twenty one to about thirty. The guys in suits weren't occupying the bar anymore, these guys had on baggy jeans, sweat shirts, and sports jerseys. One of them had the nerve to even be wearing a pair of those Fat Albert jeans by Fubu. He should have been ashamed because he looked old as hell. Those jeans are for teenagers not grown ass men.

The crowd was very hip hop, not the after five business group, like before. The ladies had on their hooch gear, complete with their fake Coach and Gucci bags and the weaves were out of control.

When I took my seat, Mara still hadn't arrived. It felt kind of good being back in our little spot, even though a lot had taken place since the last time I'd been there. I reflected back and it had been at least two months since me and the girls had been to

Pappadeaux's together. Decisions we'd made had ruined everything. Now I hoped and prayed that at least somebody would show up. I hoped Mara and D.C. missed our friendship just as much as I did.

My relationship with Michael, Mara having little Mara, and of course Courtney shattering Mara and D.C.'s friendship were amongst the things on the list that had blocked our closeness. No matter how horrible things were for us, I was determined to get us back the way we were.

"Hey, Jay." Mara greeted with a smile. "It's gotten kind of ghetto in here, huh? Is this not the night anymore?"

"Girl, your guess is as good as mine. I'm just as confused as you are."

"Can I get you ladies something to drink?" the waiter asked.

"Sure. I'd like a Swamp thing please" I said.

"Oh, you're a drinker now?"

"No I'm just in that kind of mood right now."

"Humph. You must have a booty call tonight." Mara laughed.

"Girl, I don't have to go on those anymore."

"Well, aren't we cocky."

We both laughed.

"How is little Mara. Has she grown since the last time I saw her?"

Mara laughed. "Jada, you just saw her four day ago. She hasn't changed that much."

"Well people say that babies change every day, so I thought I'd ask since I am one of the godmothers."

Mara began telling me how little Mara was sleeping through the night. She also explained that she was ready to get out of the house and start working again.

As she talked I reminisced on us back in the day on the playground playing kickball, when life was so simple.

"Mara, do you regret having her? I asked out the blue.

She got quiet. Then she took a sip of her Margarita.

"No, because I think this was all meant to be. I know that sounds off, seeming that it happened at the cost of my friendship with D.C., but I think that was all meant to be too. Hell, I think we were going to someday get into it, and our trueness was going to be tested anyway. It happens in all relationships. We are not little kids anymore, and we need to start accepting each other for who we are. We have issues that we've never even shared with one another. I mean I'm figuring things out about myself, and you guys that I had never even thought of before. But you know what? I know D.C. may hate me now, but one day we are going to be fine. One day we're going to make up and pick up where we left off. I have complete faith that we will."

"I hope so Mara" I said as I glanced down at my watch "I hope everything…

"Hi ladies," D.C. said softly

Mara stopped, put her drink down, and looked up. They stared at one another for a couple of seconds before D.C. said "Can a sista' sit down or are ya'll going to keep staring at me like I'm crazy."

"I'm glad you came" Mara said gently.

D.C. stood with out a smile, making me extremely nervous. I wondered if she was going to snap and start cursing at both of us, or just get straight ghetto and start swinging on Mara.

"Dee aren't you going to join us?" I asked gently beckoning for her to take a seat.

D.C. slowly pulled her chair out and sat down, still not saying a word.

"So Mara, have you seen Kennette at church lately?" I asked

"No. Why? She answered unenthusiastically.

"She cut all her hair off into an afro, and she looks just like a man now."

"Now she looks more like Kenneth, and not Kennette."

Of course I laughed at my joke, but no one else cracked a smile. They both sat in silence, which hadn't ever happened since we'd been friends.

I was about to give up hope when D.C. finally spoke.

"You know, you two don't have to keep tying to smooth me over with all this fake conversation. I'm not a fool you know."

Mara and I didn't say a word.

:"First of all, Mara there isn't shit right about what you did, and you have broken my heart in a way I can't describe." D.C. continued.

"I know Dee, I was…" Mara tried to explain.

D.C. put her hand up for Mara to stop her explanation. "No matter what you say Mara, the shit was scandalous, and I didn't ever think you could or would do something like that to me."

Tears streamed down Mara's face, as the people next to us stared.

"I'm so sorry Dee. That's all I can say."

D.C. shook her head in disgust as tears came to her eyes.

Mara put her head down and cried.

"Don't say that Dee. We're girls, we've been together too long to let this break us apart." I said.

"I know that Jada. But I'm hurting D.C. added.

Mara looked up. "You know Dee, what I did was not acceptable, but don't you sit over there like you haven't screwed me over before."

D.C. sat straight up in her seat.

"Do you remember going on that date with David a long time ago, and you knew I was in love with that man.

D.C. had a shocked facial expression.

"See, you always walk around here like you're the shit, stomping on peoples' feelings whenever you want," Mara continued. "You don't rule the fucking world Dee. This world can't be centered around you and your Barbie doll look."

"Oh, so this has to do with the way I look? You fucked my man because you're jealous of the way I look!" D.C. screamed. Everyone in Pappadeaux's was looking now.

"That's messed up Mara. I didn't even know you were one of the women against me too. I can't help the way I look."

"Oh, but you can help flirting with every man you come in contact with!" Mara snapped back.

"You know what. Fuck this! I came here to see if we could possibly talk this through, but I don't care now. This shit you did goes way deeper then you are saying."

"Come on you guys, let's go somewhere else and talk about this." I suggested.

"No!" D.C. said as she stood up. "Oh, and Mara for the record, I didn't think you liked David that much. I mean, you were screwing that Ramon dude too. Did you forget that! Remember you don't believe in love!"

D.C. walked away, and Mara and I sat motionless. I wanted to crawl underneath a rock, and I wished I had never arranged the meeting, because it wasn't time yet.

40
January

Jada

$\mathcal{M}$ichael ended his season with the Bulls on a good note. He did play the next three games after the bleeding ulcer incident, however he suffered another concussion in a game against the Green Bay Packers and decided to retire. He still hadn't filled out any of the paperwork, nor had he discussed it with his coaches, so I didn't get too excited.

Our relationship was going in a very serious direction, and we'd even gone to pick out rings on three different occasions. My taste in jewelry wasn't as elaborate as his, so we made the decision that when he was ready for that, he needed to be the one to pick it out. I wanted to be surprised.

It was January the fifteenth, and we were in Austin for the weekend to get Michael ready for rehabilitation. He tried to talk himself out of it, since he'd been doing a lot better, but I had seen him drink a little more after he stopped taking the pills, so I bugged him daily about us going. I even threatened to end our relationship if he didn't go.

Fortunately, that worked because I got him there two days earlier than he was due to report. I could tell he was nervous about being there, so I tried to create things for us to do in the city to take his mind off of it. He wasn't due to report until Monday, but I took him down to Austin on that Friday. We went to the outlet mall in San Marcos and shopped until he couldn't take anymore. I tried to stay there as long as I could, but as we all know a man can only shop for so long. Three hours was all he could endure.

We were back in our hotel room by six o'clock and Michael was tired. I was still a livewire and was ready to go to the movies, but he had to rest first.

He turned the television to ESPN, his favorite station, and found the news.

"Courtney Vincent, a former player with the Houston Bulls has been arrested in Tampa on drug possession charges with the intent to sell."

Michael looked at me, and both of our mouths hung in disbelief.

"The feds have been investigating Mr. Vincent and three other NFL players for a couple of months now. There has been a number of witnesses to say that Mr. Vincent was involved in drug trafficking. The Houston Police Department also reported that they have a video tape of Mr. Vincent making a transaction in Cancun, Mexico. He is now being held on a fifty thousand dollar bond."

"What the hell is going on!" Michael mumbled "I ain't never known Courtney to sell no damn drugs, let alone use the shit!"

I couldn't believe what we'd just heard.

"Have you talked to him lately?" I asked.

"Maybe two or three times after he got released, but he sounded fine. He sure as hell didn't tell me about no damn drug deals. *I was thinking, like he would tell you over the phone.* The last thing we discussed was him getting signed with the Miami Dolphins, and I assumed he had."

Michael kept mumbling about how Courtney couldn't and wouldn't sell drugs, and all I could think about was little Mara. If this were true, she would for sure never see her father. Then I thought about Mara. Had she heard too? I thought to call her, but I decided to wait until after I'd taken my shower so I could have time to figure out how I was going to tell her just in case she hadn't heard the news yet.

While I was in the shower, I thought about what would've possessed Courtney to sell drugs, especially since he'd made hundreds of thousands of dollars in the NFL. Why in the world would he want to do something like that!

Then I realized that maybe the lifestyle was too much for some brothers to handle. Most of them aren't accustomed to having everything they want, so they fear running out of money and going back to how they used to live. With Courtney getting released maybe he panicked!

I came up with a million reasons why athletes got in trouble. My final answer was pressure. It had nothing to do with their intelligence levels. It had everything to do with PRESSURE! Most of the guys have been under so much pressure to make it, because their success means success for their families and so many others that a lot of them made a lot of risky decisions. The fast life of an NFL player isn't as glamorous as people think.

Of course my outlook on athletes changed when I got with Michael. I used to think they weren't very educated, didn't know anything, and got over all the time, but he proved me wrong. Michael, by far is one of the most intelligent men I've ever met. I mean he would have to be in order to run all those plays and endure the things he endures.

NFL players, NBA players and all other athletes have my utmost respect because they had the will to make it, and they utilize their talents to ensure themselves a better life.

When I got out of the shower and was drying off, I thought about D.C. I wondered if she had heard the news yet. I knew she wouldn't care if she had. Then I had a flashback to that package that was behind her sofa. One addressed to Courtney's house, and the other to the HPD. I wondered what was in them.

"No," I said to myself. "She wouldn't have."

41

Explanation

D.C.

Well, the bulls almost made it to the playoffs, and I must say they did a hell of a job for a new team. I was quite impressed. They have everybody around this city going crazy. Every time you turn on the radio, or television all you hear about, are the Bulls.

The women in the city are out of control! A lot of them are running around town trying to meet a ball player. I haven't ever seen so many groupies come out the woodwork like I saw this year. Half of them don't even know what the hell they're doing, or how to play the game the right way. It's sad to say, but I don't anticipate too many of these players falling head over heals for a Houston woman because they're acting too immature about the whole situation.

Now my girl Jada lucked up. Not only did she meet one of the main catches on the team but she hooked him too, and not by getting pregnant. She's now wearing a nice, very elegant, classy and (excuse my French) fat ass diamond! That son of a gun IS huge.

I knew she was going to get him, because she's a nice girl. Hell, and Michael is one of those good 'ole nice guys; the kind I'm never attracted to. I tell her all the time she snagged a good one, because there aren't that many nice looking, wife free, and kid free athletes running around here nowadays that want to be in a healthy relationship. She met him at the right time.

They plan on getting married this summer here in Houston and of course I'm in the wedding. Sometimes Jada goes back and forth over whether or not to have a big wedding, or to just take off somewhere. Since her father passed she thinks it would be too emotional.

I recommended they go to Jamaica which was what a lot of folks I know have been doing. I guess the traditional shit has just gone out the window, along with a lot of other values and rules. People just don't care about relationships, family and memories like they used to.

****

Well, I finally made it to a game. It was the last game of the season, but I got here.

You should have seen Jada's face when I popped up at her seat during halftime. Of course she gave me third degree about who I got my ticket from, and how long had I known the person.

See I never told them about my rookie love, Mario.

Mario and I had been kicking it kind of tough after my accident. He was there for me when I was having a really rough time, and I realized that his innocence was just what I needed. He was going to accept me for me, and I could do the same with him.

I enjoyed Mario because he didn't try to dig up my past, and he didn't care what other guys said about me. He enjoys my company, and that is all that matters.

One thing for sure, I'm so glad I got rid of the thorn that was in my side. I mean, I'm down right elated that he's a part of the past, because he brought his tacky behind in here and caused a lot of confusion. I hate I ever messed around with him, because he was nothing but trouble from the beginning. The grief he caused me, I'll never forget.

He scarred me for life, and that is why I had to do what I did. I couldn't let him get away clean free after he'd made me get an abortion, which messed up my body, got my girlfriend pregnant, AND then had the audacity to disrespect me in the locker room by telling other guys that I was a high class ho! Hell no! He got his people mixed up and the brother has to pay.

I guess he thought I didn't figure out he was down in Cancun making drug transactions with all those so called business men he was meeting with. I didn't really put two and two together until I got back home, and looked at some of the tapes from my video camera.

I got Courtney saying and doing all kinds of crooked shit! Just to think he thought he was appeasing me after the abortion by bringing me down there while he completed his deals.

Well, look who got played. I sent all that footage directly to his NFL, ghetto wife, and one to the Houston Police Department.

It would be a shame to waste such valuable information now wouldn't it?

42
Judging

Colin

*I*t was Monday night around nine thirty when I received the phone call. I happened to be chillin' in my bedroom, with a good book by Walter Mosley when Brian called.

Brian Green is one of my clients and a linebacker for the Bulls. I had been working with him for a couple of months, and had found him to be a pretty interesting guy.

He wasn't your average preppy white boy with his long ponytail, and dangling earring. He was unbelievably funny and had a high about life I found rather cool.

Brian didn't appear to be cocky and display the attitude that most of my black clients did. He would just come to get his work out on, listen to my advice without any complaints, and go on about his business. Unlike my other African American Bull clients. Everything I advise them on, they have something to say, as if I don't know what the hell I am doing.

Brian invited me to come to a get together at his house, and since he'd been kind enough to recommend me to a few of his other athlete friends, I figured "what the heck."

When I got downtown to his loft, I called his phone to be buzzed in. The music and the people were so loud, I could hardly hear what he was saying. My initial thought was I didn't feel like being bothered with the punk rocker crowd tonight, but again, the connections I could make changed my mind and I went on up.

Once on the elevator, I began to wonder just how much money did Brian make, and what kind of ducks was he dropping to stay in such a high class spot.

I barely stepped one foot off the elevator when I heard the loud rock and roll music. "I'm not in the mood for this tonight" I thought.

I noticed the nice professional paintings that were neatly perched on the wall, as well as the expensive light fixtures.

Number six thirty was of course the loft that had the three blondes dressed in bikinis and heels, standing in front of it.

"Good evening," I said in my polite, yet professional voice.

"How are you?" They all responded in unison.

I proceeded in opening the half cracked door, and all I could see were more Caucasian women, half dressed, and a lot of large bodied white boys drinking and talking loud. There wasn't a black soul in sight.

I said excuse me a million times as I made my way through the small unit, trying to locate the host of the jungle party.

I spotted him out on the balcony with two other guys and a woman.

"Hey, I didn't know you were having a party," I said once I got out there "I thought this was a small get together."

"Oh, hey Dude. I didn't know you were here." Brian greeted, loudly in my ear. "You know I have a party every Monday night. What the hell, we don't have practice tomorrow anyway. Plus, I already passed my drug test."

Everyone on the balcony laughed, but I didn't find the humor.

"Hey, let me introduce you to a few of my friends."

Brian did his introduction thing, and I stood, thinking it was time for me to break out of there because it was too loud and the cops were bound to burst in at any minute. The guys that were with Brian were staring at me like I had dirt on my face, which made me feel even more uncomfortable, while pissing me off at the same time.

"Are you from around here?" one of them asked.

"No. I'm from Charlotte, and yourself?"

"I'm from the Houston area," the muscular man responded.

I stood in front of them not interested in developing a conversation, and that's when I decided to leave.

"Hey, let's go back in and get some more liquor" Brian suggested, as he stumbled back inside. Everyone followed him, and I observed the activities through the glass door. Everyone was drinking, smoking, popping pills, and there was even a small table of cocaine users hidden in a corner. It was way to wild for me, and not my type of party.

"Come on man," Brian said loudly as he came back outside and grabbed my arm.

"Brian, I'm getting ready to get out of here. I have an early client tomorrow."

"No way dude! You at least have to have a drink with me before you go."

Before I could say yes or no, Brian handed me a shot glass of something clear. Everyone in the room seemed to be looking at me.

"Come on guy, drink up!" Brian said, this time in his deepest manly voice.

Not thinking, and feeling the pressure of my manhood being tested, I threw the drink down my mouth.

Everyone started cheering, and Brian had this devious grin on his face, which instantly made me leery of what I'd just swallowed.

"There you go dude! Now you can relax and enjoy yourself."

I smiled, but I still had the front door in sight. I was not going to hang around with them any longer.

On my way to the door, I started to get a little dizzy. I thought it was because I hadn't had a straight drink in a while, but when I felt light-headed, I took a seat on the floor near the door.

I put my head on my knees, in hopes to get myself together, but when I looked up, the room was still spinning.

The music seemed louder, and the people were almost in 3-D. I looked in the kitchen, and I noticed two men tongue kissing each other. I blinked a couple of times to make sure I was focusing right, and when I looked again, they were still at it.

"Man I got to get out of here" I said to myself.

"Hey, are you ok?" a voice of a young lady said.

I turned to my side, and it was one of the Barbie doll clones that was on the balcony with Brian earlier.

"No I'm not. I think there was something in my drink" I tried to explain.

The girl laughed. "No there wasn't silly, you're just drunk."

"No I'm not! I said a little louder. "Brian drugged me!" The girl helped me to my feet, and needless to say that's all I remember.

****

When I opened my eyes the next morning, I was in between two naked white boys, Brian being one of them.

Panic immediately set in, and I sat up. I looked down only to see that my pants were undone. I closed my eyes, again hoping that when I opened them, the nightmare would go away.

Unfortunately, when I opened them, I was still half dressed in a room full of naked ass white men!

"Fuck!" I said loudly, not waking up one of them.

I immediately tried to find my things so I could get the hell out of there.

Thank God, my keys were in my pants pockets, but I didn't know where the hell my shoes or shirt were.

When I got to my car, my head was spinning. "What the hell had I done?"

I rested my head on the steering wheel, to try to clear my mind. A tear came down my face, because I didn't know what to do next. Had they had sex with me, or did I do something to them?

My mind was racing at a hundred miles an hour, and I couldn't get it to stop.

Then a car pulled in next to me, and I instantly tried to get myself together.

A huge brother in a 740 BMW, got out, and looked at me. Our eyes locked, and I'm sure he could read panic in mine. He got out the car and came to my side and knocked on my window. "Are you alright man?" He asked.

I shook my head no, as I tried to maintain my composure.

"Hey man, you need some help?" the huge man asked again.

"Yeah man. I'm all fucked up." I managed to say

"Shit I see. You want me to drive you to your crib man, cause you don't look like you're in no shape to get there."

"Yeah man. That would be cool." We got into his truck, and my head was still spinning.

"Do you know where you live bruh?" he asked with a deep chuckle.

"Yeah, somewhere off of I-10."

"Aw, you're far out there. Well, we can't take you anywhere until you figure out where you live on I-10."

"Just give me a minute man. I'll get it."

The brother sat there for a moment, looking at me like I was crazy, then he introduced himself.

"Hey. My name is Mario. Mario Jackson," he said, sticking his hand out for me to shake it. "What's yours?"

Instantly I knew who he was. He was the first round rookie from Detroit.

"Colin. I'm Colin man."

"Nice to meet you Colin" He said politely. "Check it out. I'm about to run up here real quick and get my girl, Deidre and then I'll take you home. Is that cool?"

"Yeah man. That's cool."

I closed my eyes once again, relieved he'd shown up, and pissed at myself for being wrong. I had been just as judgmental as the rest of the world against black athletes, and I had the shit all wrong. Way wrong!

Epilogue

Jada

$\mathcal{M}$ichael and I were finally at the altar. We stood before Reverend Moore with our hands intertwined, and our eyes locked on each other. We were so in love.

If a person were to stand next to us, I have no doubt he would be able to feel our connection.

The church was full of pink and yellow roses; my favorite flower.

White candles lined the aisles, flickering each time a hint of air hit them. It had been a struggle making my wedding plans because everything I requested, momma disagreed.

Dealing with my mother and my aunts, to plan for the wedding drove me insane.

I wanted to go to an island, but they thought that was a disgrace so I went along with the traditional way.

Mara and D.C. were both bridesmaids, and believe it or not, they were extremely cordial to each other during the rehearsals. It seemed like they were trying extra hard to get along for my sake.

"Jada and Michael have words they would like to say to one another," Reverend Moore announced to our audience of a hundred and fifty."

I cleared my throat as softly as I could, then I took a deep breath. I was so nervous.

Michael's beautiful dark eyes had a glaze over them, which made my heart sink because I knew at any moment he was going to cry. I loved the fact that he showed his emotional side to me, instead of keeping his guard up all of the time like most men do.

Michael, this is the happiest day of my life. You have taught me to believe in love again and to trust. Since the day I laid my eyes on you, I've had butterflies in my stomach. You are the smartest, most loving man beside my father that I have ever met, and I wish he were here to meet you. He would be so proud of my decision."

Tears were gently cascading down my face as my voice quivered to finish. *"I'm never going to leave your side. I am here with you, by you, until death do us part. You can trust and depend on me because I love you, and I'm glad God brought us together."*

I wiped away a few of Michael's tears and gave him a reassuring smile to let him know I appreciated his emotions.

Then Michael cleared his throat, and I knew he was going to have me and the audience in tears.

"Jada," he began in a shaky voice *"You have given me a feeling that I haven't had my entire life. I have never felt this way about anyone. When I see you I get this warm, bubbling feeling inside of me that I can't explain.*

I heard a few laughs from the audience.

"Sometimes I can't believe you are mine." He continued *"Thank you for believing in who I am, and being supportive. I know I can be a lot to deal with, but you have proven to me that you're not about games; you are about what's in your heart. I*

will cherish you and what we have until I take my last breath. You being in my life means more than anything to me."

I knew my mascara and makeup were a mess, because I couldn't stop my tears from flowing. Michael wiped them away, and gave me that same reassuring smile I'd given him.

We turned back to the Reverend so he could pronounce us husband and wife.

"Now you may kiss the bride."

Michael planted a soft, sensual kiss on my lips, and I melted inside.

"I love you baby" he mouthed to me before turning to face the crowd.

The audience was clapping and making cheerful noises when we turned to face them. Everyone I noticed had a pleasurable smile on their face. It was a beautiful and heartwarming moment for me.

I walked down the aisle, as everyone threw rice at us, and I noticed Mara and D.C. hugging, and Mara wiping tears from her eyes. I wondered what that was about, but it brought my heart joy that they were being civilized to one another.

When we approached the last pew of the church, I saw a lavender church hat that caught my eye. When the woman looked up and I saw the tears flowing uncontrollably, I became breathless. Why would Angela come to my wedding? The nerve of her! Was she about to torture us for the rest of our lives? The tricks she played with Michael were over. He was no longer FAIR GAME!